MATTIE
AND THE
MACHINE

by Lynn Ng Quezon

SANTA
MONICA
PRESS
TEEN

Published by: Santa Monica Press LLC
P.O. Box 850
Solana Beach, CA 92075
1-800-784-9553
www.santamonicapress.com
books@santamonicapress.com

Printed in the United States

Santa Monica Press books are available at special quantity discounts when purchased in bulk by corporations, organizations, or groups. Please call our Special Sales department at 1-800-784-9553.

ISBN-13 978-1-59580-118-0

Publisher's Cataloging-in-Publication data

Names: Quezon, Lynn Ng, author.
Title: Mattie and the machine / by Lynn Ng Quezon.
Description: Solana Beach, CA: Santa Monica Press, 2022.
Identifiers: ISBN: 978-1-59580-118-0 (print) | 978-1-59580-773-1 (ebook)
Subjects: LCSH Knight, Margaret E., 1838-1914--Juvenile fiction. | Inventors--Juvenile fiction. | Children as inventors--United States--Biography--Juvenile fiction. | Looms--United States--History--19th century--Juvenile fiction. | Historical fiction. | BISAC YOUNG ADULT FICTION / Historical / United States / 19th Century | YOUNG ADULT FICTION / Technology | YOUNG ADULT FICTION / Historical / United States / Civil War Period (1850-1877) | YOUNG ADULT FICTION / Girls & Women
Classification: LCC PZ7.1 .Q35 Ma 2022 | DDC [Fic]--dc23

Cover and interior design and production by Future Studio

To my husband Ron,

Thank you for being my co-researcher, my loving patron,
and my biggest fan.

Chapter 1

THE BAG DIVISION'S SIX MACHINES ARE, AS OLD JAKE USED TO say, pernickety as a moody racehorse. When everything is perfect, they run like a dream, whisking out paper bags by the thousands. But one thing goes off kilter, and they chew the paper feed to bits. And with these machines, a hundred things can go wrong.

Fortunately, I've gotten quick at figuring out what's wrong.

Ida's gray-streaked head shakes with amazement as I wriggle out from beneath Machine 3 with a cracked bevel gear in hand. "Mattie," she says, raising her voice over the factory clatter, "I swear you got a sixth sense with mechanical things."

"It's just practice," I say, easing my legs out. "If you took them apart as much as I do, you'd get good, too." While my height comes in handy working with the factory's overhead line shaft, it makes crawling under things difficult.

"No, you have a gift," Ida insists. "Old Jake never fixed things this quickly."

That's because Old Jake liked beer for breakfast and rum in his noon coffee.

I don't say that out loud, of course. It's disrespectful to speak ill of the dead. Not to mention, Jake's the reason I'm no longer an ordinary hand like the other women at Columbia Paper. Most mechanics would laugh at the thought of training a young girl, but Jake taught me his trade and taught me well.

For that, I'm grateful. Maintaining machinery, adjusting and replacing their myriad parts—that's much more satisfying than simply bundling the bags they make. Plus, the extra twenty-five cents I earn a day has been a godsend with my brother still unable to work.

So I silently thank Jake, God rest his drunken soul, and

refocus on the task at hand. "Well," I say, smoothing my calico skirt and apron, "I might be fast, but even I can't fix your machine without the right gear, Ida." I tilt my head toward the worktables, where a dozen workers are folding Columbia Paper's specialty square-bottom bags by hand. "You might as well join the folders while—"

Suddenly, the factory bell peals, piercing the workroom clamor. Folders and machine operators alike halt to exchange bewildered looks at the oddly timed burst.

"That's strange," says Ida. "Lunch isn't for two more hours."

The door bangs open, and Mr. Lovelace's balding pate and muttonchop whiskers thrust inside the room. "Machines off," he bellows. "Everyone in the delivery yard now. Hurry it up, girls."

"Ladies," Ida grumbles as he waddles off. I sigh and hasten to shut off the machines. To a foreman like Mr. Lovelace, it doesn't matter if you're a widowed mother of two like Ida or a six-foot-two-inch giantess like me. If you work in a factory and wear a skirt, you're a girl.

Within moments, the Bag Division's twenty workers file out of the workroom's dust and into the September sunshine. It's a perfect New England morning, the gold and scarlet of Springfield's woods a dazzling contrast to Columbia Paper's gray brick buildings. The crunch of fallen leaves mingles with the groan of millrace waterworks as we tramp from the bag-making annex, past the length of the massive paper mill complex, to the delivery yard.

We arrive to find the women of the Paper Mill Division already assembled before the factory office. Their expressions are drawn, and restless hands fidget over their aprons. As we line up behind their orderly ranks, Fannie Foster, a buxom bag worker my age, tugs my sleeve. "Mattie, look," she says, pointing to the road that services the yard. "Isn't that Mr. Pope's?"

Next to the blue-and-white sign welcoming all comers to the Columbia Paper Company is a four-wheeled carriage. Its polished wood and brass sparkles, and the factory's office lad nervously holds the heads of its equally stunning Hackneys. Only the wealthiest man in Springfield could afford such finery, and any lingering doubt is dispelled by the initials emblazoned on the carriage panels: AJP.

My stomach flips. This could be good. Or very bad.

"Maybe it's true," Fannie whispers. "Maybe Mr. Pope—"

"Hush," I snap. "No sense speculating about things we know nothing about."

Fannie's mouth clamps shut, but around the yard, other voices buzz like persistent mosquitoes:

"When did we see Mr. Pope last? Five months ago? Six?"

"Man can't be the same after an illness like that."

"He's seventy. Of course he wants to retire, and the owner of Holyoke's mill been eyeing ours for sure."

"It is his carriage, but could be kin bringing bad news."

My hands clench. *Don't be burying him before his time with your gossiping.*

I've been working in factories since I was eleven, and Mr. Pope's the best employer I've known. He's fair, doesn't put on airs, and treats the hundred women at Columbia Paper with fatherly regard. Most owners avoid the smell and noise of their mills, but Mr. Pope, a onetime factory worker himself, would ride in on his gray mare every Tuesday to inspect things in person.

At least, he did so until he fell ill last spring.

I murmur a prayer on his behalf. But even as I ask God to restore Mr. Pope, I know my motives are selfish.

My place as a mechanic is as much due to Mr. Pope's goodwill as my own skill. After all, in a factory, women are hands and operators only; mechanics, engineers, and overseers are all men. So when Old Jake died last winter, Mr. Lovelace laughed in my face when I asked to keep helping with the machines.

But Mr. Pope heard him laughing, too. When he found out

what I wanted to do, he shocked us all by telling Mr. Lovelace to hold off finding a new mechanic, and offering me a month-long trial that turned into a permanent position.

Entrusting a fifteen-year-old girl with a man's job takes an open mind, and that's rare among factory owners. If anything happens to Mr. Pope, I'll likely find myself an ordinary hand again. Or worse, out of work. With both Mother and Charlie depending on me, the thought of losing my pay—even for a spell— puts me in a cold sweat.

Just then, the office door opens, and Mr. Lovelace and the other overseers exit onto the wooden porch overlooking the yard. Silence falls at their grim faces. Anything that makes them look like that can't possibly be good for the rest of us.

My stomach is twisting into knots when there's a gasp at the front of the crowd. I crane my neck to see what's happening, and Mr. Pope's towering figure emerges onto the porch.

Applause breaks out, as does relief. The way the overseers looked, I expected a funeral announcement, not Mr. Pope smiling and waving.

However, even though he's in his usual tweeds and bowler, he's not his usual self. His suit jacket, once tight on his bearlike body, hangs loose, and the cheeks behind his bushy white beard look peaked. His posture is hunched, and I realize he's leaning on a cane, something he never used before.

But when his mouth opens, his voice booms, resonant as it ever was. "I thank you for that warm welcome, friends, and you have been friends indeed these last six months. Your prayers have blessed me, your well wishes encouraged me, and your diligence sustained me. I have always considered Columbia Paper a family, and you proved it by keeping this house together in my absence. For that, you have my gratitude."

He bows, taking off his hat, and we applaud once more. The tension in my stomach unwinds. If Mr. Pope is here thanking us, that can only bode well. Yet the foremen remain somber as mourners at a wake.

"However, I wish to offer more than gratitude," says Mr. Pope, replacing his hat on his head. "I may have been ill, but I was not unaware of the talk flying about. Talk of the company floundering or failing entirely because your captain was not at the helm. And though we were not shipwrecked, I will not deny those were real possibilities. Nor will I deny the tremendous anxiety you suffered. But I am here now to offer the assurances I can."

My hopes lift. Mr. Pope has practically announced his return, and I beam alongside my coworkers as he continues. "The future is an inscrutable thing. The long war with the South taught us all that. Yet a good captain always plans ahead that his ship might weather any storm. To that end, I have made a decision: Today, I retire as head of Columbia Paper."

Chapter 2

I blink, confounded by Mr. Pope's words.

"Mattie," Ida whispers, her brow furrowed, "did he say 'retire'?"

Mr. Pope's voice slices through our bewilderment. "This may seem a strange course for a man recently restored to health, but my illness was a harsh reminder that we cannot fight age. While I will remain Columbia Paper's champion so long as I draw breath, it is best that I pass the company's oversight to one vigorous enough to bear it."

With that, Mr. Pope turns and gestures. The men behind him shift, and a thickset figure with a hooked nose and handlebar mustache steps forward to join Mr. Pope.

I gape. I'd been so focused on Mr. Pope I hadn't noticed this stranger. And the more I look, the more uneasy I get. Unlike Mr. Pope's homey air, this man is frosty polish in his frock coat and stovepipe hat. Between his fierce features and tailored black finery, he resembles a haughty raven.

As the stranger eyes our ranks like a horse trader sizing up a purchase, Mr. Pope says, "It is my pleasure to introduce my grandson, Charles Yates, new head of Columbia Paper."

A round of polite applause goes up. In front, the foremen's smiles are strained. Mr. Lovelace looks as if he's grinning through a toothache as Mr. Pope continues. "Charles represented Massachusetts well as captain in the Twenty-Seventh Regiment. I have no doubt the leadership he demonstrated in our Union's service will ensure the future of Columbia Paper."

"Thank you, Grandfather," Mr. Yates says briskly as Mr. Pope steps back. "And indeed, I have made plans to secure the company's future. Plans I intend to implement in short order."

My heart hammers in my chest. Not only do we have a new head, but one ready to unleash change. Which can mean anything from altering our work process to dismissing employees.

"In the two years since the war ended, the demand for paper has steadily increased," says Mr. Yates, hooking his thumbs into his waistcoat. "Newsprint, manila products, wrapping paper—all things that uplift our country and help it prosper. Columbia's output, however, has not kept pace with that demand. That is opportunity we have not seized. But it is opportunity we *must* seize—for the sake of the company and our nation."

Ida scoffs under her breath. "Since when has the fate of the Union rested on paper mills?"

I ignore her, listening intently to Mr. Yates. This fellow might have an overweening sense of self-importance, but my immediate fate does rest in his hands.

"Therefore, Columbia Paper is expanding." Flinging an arm in the direction of the bag workroom, Mr. Yates declares, "In a month, we will demolish the bag-making annex to make way for a second paper mill. God willing, the new mill will begin production a year from now. As for the Bag Division, it will relocate to a larger facility in order to double bag production. I've already secured a property on Market Street near the train depot for this purpose."

Excitement instantly trills through the Bag Division. After all, the bag-making annex is merely a drafty shed that was turned into a workspace when the factory brought the bag machines two years ago. If we can move into a proper building before winter, that's already cause for celebration. The fact that it's in the middle of town where most of us live rather than the outskirts has us giddy.

"If it's by the depot, I could eat lunch at home with the children," says Ida, clasping her hands to her chest.

"And I could get more sleep," says Fannie. "Sounds too good to be true."

"If he's secured the property, it must be true," says Ida. "And if he's doubling production, he'll be hiring. Fannie, you said your cousin was looking for work. Tell her—"

"I realize," booms Mr. Yates, silencing the chatter, "that these changes may cause disruption. But fear not. I will keep watch to ensure that all goes smoothly. Indeed, I intend to give this company the attention it's lacked the last several months. As such, Columbia Paper's office will also move to Market Street. Mr. Lovelace will oversee the new construction and the Paper Mill Division here, but I will manage the company's business affairs and the Bag Division in town."

That's why the foremen are nervous. Most have worked under Mr. Pope for years, and during his absence, they grew used to acting on their own. Now, they are back under scrutiny, with someone who will watch more closely than Mr. Pope.

I share their nervousness. Company owners pay little heed to mechanics, but a female mechanic is a particularly irregular anomaly. I cross my fingers, praying that the new boss's declaration to oversee the Bag Division is bluster and he ignores us to smoke cigars at his desk.

"Any great endeavor is impossible for a single person alone," Mr. Yates continues. "As every military man knows, success requires a disciplined troop. Therefore, I ask your full cooperation. Cooperation in following your assignments and cooperation in collaborating with the twenty men who will join the Bag Division this January."

I start at his words. *Men? As factory hands?*

The other bag workers look as thunderstruck as I feel. Ida presses a hand to her forehead. "Good Lord Almighty," she mutters. "Change is surely blowing our way."

Chapter 3

COLUMBIA PAPER'S NEW MARKET STREET FACILITY INCLUDES two identical buildings for the Bag Division. The brick structures have the same overhead shafts, the same steam-powered engines, the same number of bag machines and worktables. The only difference is the West Workroom clamors with activity, while the East Workroom quietly awaits its male workforce.

That wait ends today.

I oil the gears of the East Workroom machines, then load a roll of paper onto Machine 11 for a test run. It worked fine yesterday, but better sure than sorry. I've only one chance to make a good first impression on the new arrivals, and I don't want to bungle it.

Meanwhile, Ida and Fannie calibrate the worktables with equal care. Our square-bottom bags must be uniformly hand-folded, so we use custom-built tables for the task. Each is equipped with a rectangle of sheet steel that provides a consistent edge to fold bag bottoms. As Ida and Fannie inspect the folding plates and the twelve-inch vertical bars that attach them to the tables, they chatter about the topic the factory has buzzed over the last three months: What are our new coworkers like?

"I hope they're mannerly," says Fannie, sliding a folding plate to the top of its spring-loaded connector bar and then lowering it to rest on the tabletop. "Be nice if they were handsome, too. We only ever see old, bald men here."

Ida clucks her tongue, the sound echoing in the near-empty workroom. "Don't get your hopes up. All we know is they're poor and have had a bad time of it."

Despite the incessant speculation, we've only confirmed three facts about the new workers. One, they are young. Two, they come from a Maryland backwater called Oak Creek. Three, while they were away with the Union Army, Rebs overran their home, and at the war's end, they returned to ruined wells and torched barns.

My heart went out to them when I learned that. Although Mother and I didn't have much, we managed to provide Charlie with rest and solace when he returned broken from the war. Those Marylanders went from fighting Rebs to fighting to keep body and soul together. Rebuilding was difficult without the tools and equipment the Rebs destroyed, and two years after their return, Oak Creek was still in shambles.

That's where Mr. Yates stepped in. Apparently, he'd captained the men when their platoon was incorporated into his Massachusetts regiment. Gossips say he cajoled his grandfather into handing over Columbia Paper just so he could help his old subordinates. Whether or not that is true, this is certain: the instant he got the funds to expand the Bag Division, he sent offers of work to Oak Creek.

Fannie's expression turns thoughtful. "It did surprise me that Mr. Yates hired the whole lot of them. I didn't think he could be kind, considering he's such a screw—"

"Fannie!" Ida and I hiss. Ida slaps a hand over Fannie's fool mouth while I scan the door and windows. Fortunately, all the other workers are in the West Workroom across the delivery yard, and the only soul outside is the young new bookkeeper Mr. Mowe, who's too busy sweeping snow off the office porch to pay any mind.

As I breathe a sigh of relief, Ida releases Fannie and cuffs her. "Watch your tongue, girl," Ida mutters. "You want to get sacked?"

Fannie's face burns red. Whereas the old bag-making annex was far and away from the company big bugs, the East and West Workrooms are within spitting distance of the new office. And stationed inside that office is Mr. Yates, who—true to his word— has been overseeing the Bag Division.

While the boss doesn't bustle about the factory like Mr. Lovelace, neither is he idling at his desk. When we are diligently working, he's nowhere around, but if someone gets distracted or arrives late, he has an uncanny way of showing up. As for his reprimands, they are both public and humiliating.

Fannie's lucky he didn't catch her. Very lucky. Abashed, she resumes inspecting worktables with a buttoned lip and renewed zeal. Ida shakes her head and turns to me. "And what do you think, Mattie? What do you think these boys will be like?"

I shrug as I adjust Machine 11 to make two-pound size bags. "All I know is that seeing a workroom full of men will take getting used to."

Ida grunts in agreement. We both became factory workers during the war, when New England men volunteered by the thousands to fight for the Union. Those who didn't enlist often ventured West. So although men still supervised us and fixed machinery, we'd grown used to working solely alongside women.

However, peace has brought change, and I'd certainly rather these men join us here than wage war on the battlefield.

I'm connecting the belt from Machine 11 to the overhead line shaft when a rapping catches our attention. Mr. Mowe's tall form fills the doorway. "They're here," says the junior bookkeeper, spectacles fogging in the relative warmth of the workroom. "Bundle up, and we'll meet them in the yard."

My gaze flits to the window. Sure enough, coming through the main gate is a group of men, with Mr. Yates's imperious figure in the lead.

Ida tosses me a rag to wipe the oil from my fingers. "The wait is over," she says, donning her shawl. "Let's give those boys a warm Springfield welcome."

Beneath my plaid shawl, my hands wring, restless as a pail of eels, while Mr. Yates introduces Ida, Fannie, and me as "three of our factory girls." I'm not used to so many eyes on me. In addition to the Marylanders, I sense stares coming from the West Workroom. The other women are supposed to continue working as usual, but curiosity is clearly getting the better of them.

If Mr. Yates is aware of their distraction, he doesn't show it. His gaze remains square on the newcomers. But though he's gone out of his way to help them, he doesn't exhibit a particle of sentiment. He's his usual brisk self as he explains the weekly paydays, the bell schedule, the ten-hour days, the six-day work week.

As for the men, their expressions are difficult to read, swathed as they are in scarves, upturned coat collars, and battered hats. However, they radiate respect toward their former captain as they stand in two perfect lines, ramrod straight. I, on the other hand, am doing my darndest to slouch without looking like it.

Mr. Yates might be the old boss's grandson, but he didn't get his height from Mr. Pope. I didn't realize at first because of his stovepipe hat, but Mr. Yates is at least a half foot shorter than me. At the tender age of fifteen, I haven't much experience with the masculine sex, but I do know that men don't like women looking down at them.

I haven't given Mr. Yates cause for complaint—I've made doubly sure my work is flawless since he arrived. Yet annoyance fills his eyes whenever I come into his sight. It's unfair; I didn't choose to be tall. But he's the boss, and I need my pay. So I keep my distance, avoiding the office and staying at the rear during assemblies.

There's no hiding now. The fact that I'm here on his orders is no comfort. So it is an immense relief when Mr. Yates concludes, "Unfortunately, I must leave to address an urgent matter at the paper mill, but these three will show you the ropes. I know they're girls, but they're capable of that much."

As Ida bristles at that last remark, the boss heads out of the yard, Mr. Mowe following him close behind with an armload of documents. I eye the rangy accountant's upright posture with envy. *Must be nice not having to hide your height.*

As I straighten my aching back, Fannie says to the newcomers, "Let's get you inside."

We lead them to the East Workroom. They hang their hats and coats in the entranceway, and when the layers come off, I'm taken aback by what's beneath.

They are young. And thin. At least two hobble on a wooden leg. Some bear scars. Others are missing teeth. All have been roughened by wind and weather. Just one glance, and I know the stories of their hardships were no exaggeration.

Yet, as they take in the factory, hope lights their faces. As if they're the liberated tribes of Israel, and the East Workroom is their Promised Land.

Ida nudges me. "Go on, Mattie."

"Right," I stammer. We'd drawn straws beforehand to decide who'd do the explaining, and I got the short one.

My mouth goes dry as I step forward. I'm terrified I won't be able to train these men the way the boss wants. However, their eyes reflect only anticipation. No one seems to mind that an oversized girl is teaching them their job.

Heartened by that small mercy, I clear my throat. "We make two kinds of bags here. The first is the flat bag. These are the kind shopkeepers use for candies, buttons, and such. We make them using Machines 7 through 11." I gesture toward the row of bag machines. "Please watch."

They gather around as I throw the switches on Machine 11 and engage power. The machine whirs to life, and the men whistle in appreciation as it draws paper in one end and drops perfect bags out the other.

"The machine first turns the paper from a sheet into a tube, then sends it through rollers," I say, pointing out each process in turn. "Once a bag's length of tube comes through the rollers, a blade cuts it off. At the same time, the other end gets sealed with paste, and the bag falls into the delivery bin."

I take an armful of newly made bags. "Your job as operator is to bundle these bags. We bundle them in sets of one hundred." I demonstrate how to tie the stack with twine. "You must also replace the paper rolls and refill the paste reservoirs. All our supplies are on those shelves." The men's eyes follow my arm as I point to the back of the room.

"So," I say, switching off the machine, "any questions?"

The men stare mutely back. According to Mr. Yates, they have no factory experience, so I thought they'd be bursting with questions. I can't tell if they've truly no questions, or if they're so confused they don't know where to begin. I'm wondering if I've inadvertently insulted them when a tentative hand goes up.

It belongs to a broad-shouldered fellow with a mop of dark brown curls. Judging from the wispy mustache on his upper lip, he's a couple years older than I am. Judging from the inquisitive look in his dark eyes, he's curious, not insulted. "Yes," I say, a little too brightly.

"You said we'd be using Machines 7 through 11," he says in a voice rich and deep as molasses. "Does that mean that one's no good?" He points to the last machine in the row, which has a yellow "12" painted on the frame.

"Oh no, Machine 12 is fine," I say, relieved that I wasn't incomprehensible. "It's used to make our second bag, the square-bottomed kind. Shall I explain?"

The men nod, and I power Machine 12 on. "This machine works similar to the others," I say, as it draws paper from its roll. "But there's no pasting mechanism at the end, so what comes out are flat paper tubes." I lift a finished tube and separate the sides to show that both ends are open. "These we must fold by hand."

I scoop up several dozen tubes and take them to a worktable.

After tapping their edges to form a tidy stack, I lift the table's folding plate and slide them underneath. "To make the bag bottoms uniform, we use a folding plate," I explain.

Once in place, the stack extends four inches beyond the plate's edge, and I insert my index fingers through the opening of the topmost tube. "First is the diamond fold, which goes like so." I pin down the bottom lip of the tube with one finger while the other finger pulls the upper lip against the folding plate. The motion flips the paper into a diamond shape, and I crease it in place.

"Next," I say, "you fold down the top point and the bottom point." The second and third folds turn the diamond into a flattened hexagon, and I secure them in place with paste from a pot on the table.

"That makes a square-bottom bag," I say, slipping it out from under the plate and opening it to show the square bottom. "They're more expensive than flat bags, which means they're less common, but some shops like them because they hold as much as a box and they're quicker than wrapping paper and twine."

"So," Fannie pipes up, taking an armful of tubes from Machine 12, "are you gentlemen ready to fold bags with us?" She flashes a winsome smile, and the newcomers belt an enthusiastic "Yes!"

As Fannie giggles appreciatively, several men make sheep's eyes at her. They've been here less than a quarter hour, and half are already in love with her. I'm awed by the power of Fannie's feminine charm. Ida mutters something under her breath about youthful nonsense before saying, "Let's begin, then. Half of you can try the machines with me. Miss Foster will help the rest fold square-bottom bags at the worktables."

Ida's tone brooks no foolishness, and the men immediately separate into two groups. However, the curly-haired fellow raises his hand again. "Ma'am," he says, tipping his head respectfully, "I don't mind folding bags, but Mr. Yates said I was to train to be a mechanic."

"Oh yes, the new mechanic, I forgot," says Ida apologetically. "You follow Miss Knight, then."

As Ida turns her attention to the men at the bag machines, the mechanic-to-be offers me a handshake. "Pleased to meet you, Miss Knight."

"Just Mattie is fine," I say, shaking firmly. "And you are?"

"Frank Niebuhr. And just Frank is fine."

His smile is quick and friendly, and I immediately warm up to him. "Well, Frank," I say, "if you'll come this way."

As I lead him to the supply shelves, I notice he walks with a pronounced limp. With every stride, his body lurches side to side. However, he doesn't use a cane and has no trouble keeping up with me.

I gesture toward the shelves of tools, pulleys, belts, and oil-cans, and the wooden drawers that hold spare parts. "Everything you'll need to fix anything will be here. Grab that toolbox, and I'll take you to the engine room."

Frank slides the heavy toolbox off the bottom shelf and lifts it easily. "So what is the mechanic like?" he asks.

An icy gust blasts my sunny mood. "I beg your pardon?"

Frank scratches the back of his neck, looking antsy. "He's teaching me, so I want to get off on the right foot. I was hoping you might tell me what kind of man he is."

I stifle a groan. "Frank," I say slowly, "I'm the mechanic."

He stares back as if the gears of his brain have jammed. Then a blush flares from his collar to his ears. "I guess I really got off on the wrong foot just now," he says, head hanging.

I'm taken aback. I thought he'd laugh in my face or protest that a girl can't possibly be a mechanic. Instead, Frank is genuinely abashed. Which means he might actually respect what I can do. Hoping against hope this is the case, I say, "Well, I'll consider it water over the dam as long as you're willing to learn from me now."

His face brightens, and my spirits lift at his "Yes, ma'am!"

Chapter 4

THE FIRST THING OLD JAKE TAUGHT ME WAS HOW TO CHANGE bag size settings. Our machines can make half-pound to ten-pound bags, but must be adjusted to switch from one size to another. That's a mechanic's job, so while Old Jake made adjustments, most operators took a water break or used the necessary. I, on the other hand, would watch in fascination as he worked. One day, he got fed up with my staring and snapped for me to make myself useful and unscrew the machine's tube-former. I did so straightaway, and Old Jake discovered he had someone eager to do his bidding—so long as it had to do with machines.

After that, he showed me every trick he knew, but it wasn't out of a shared passion for machines. For him, being a mechanic was simply a way to earn a dollar. If I could manage the machines while he snuck a nip of rum by the millrace, all the better. So he always taught me what I wanted to learn, answered my questions thoroughly, and checked my work closely, but Old Jake never exhibited enthusiasm for the machinery he manipulated.

Frank is not like that.

He gazes longingly at the East Engine as he shuts it down for the day. "This beauty's amazing. If we could wrangle one home, cutting lumber would be easy."

"Oak Creek has an actual creek, doesn't it?" I ask as the engine's roar tapers to silence. "If there's running water, you can power a sawmill without steam."

Frank shakes his head. "Oak Creek's got hardly enough to water an ox, let alone turn a turbine. If it's getting power, it'll have to be steam." He contemplates the engine room piping. "Any chance we could take a gander at the boiler?"

While our Market Street workrooms are close to the depot

and telegraph, they are removed from the nearest millrace. In lieu of water power, the manufacturers on our block share steam piped from a common boiler. In truth, I've wanted a look at the boiler building myself. But . . .

"We need Mr. Yates's permission to leave during work hours," I say. "We also need him to make arrangements with the boiler engineer for us."

"Is that all?" Frank cocks his head. "Then I'll ask the Captain next time I see him."

From the way he grins, he's confident he'll get his way. Part of me is jealous, but more of me is grateful for that confidence; I'd never have the gumption to ask Mr. Yates, and if Frank succeeds, I reap the rewards, too.

We leave the thick walls of the engine room for the work-room proper. Quitting bell rang several minutes ago, and everyone else has already left. With the engine off, the only sound is the clink and thud of our tools as we return them to the supply shelf. Out of the corner of my eye, I note that Frank is putting everything in its proper place. Once he slides the last drawer shut, I say, "Frank Niebuhr, I do believe you're ready to take charge of this workroom."

His eyes snap up at me, aglow with excitement. "You mean that?"

I nod as I unpin my apron. Over the last two weeks, Frank's been my shadow from starting to quitting bell. As I guessed, his limp doesn't interfere at all. If anything, he's a natural mechanic. We've taken two machines apart and reassembled them, and he quickly grasped how the parts meshed together. He's also good with tools; apparently, when anything in his platoon broke, he was the one to fix it. Little wonder Mr. Yates thought he'd make a good mechanic.

"I'll be across the yard if a machine throws a conniption fit, but I'm sure you'll do fine on your own," I say, holding out my hand.

But as I give him a hearty congratulatory shake, I feel a little sad. With Frank able to oversee the East Workroom alone, I'll return to the West Workroom. That means we'll only see each other in passing from now on.

Just then, approaching footsteps thump outside, and Ida's head pokes through the door. "There you are, Mattie! I've been looking all over for you."

"Is something wrong?" I ask, reaching for my coat. "Did I forget something in the West Workroom?"

"No. It's just . . ." Ida hesitates, twisting her shawl tassels. "Eliza gave Sam some old tracing cloth today. He's so excited, he begged for you to come tonight. I know you've had a long day, but . . ."

"I'd be delighted." Turning to Frank, I say, "Sam is Ida's little boy. I promised I'd help him make a kite once he got all the pieces."

"A kite?" His gaze flits to the grayish snow piled in the delivery yard. "It's February."

"Making it now will give him something to do by the fire, and once the weather clears, he'll be ready to play," I say, donning my hat and mittens. "Well, Frank, good night—"

"Can I help?"

I start at Frank's offer. Ida looks equally surprised as she replies, "That's kind of you, but I couldn't possibly impose—"

"It's no imposition. Making a kite sounds fun." Frank flashes his cocksure grin. "Will you let me join?"

My heart dances at the prospect of more time with him, and I grin back. "Sure."

❄ ❄ ❄

A brisk five-minute walk later, we arrive at Ida's house on Pynchon Street. The front of the two-story wood-frame house is dark, and Frank and I follow Ida around to the back. "My mother-in-law takes laundry," she explains to Frank, as we pass washtubs and pails stacked beneath a lean-to. "The weather being what it is, we got clotheslines everywhere inside except a small space in the kitchen."

He frowns. "Your husband died fighting for the Union. Don't you get a pension?"

Ida lets out a bitter laugh. "It's barely enough for one, and we've four mouths to feed. Fortunately, Mother Sarah is still strong. So long as she stays strong, we can send Clara and Sam to school instead of to work."

We enter the back door to the smell of simmering pea soup and drying laundry. But sitting at the kitchen table is only one child, not two, and beside the little boy isn't old Mrs. Leavilte but a fine-boned young woman in well-tailored plaid dress with a yellow bow over her bosom.

"Eliza, what are you doing here?" I say, as Sam scurries to his mother for a kiss. "Don't tell me you left Uncle Thomas to starve?"

She giggles. "Nothing so cruel and unusual. Two of his armory friends came to call, and they went to sup at Ripley's tavern tonight. I knew Ida was asking you over, so I figured I'd join, too. Besides, I found ribbon scraps this afternoon." Her slender fingers lift a piece of twine with multicolored bows tied along its length. "I thought they'd make a good tail."

"They would indeed." I turn to Frank, who's wiping his boots on the doormat. "Frank, this is Eliza MacFarland. I share a room with her at her uncle's house across the street."

"Frank Niebuhr," he says, stepping inside. "I heard there was kite-making afoot and asked to join. A pleasure to meet you, Miss Eliza."

Eliza jumps as if she's been bit. "How do y-you do?" she stammers, flushing crimson.

I stifle a sigh. Eliza is the daughter of a Boston headmaster and the smartest girl I know. She's also the timidest. When she gets nervous, her wits scatter, and she stutters. Badly. As such, she could never show off her booklearning at spelling bees and recitations. Her parents dearly want her to be a schoolteacher like her older sister, but because of her nerves, she's failed the teacher's exam three times now. Which is a shame because when Eliza's calm, she's exceedingly well-spoken.

As Eliza tentatively exchanges a handshake with Frank, Ida asks Sam, "Where are Clara and Nana?"

"Upstairs," he says. "Clara ran out when Nana said not to, and *bang*! Blood got everywhere—"

"C-Clara fell and b-bloodied her nose," Eliza cuts in. "Mrs. Leavilte is c-cleaning her up."

Ida groans. "I'd best lend Mother Sarah a hand. Be right back."

I wave her off. "We'll be fine. After all, we've a kite to make." I ruffle Sam's blond hair.

As Ida sidles out between lines of drying linen, I clap my hands and say, "Now, where's that tracing cloth?"

While Sam helps Eliza clear the table and lay out the fabric she brought, I go to the stove. Amid the herbs and pots hanging above the simmering soup are several spruce sticks, each about a yard long. I take them down and give them to Frank. "These should be good and dry. Pick the best three and whittle them to three-eighths by a quarter inch."

"Yes, ma'am." Frank gives me a jaunty salute, then turns to Sam. "Hello, little fellow," he says, bending to meet Sam's eyes. "I don't suppose you can find me a knife?"

"Here," I say, taking out my jackknife. "I just sharpened the blade, so it should do the job fine."

I coax the knife's stubborn hinge open and offer it to Frank, who stares as if I've conjured a live goat from my pocket. "Mattie, do you carry a knife all the time or just on special occasions?"

Eliza laughs. "Mattie wouldn't be Mattie if she didn't have a tool or two on her," she says, more relaxed now. "In fact, I daresay she and I would never have met if that wasn't so."

Frank's confusion turns to curiosity. "Sounds like a story there," he says, taking the knife and dropping onto a chair.

"It's nothing," I huff, rummaging through the Leavilte sewing basket for fabric shears. "I only did what any other person would do."

"See, I moved here last winter," says Eliza, ignoring me. "Uncle Thomas broke his leg slipping off his porch, and my parents sent me to help. But I'd never been to Springfield, so Ida kindly sent little Sam through the snow to the depot to fetch me and my baggage. Isn't that right, Sam?"

Sam nods emphatically. "I brought a sled for her things. She had three boxes this big!" He flings his arms wide.

"The amount I brought was excessive," says Eliza with a touch of embarrassment. "But I didn't know how long Uncle would convalesce, and Mother insisted I . . ." she trails off before continuing. "Well, anyway, we would've had trouble carrying just one trunk, but the sled slid along with all three nicely. However, we'd only gone a block when—"

"Crash!" cries Sam. "All the boxes fell."

"Just so. The sled had broken. So there I am in an unfamiliar town, my worldly possessions spilled upon the snow, with no idea how I would convey them to Uncle's house, when, lo!" Eliza clasps her hands in a dramatic pose. "Out of the post office, a savior appeared. Mattie whipped out her tools, and within two shakes of a lamb's tail, she'd resurrected the sled."

Frank's eyes twinkle at Eliza's theatrics. I groan. "She's exaggerating," I say. "It was only a runner that had come loose. Anyone could have fixed it."

"It was a divine appointment, as far as I'm concerned," declares Eliza, hands on her hips. "Because I didn't merely get help, I got a dear friend."

"In that case, I got the better part of the bargain." Turning to Frank, I say, "Up till last May, I was boarding at Mrs. Dwight's, where it's four to a room and dinners are boiled cabbage and brick-hard bread. Then Eliza convinced her uncle to let me move in. Now I pay a third less, and I room with an angel and eat like a queen."

Eliza sniffs. "Now you're exaggerating."

"And she does my laundry and mending to boot," I go on. "Speaking of which, if you need mending, Eliza takes in sewing. She's the best seamstress I know. See that dress she's wearing? She made it entirely herself."

Frank stops whittling. "Is that right?"

Eliza's cheeks color at his admiring look. "M-Mattie, stop. I'm sure F-Frank's mother or sweetheart is s-sewing his shirts."

Frank laughs, the sonorous sound filling the room. "If only that were so. It's only my Pa and four younger brothers in Oak Creek, and they can't sew a stitch. As for a sweetheart, the Good Lord hasn't blessed me with one yet, so you will get a shirt order once I got the money, Miss Eliza."

Eliza squeaks out thanks, delighted at the prospect of a new customer. My heart pounds, too, but not because I'm happy for her. Like Eliza, I had assumed Frank was spoken for. The knowledge that he's not makes me giddy.

Stop, snaps the sensible part of me. *Just because he's got no sweetheart doesn't mean he's interested in courting, let alone courting a factory girl taller than him.*

Yet I can't stop smiling the rest of the evening.

Chapter 5

FEMALE CHATTER FILLS THE WEST WORKROOM ENTRANCEWAY
when I arrive. It always buzzes while we trade our coats and shawls
for work aprons, but this morning's noise is giddier than usual.

That's because it's Valentine's Day.

"Mattie, look!" Fannie skips away from a group giggling over
romantic tokens to show me a handful of heart-covered cards. "I
suspected one of those Maryland boys might be sweet on me, but
four?"

She squeals with delighted surprise, but I'm not the least astonished. I've seen how the Marylanders' eyes follow her. She's
sure to have more valentines by quitting bell. "Be gentle if you
need to break some hearts," I say. "We don't need a brawl in the
yard over you."

Fannie laughs. "Mattie, you're so silly," she says, tucking the
cards into her apron pocket. "Now, where's your card? I want to
see."

"My card?" I blink, wondering how she knew. "It's not much
to look at."

"Show me." Fannie clamps onto my arm, chanting a singsong
"Show me, show me . . ."

"Fine." Shaking her off, I reach into my coat pocket and hand
the card over.

Fannie's brow puckers at the sloppy flowers painted on wrinkled brown paper. The furrows deepen as she reads the block letters penciled across the top. "Happy sixteenth birthday, Mattie?
Thank you for the kite?"

"My boy made that." Ida puffs up like a proud hen. "Sam's
handwriting needs work, but he spelled it right."

Fannie nods. "I see . . . wait!" She whirls back to me. "Today's your birthday?"

I shrug as I pin my apron. "Holidays can be birthdays."

"Then Frank Niebuhr definitely should've gotten you something," she cries, stamping her foot.

Heat sears my cheeks, and I pluck the card from Fannie's fingers. "Fannie," I say in a low voice. "There is no earthly reason Frank *should* give me anything today."

"But you two are thick as thieves," Fannie insists. "You're always talking."

"About work."

"He walked you home every night last week."

I brandish Sam's card. "Frank walked me *and* Ida to her house. We were making toys for her kids."

Fannie begins another retort, but the bell cuts her off. "Time for work," I say, leaving her with her jaw hanging.

I quickly put distance between us. I don't begrudge Fannie and the others their valentines, but I have more important things to dwell over. Mother's letter in yesterday's post was a stark reminder of that.

When I left school for the factories, it was supposed to be temporary. Just until the war ended and my brother retook his place as the family breadwinner. But when Charlie finally returned, he was broken in body and spirit. So I continued working while Mother nursed him. Two years later, his body is restored, but his spirit ... according to yesterday's letter, nightmares still plague him, and when Mother brought him to a carpentry shop in hopes of getting him hired, he collapsed into a sobbing, quivering heap.

Mother's applied for veteran's aid, but red tape bogs her at every turn. She can't leave Charlie alone, so she sews piecework at home, but it's not enough to make ends meet.

That means I must make up the difference.

Squaring my shoulders, I grab my tool box and set about to do exactly that.

❄ ❄ ❄

I was right. By day's end, Fannie has two more valentines.

I laugh to myself as six Maryland men position themselves around her after quitting bell. One of Fannie's would-be sweethearts had asked to walk her home, and immediately the whole lot clamored to do the same. Fannie being Fannie, she didn't know how to choose, so they decided to all walk together.

As they leave, looking like the Queen of England and her honor guard, I think, *This is certainly a memorable Valentine's Day for Fannie.*

I can't say the same for myself.

With a sigh, I finish sweeping the paper bits around Machine 5. Its cutting blade had jammed an hour before lunch, and by the time we shut it off, thirty feet of paper had snarled its inner workings. So I spent most the day disassembling, clearing out, and reassembling the machine.

As I pluck paper shreds from my bun, I remember how Fannie hounded me about Frank. If circumstances were different, I might daydream about him, just a little. But the reality is, I have a family depending on me. He does, too. Instead of getting heartsick for the impossible, I'll be grateful for what I do have: a friend who shares my fascination for machines.

I get ready to leave, but as I button my coat, Frank bursts into the workroom. "There you are, Mattie," he cries. "I thought I missed you."

"Machine 5 was a mule today," I say, putting on my hat. "Had to take it apart and wanted to make sure it worked right before I left."

A frown replaces Frank's frazzled look. "You should've told me. I would've helped."

"My machine, my problem." I cock my head. "Anyway, did you need me for something?" The Leaviltes are helping finish a wedding quilt this week, so Frank and I aren't going to Ida's tonight.

At my question, nervousness invades his features, and he fidgets, hemming and hawing. Puzzled by his antsiness, I say, "Frank? What's wrong?"

He stiffens, as if bracing to leap off a cliff. Then, with uncharacteristic timidity, he takes a small wrapped object from his pocket and places it in my hands.

My eyes go wide. Penciled on the brown paper are the words: Happy Birthday.

I swallow hard. "How did you know?"

"Open it."

A blush flames his cheeks, and I can feel my own face and ears burning. The cold, empty workroom suddenly feels too close, too hot. Unable to hold his gaze, my eyes drop to the parcel. I peel the wrapping with fumbling fingers and gasp.

Nestled in the paper is a jackknife. It's the same size as the one in my pocket, but there the similarities end. Mine is nicked and pitted, the point long since honed away, the wooden handle scratched. This one gleams with a virgin shine and boasts not one, but two blades. Its rounded contours rest comfortably against my palms, as if begging to be used. And carved into the handle's otherwise pristine finish are the letters "MK."

My knees go weak. "Frank . . . it's beautiful. But why?"

He cracks a smile, seemingly relieved. "Why?" he says, rubbing the back of his neck. "Because as good as you take care of your jackknife, it's bound to break any day now. And I figured having a pen blade along with the hawksbill one would—"

"No, no." I shake my head. "I meant why give me anything at all? We've only just met."

His dark gaze softens. "Maybe that's true," he says, reaching to cup his hands around mine. "Maybe we haven't known each other long. But I would very much like to know you better, Miss

Mattie Knight."

A hurricane whirls my stomach. I'm keenly aware of his touch, the warmth of his calloused skin. Giddiness threatens to overwhelm me as we stand, my hands in his.

Then he folds my fingers over his gift and withdraws with a whispered "Happy birthday."

The next thing I know, he's gone, his uneven footsteps fading in a rapid retreat.

I stare out the open doorway, my mind blank as a fresh sheet of paper. The February wind snatches my hair, but I don't feel a chill. All I'm aware of is the hammering of my heart and the memory of our hands pressed together.

"Mattie?"

I jump at Mr. Mowe's voice. His tall frame bundled in a shapeless wool coat, he tramps over from the office with the workroom keys. "Are you all right?" he asks.

My stalled brain jolts back into high speed. "I'm fine," I blurt, pocketing the jackknife.

The concern in his bespectacled gaze only deepens. "Are you certain? You've been standing here a good two minutes."

Two minutes? But I mask my shock with a smile and say, "All's well, Mr. Mowe. Good night." And before he can pry further, I rush off.

As I exit the factory grounds, my fingers curl around Frank's gift in my pocket. Joy thrills my being, and I fly down the gaslit streets. I want to shout, to sing, to laugh aloud. I'd presumed this birthday would be another mundane workday, but it is the best day in my sixteen-year existence.

I would very much like to know you better, Miss Mattie Knight.

I'm breathless when I reach the front gate, and not just from the sprint home. Fannie was right. I didn't dare hope to be more than Frank's friend, but he sees me as special. Special enough for a gift so lavish—

Suddenly, cold realization spears my reverie. Snatching up Frank's gift, I hold it beneath the glow of a streetlamp. I scrutinize the knife, the maker's stamp on the tang. Quick calculations run through my mind, and at the end of those sums is crushing guilt.

I dash inside. Uncle Thomas's coat, cap, and cane are gone from the entryway. However, Eliza's bonnet and cloak hang in their place, and light emanates from the upstairs room we share. I bound up the carpeted steps, taking them two at a time.

I burst in to find Eliza in the narrow space between our beds, sorting bolts of linen on the braided rug. "Welcome home," she says brightly. "Uncle's at an elders' meeting, so supper is—"

I thrust the jackknife under her nose. "Frank gave me this," I say, my breathing ragged from exertion and panic. "For my birthday."

She blinks. Then a giggle escapes her. "It's hardly a romantic token, but he knows what suits you—"

"I can't keep it." I place the jackknife atop our dresser with a definitive clunk. "It's not right."

Eliza's eyebrows knit as I sink onto my bed. "Why? I thought you were fond of him. And he seems like such a fine young man."

"Which is why I can't let him do this." I grip my head in my hands. "Eliza, the knife . . . it's too much. He's got a father and brothers depending on him. He can't afford to give me this."

I would know. The wages at Columbia Paper are sufficient for a single person, but those with dependents must walk a tightrope to make ends meet. Not to mention, Frank and his fellow Marylanders began at a deficit. Because they owed Mr. Yates for travel expenses and their first two weeks' lodging, they didn't receive their first pay until last Saturday.

I glance at the jackknife, and conscience stabs again. A penny Valentine card, like those Fannie got, is one thing, but a fine knife . . .

"Even if Frank sent nothing home, he wouldn't have enough

for that knife," I groan. "He's boarding at Mrs. Parish's, and you know she charges five dollars a week. I'd feel badly enough about him spending on me instead of his family, but he can't be borrowing because he's sweet on me."

"Mattie—"

"The right thing would be to return it," I continue miserably. "But he marked my initials on the handle, so the store won't take it back. And I've got no savings to—"

"Mattie!"

Eliza grips my shoulders hard, startling me silent. As I gape, she heaves a sigh. "Mattie, I assure you, Frank's circumstances aren't as dire as you imagine."

My brain racks. "How? We have the same job, and I can't afford that knife on $1.25 a day."

"True," says Eliza. "But Frank's not paid your wage. He's paid a man's wage."

My train of thought derails with a crash. "What?"

"If you need convincing . . ." Eliza takes an envelope from her handbag and hands it to me. "I was actually at Mrs. Parish's at noontime. Frank told his friends about me, and two wanted to place orders. This is what we agreed on."

I open the envelope, and my world turns upside down.

Chapter 6

THE FOLLOWING MORNING IS CRISP, A NEW LAYER OF FROST glazing the company office's low-pitched roof. But I don't feel cold. In fact, I'm hot enough to burn down all of Market Street.

Stomping up the porch steps, I shove open the front door—and collide into Mr. Mowe.

"Oh, I'm terribly sorry . . . Mattie?" Alarm floods the junior bookkeeper's face when he recognizes me. "Is something wrong? Has a machine broken?"

"Something is wrong, but not with the machines," I say, my gaze flicking over his shoulder to scan for the boss. "I wish to speak to Mr. Yates. Where is he?"

"Out. They finished demolishing the old bag annex yesterday, and he's inspecting the site before the paper mill expansion begins. He should be back any moment though, so please have a seat." He points to a chair beside a door that bears a plaque engraved with Mr. Yates's name. "Now if you'll excuse me, the office lad is sick, so I've got to fetch the post." With a tip of his battered felt hat, he exits the building.

I cross the room to the chair. In contrast to the workrooms, which are only heated enough to take the edge off the cold, the office is cozy, and the aroma of coffee emanates from the kettle steaming upon the potbelly stove. As I shrug off my coat and sit, the senior bookkeeper and the two office clerks watch from behind their desks as if I'm a dragon who's emerged from the henhouse. After all, I never come near the office, except to receive my pay on Saturdays, and I've never actually stepped inside.

Under different circumstances, their stares would've cowed me, but I glare back with righteous indignation. Their eyes immediately drop to their papers. That gives me no satisfaction, though. Rather, wrath mounts at the thought of the figures inside their ledgers.

Of the higher wages allocated to the East Workroom men.

I couldn't believe it at first. I still don't want to. But the sums on Eliza's order sheet and the coins she received in payment don't lie. Flabbergasted, I went to old Mrs. Leavilte, who takes laundry for the matrons boarding the Marylanders, and she confirmed what Eliza told me.

Instead of the dollar-a-day wage the women receive for making bags, the male bag workers get $1.30. That's five cents more than my wage as mechanic!

The scrape of the front door interrupts my stormy thoughts. In a twinkling, the office staff is on its feet, chorusing, "Good morning, Mr. Yates."

The boss responds with a perfunctory nod. With the air of a commander addressing his troops, he says, "Gentlemen, preparations have passed muster. We can finalize the contracts for the mill expansion. Bring me all relevant paperwork along with the summary sheet for this week's payroll."

At that last word, I jump up. "Mr. Yates—"

"And you, girl," he adds offhandedly as he removes his lambskin gloves, "bring me a cup of coffee."

I bristle. Before I can think better of it, I snap, "Mr. Yates, I am a mechanic. I'm paid to run machines, not bring you coffee."

The atmosphere in the room turns glacial. Mr. Yates faces me, his hawkish nose flaring in disapproval. I merely lift my chin and glower from my superior height. Meanwhile, the office staff pale as if they've been caught between two dueling gunmen.

Finally, Mr. Yates breaks the silence. "The girl mechanic," he says coolly. "I see. Since you are not here to distribute coffee, I assume you have other business with me."

"You assume rightly," I respond with equal frost.

Mr. Yates purses his lips, then strides to his office door.

"Excuse me, gentlemen. We'll resume as soon as I'm done speaking with Miss . . ."

"Miss Knight," I supply.

"Right." Mr. Yates unlocks the door with a brass key and waves me in.

The small room beyond is as primly pretentious as the man who occupies it. Curtains of lace and blue velvet adorn the window, and a matching plush carpet covers the floor. The morning light sparkles off the brass handles of a towering cabinet letter file and the polished face of a pendulum clock.

Mr. Yates shuts the door, and as he takes the leather wingback behind his oak desk, I realize, to my annoyance, that it's the only chair in the room.

I glare down my nose at him. If he's not courteous enough to offer a seat, I've no qualms letting him feel the shortness of his stature.

"As you can see, Miss Knight, I'm a busy man," says Mr. Yates, removing his pocketwatch and winding it. "State your business and be quick about it."

With equal brusqueness, I say, "Mr. Yates, I have it on good authority that you are paying the East Workroom men thirty percent more than the West Workroom workers."

He doesn't bat an eye. "What of it?"

"It's unfair. They've been here scarcely a month. Some have only just got the hang of—"

"Miss Knight," says Mr. Yates, with the forbearance of a schoolmaster instructing an especially dull pupil, "you are young, so I will forgive your ignorance and enlighten you to common business practice. And common business practice is that men's wages are higher than women's."

I bite back a scream. I'm well aware of the practice. I've known it since my first job at the Amoskeag Mill back in New Hampshire. Women got three-quarters the men's pay, and children only half that amount. The mills justified it by saying the men had the harder task hauling raw cotton and finished bolts than the women operating the looms or the children sweeping and doffing bobbins. And it was difficult to argue with the mills because our tasks were divided by age and sex.

That is not the case here.

"Is it not also common business practice to pay the same wage to workers at the same task?" I retort. "Everyone in the East and West Workrooms are doing the exact same job. And if you compared bag output—"

Mr. Yates snorts. "Surely you don't expect me to believe a factory of women is as competent as one run by men? Science has proven the physique of the sterner sex is designed for the rigors of the working world, whereas the fairer sex lacks such stamina. And the clothes you women wear . . ." He sniffs. "Entirely impractical in an industrial setting."

I'm seized by the urge to strangle him by his striped silk cravat. If I could exchange my skirt for trousers without drawing wholesale condemnation, I would. "Mr. Yates, with all due respect—"

"Not to mention," he adds, returning his watch to his waistcoat pocket, "women lack mechanical aptitude. Leave a woman unsupervised with factory equipment, and she's certain to break it."

"I beg your pardon," I growl, "but I am this factory's mechanic. Every bag machine here, I set up by myself. I maintain them. I fix them. They run because I make them run."

"Perhaps so. Perhaps you are an anomaly among womankind. You're certainly anomalous in another respect." His eyes make an exaggerated sweep from my boots to the top of my six-foot frame. "However, even if you've attained some mastery over machines, they still work best under a man's touch."

"Might I remind you," I grind out, "Frank Niebuhr only knows what he knows about this factory because I taught him."

"And I have full confidence that his skills will exceed yours in the near future."

My vision goes red. But before I explode, Mr. Yates says, "You speak as if I was indebted to you somehow. As if you were indispensable to this company. If you are under that particular impression, I advise you to rid yourself of that notion, lest you find yourself without employment."

The rage searing my veins chokes and fizzles into dismay. Regarding me like a troublesome nag he's tempted to shoot, Mr. Yates huffs, "My grandfather was a good businessman, but age has made him maudlin. The thought of his faithful employees suffering on account of company changes so agitated him, I had to promise not to alter the existing workforce before he handed it over. As a man of honor, I will uphold my promise, but given the choice, I would've hired a real mechanic and returned you to a factory girl my first day."

Before I can feel any sort of relief, he adds, "However, stir up trouble, and you will no longer be deemed a 'faithful employee' protected by that promise. Am I clear?"

His eyes bore into mine, daring me to contradict him. I can only lower my head and reply, "Very clear, sir."

As I stare at my boots, hating my powerlessness, Mr. Yates sighs and leans back in his chair. "It's incomprehensible to me why a girl would get so agitated over wages, and even less comprehensible why you're set on being a mechanic."

Frustration claws my throat. I doubt I could make him understand my fascination with machines when most women find it perplexing. But perhaps I can make him understand what a difference equal pay would make.

Keeping a humble tone, I say, "The thing is, sir, I have two dependents. Even a few more cents a day would mean a great deal to us."

"What dependents could a girl like you have?" he scoffs.

He was a Union captain. He's helping his old troop. Appeal to his sense of charity.

"My mother in New Hampshire is a widow. As for my brother, Charlie, he enlisted the day he turned eighteen, and he returned to us unable to work. And because he joined a Massachusetts company instead of a New Hampshire one, he's had trouble getting a veteran's pension."

The boss's glare softens a touch. "I've heard pension applications for out-of-state enlistees have been mired in red tape," he says after a pause. "If you explain his circumstances more fully, perhaps I can petition the state Pension Commission on his behalf. In the meantime, he can work in the East Workroom as a bag folder. Provided that, of course, he has both hands."

Hope sparks in my chest. "I appreciate that, truly I do," I say. "But even though Charlie's got his two hands, he can't work. You see, he's got Soldier's Heart."

The sympathy on Mr. Yates's face vanishes. "Then, Miss Knight," he says, rising abruptly, "I've nothing more to say other than your family had better stop coddling your brother."

He starts to leave, but I block his path. "Wait," I say, bewildered. "Why—"

"Let me be blunt," he cuts me off. "A real man provides for his family. What your brother needs is not charity but a hard kick in the pants."

My hands clench. "How can you say that? My brother served this country—"

"As did I," Mr. Yates retorts. "As did every man in the East Workroom. We all fought, suffered, and bled out there. Some even lost a leg. And when it ended, we resumed our responsibilities as husbands and sons."

"Charlie's tried to do that," I insist. "But he gets overwhelmed. His nightmares—"

"As far as I'm concerned, the proof of a man's character is in his actions. Has Frank Niebuhr told you how he got his limp?"

I blink at the mention of Frank and shake my head. Although I have wondered about his leg, I thought it would be rude to pry.

"He was only thirteen when the Oak Creek men enlisted, and, determined to go along, he volunteered as a camp helper. One day, their regiment got word of a skirmish outside camp. A surgeon was dispatched to treat the wounded, and Frank rode along to assist him. On the way, enemy riders spotted them and gave chase.

"Had Frank fled in that instant, no one would've blamed him. He wasn't a soldier; he wasn't even receiving pay. But he knew men were depending on that doctor. So he told the doctor to ride ahead while he distracted the Rebs. Thanks to Frank, he made it safely, and lives were saved. But it came at a cost. A Reb shot Frank's horse, and his leg was crushed when it fell."

Mr. Yates pauses to let his words sink in. And indeed, I am stunned. I suspected that Frank sustained an injury, but never imagined those circumstances.

"Frank Niebuhr is a man of integrity and courage," Mr. Yates declares, his voice ringing with judgment. "His limp testifies to that. But an able-bodied man who would burden his widowed mother and unwed sister? I see only proof of sloth and cowardice."

My brother's not a coward, I want to scream. But I can't. Because what the boss says is true. The trembling wreck in my mother's home bears no resemblance to the brave, strong man who marched to battle. And because Charlie's wounds cannot be seen, I have nothing solid to counter Mr. Yates's accusation.

The fight drains out of me, and Mr. Yates shoulders past. "Now if you'll excuse me, I have a company to run. And you'd best return to work before I deem it proof of your indolence."

He throws open the oak door, and a tumult assaults our ears. The senior bookkeeper and clerks are clustered around Mr. Mowe in the entryway, all talking at once.

"What's going on?" booms Mr. Yates, silencing the commotion. "This is an orderly place of business, not a county auction."

Mr. Mowe, still in his hat and coat, steps forward with an open letter. "Sir, we have a problem."

My ears prick up at the word "problem." It is un-Christian to wish ill upon another, but at this instant, I hope all the plagues of Egypt descend upon Mr. Yates.

Curious, I take my time donning my coat. As I fasten the buttons as slowly as possible, Mr. Mowe says, "Jordan Marsh and Company sent this. They want to purchase bags for their department store starting next month."

"Sounds like good news to me," says Mr. Yates, taking the letter from Mr. Mowe. "How is a new client a problem?"

Mr. Mowe points to the bottom of the sheet. "They don't want flat bags. They only want square-bottom ones. In these quantities."

Mr. Yates's eyes bulge from their sockets. As I wonder what numbers unsettled him so, Mr. Mowe adds, "Apparently, your sales talk worked too well. From the looks of it, Jordan Marsh is doing away with boxes and wrapping paper entirely in favor of square-bottom bags."

"Well," says Mr. Yates, recovering swiftly, "it does exceed current capacity, but this is a good problem and not an unsolvable one. We can shift production from flat to square-bottom bags, and I'm certain East Workroom output can increase to meet this demand."

I suppress a snort. *Already crediting your men with success, are you?*

Despite the boss's confident reassurance, Mr. Mowe's brow remains pinched. "If the East Workroom rises to the challenge, that resolves this situation, but there's a good chance we'll encounter trouble down the road if a new trend begins."

Mr. Yates frowns but gestures for the young bookkeeper to

explain. "Jordan Marsh sets the fashion for Boston stores," says Mr. Mowe. "If all our Boston clients start changing their orders of wrapping paper and flat bags to square-bottom bags, the bag folders won't be able to keep up."

"One more thing," says the senior bookkeeper, waddling up with a leatherbound ledger. He riffles through the pages and holds it up to Mr. Yates. "The profit on flat bags is nearly double that of square-bottom bags. If the flat bag machines stand idle while workers hand fold square-bottom ones, then . . ."

His pencil scratches something into the margin, and Mr. Yates's arrogant air evaporates. Grimmer than I've ever seen him, he holds a hushed exchange with the bookkeeper over the ledger, scribbling figures all the while.

"That would be a quandary," says Mr. Yates a few moments later. He straightens with a scowl. "If only the confounded machines could make square-bottom ones, too."

At those words, inspiration strikes, dazzling as a lightning bolt. *If the man needs proof to acknowledge a woman's skill, I'll give it to him.*

"Mr. Yates," I call out, startling the men. As they frown, clearly baffled that I'm still in the room, I approach the boss and smile. "May I offer a proposition?"

Chapter 7

At church the next day, Reverend Parsons preaches on the Apocalypse. While I've occasionally imagined reuniting with my father in Heaven, I've never thought much about End Times.

But when Fannie sees me in the Fellowship Hall after service, she charges over as if I've unleashed all Four Horsemen and the Harlot of Babylon upon Springfield. "Mattie, I heard about your deal with Mr. Yates. What were you thinking?"

I groan into my coffee cup. I knew word would spread through the factory quickly, but I didn't think Judgment Day would arrive till Monday. The gossips are more industrious than I thought.

Beside me, Eliza tilts her head as she nibbles on her coffeecake. "What are you raving about, Fannie?"

Fannie whirls on her. "I'm talking about the bet she struck with the boss!"

Eliza chokes into a coughing fit. As I slap her on the back, I glare daggers at Fannie. "Not so loud," I hiss. "Are you trying to get me into trouble?"

While gambling is not listed as a sin in the Good Book, the First Congregational elders deem it a gateway to perdition, and chief among them is Uncle Thomas. Fortunately, he's whisker-deep in his own coffeecake and oblivious to all else. Thus, I'm spared his disapproval and a lecture about the evils of gambling.

I am not, however, spared Eliza's dismay. "Mattie, is that true?" she gasps once her throat clears.

"It's more a proposal than a bet," I say, wishing I could permanently fasten Fannie's mouth shut.

Eliza crosses her arms. "Explain this 'proposal,' then."

Huffing in frustration, I say, "Yesterday, I told Mr. Yates it was unfair that the men get paid more than the women. He said it was fair because men are better with machines. So I said I'd prove him wrong by building an improved bag machine."

Eliza blinks. "An improved bag machine?"

I nod. "You know the square-bottom bags we fold by hand? I'm going to make a machine that makes them from start to finish."

"That's not all," Fannie interjects. "She's contending against Frank!"

Eliza gives a start. "What does Frank have to do with it?"

Nothing. At least, he wasn't supposed to.

The original stakes I proposed were equal wages, if I succeeded in making a working machine. However, Mr. Yates added his own condition, one I could not rightly refuse.

"Mr. Yates said I couldn't claim to be the better mechanic without a fair competition. So he's having Frank build a machine also, and we'll contend at the company's anniversary party in September. The machine that makes the most sellable bags wins, and if I win, Mr. Yates will pay the women same as the men."

"And if F-Frank wins?" says Eliza, her stutter creeping into her voice.

"I return to being an ordinary hand. But," I add when Eliza pales to the whiteness of her lace collar, "I do not intend to lose."

Fannie shakes her head. "You've lost your mind. You've made a good thing of your mechanic job, and I know your family needs the extra pay. I can't believe you're risking it like this."

I clench my jaw. Mr. Yates clearly thinks I'll fail. My blood boils remembering his mocking offer to buy my machine, should I win. But I expected my friends to have more faith. Judging from Fannie's exasperation and Eliza's disbelief, they also need convincing.

"It's not a risk," I say. "I would never have proposed it if I didn't think I was able."

"This is different than replacing broken parts," Fannie protests. "You have to invent something completely new."

"But Mattie has experience inventing things," Ida cuts in, striding over with her four-year-old daughter in tow.

Clapping a hand on my shoulder, Ida counters the younger women's doubt with the conviction of a revivalist preacher. "I'll have you two know, you stand in the presence of the inventor of the loom-shuttle restraining device," she declares.

"Restraining device?" echoes Fannie. Eliza's face screws in incomprehension.

Ida sighs. "Neither of you worked the cotton mills, so I'll pardon your ignorance. Suffice to say, it is an invention that has protected many a worker from harm. And if Mattie can conceive and create such a device, she'll surely find a way to fold square-bottom bags by machine."

Eliza's eyes glow with newfound respect. Fannie's frown, however, remains. "What about Frank?" she says.

I shrug. No one knows better than me how quickly he picked things up in the factory. "He's a smart young man. I suspect he'll give me a run for my money."

"That's not what I mean," Fannie cries, looking fit to burst a corset stay. "Frank's sweet on you. Do this, and you'll lose your only chance at a beau."

Ida elbows Fannie hard. "Don't talk about Mattie like she's a flea-bitten mongrel who can't find a home."

"I didn't mean it like that!"

Suddenly, Eliza seizes my arm. "M-Mattie," she says, pointing toward the hall entrance with her free hand. "L-look!"

I turn around and nearly drop my coffee. Standing at the threshold in his Sunday best is Frank Niebuhr. He spies us the same instant we see him, and we fall silent as he limps across the crowded space to our corner. "Hello, ladies," he says, tipping his cap.

Cotton fills my lungs. Although the greeting goes to us all, his eyes lock on me.

"Frank, what a surprise," Fannie squeaks, smiling nervously. "I thought you attended the Baptist Church."

"I do," says Frank, his manner uncharacteristically stiff. "But I dropped in because I hoped to find Mattie here. Mattie, can we talk? In private?"

"Of course." The words come out automatically. Just as automatically, I follow him out of the Fellowship Hall. My mind, however, is a whirlwind.

I haven't seen him since Valentine's Day, and now we're on opposing sides like Romeo and Juliet. As an employee, Frank's obliged to follow the boss's orders, so I'd never hold it against him. However, from his grim expression, I'm worried his heart might've gotten the better of his head. *Did he refuse Mr. Yates? Did they fight? Is Frank in trouble?*

As we exit to clear, crisp skies, I pray that Frank hasn't been dismissed on account of me. On the other side of the wrought iron fence that separates the church grounds from Court Square, Sam and his friends race across the mud with his new kite. It catches the breeze, soaring skyward, and I wonder if Frank and I can rise above what comes.

He halts at a quiet spot in the church garden. "Mattie," he says, facing me. "The Captain told me last night what you said to him."

I steel myself. *Whatever comes, we can bear it together.*

"Good Lord," Frank snaps, "are you trying to get yourself sacked? What were you thinking, mouthing off like that?"

Frank's words hit like a kick to the stomach. "What do you mean, mouthing off?" I gasp.

"Wait . . ." He backs up a step, consternation invading his features. "Don't tell me you actually meant everything you said about equal wages."

"Of course I did," I blurt. "Why shouldn't I mean it?"

His bewildered expression hardens to flint. "Because it's ridiculous," he says, his low drawl honed razor-sharp. "That's why."

My heart shatters. I'd believed Frank would be my knight in shining armor, champion to my cause. Instead, he's cut from the same cloth as Mr. Yates.

But the shock of heartbreak is almost immediately overshadowed by anger. "You realize," I snarl, hands fisting, "I was the one to show you the ropes, not the other way around."

"And I respect your skills, honest I do," he says with maddening sincerity. "But your skill and our wages are two separate things. It's just as the Captain says. Men getting higher pay is the natural order of things."

"How so? Customers don't pay extra for a paper bag because a man made it."

As I fling my retort, passersby on the square glance our way. Even Sam and his friends have stopped to gawk. But I'm too furious to care, and that fury surges when Frank says, "Don't talk nonsense. It's a man's responsibility to be the family breadwinner. Everyone knows men work harder to live up to that. That's why we get more."

"I am my family's breadwinner," I snap. "I work just as hard to support my widow mother and my brother."

The indignation in Frank's dark eyes softens to pity. The switch is so unexpected it takes me aback. "The Captain told me about your brother," he murmurs.

"Then you should understand—"

"What I understand is that your brother's failing you and your mother."

It takes all my self-control not to slap him. "Enough," I say, turning on my heel. "I don't have to listen to—"

Frank seizes my wrist, forcing me to face him. "You think I don't know what your brother went through? Well, I do, and a whole lot better than you."

His grip tightens to a painful degree, but I can't cry out, much less tear away. Torment contorts his face into one I scarcely recognize, and his tortured gaze paralyzes me as he rasps, "I saw friends shot to bits. I've had guts rain on me. I've smelled so much gangrene I thought the whole world was rotting. It was hell, Mattie, and not a soldier alive wasn't crushed by it. Even after we came home, those ghosts followed us back."

He lets go of my wrist, letting his hand fall to his side. "But you know what? Me and the others, we pulled ourselves together. Oak Creek was ruined, and our families needed us. If we didn't help, they'd starve." He turns aside, shoulders sagging. "It wasn't easy. Not for any of us. Did you know Clem and Luke still feel their missing legs? They say the pain's so bad sometimes it keeps them from sleeping, even though their legs are long gone. But they're working with the rest of us because their folks are relying on them."

Frank looks up at me, condemnation in his eyes. "That's why I've no respect for a man who'll weigh down his family. I'd sympathize if he was blind or crippled or if he'd just returned from the fighting. But the war's been over more than two years. If he's not pulling his share, he's a deadbeat who cares nothing for you."

"He does care!" Tears well up, but I blink them back, refusing to let Frank see me cry. "When my father died, Charlie went straight to work. He provided for us until the day he enlisted. I don't know why he's not back to himself, but I cannot abandon him."

Frank's gaze wavers, then drops. "You're a good person, Mattie," he sighs. "I admire that. But a girl's supposed to rely on her menfolk, not the other way around. It's not right."

"I choose to support him," I say, willing him to understand. "And I've been able to with my own hands. If you truly wish to help me, ask Mr. Yates to match our wages."

His brow darkens. "No."

"Frank—"

His hand whips up, cutting me off. "Mattie, I didn't come to argue. I came because this harebrained deal will only hurt you. Now, I talked it over with the Captain, and he's willing to forget it all and keep you as mechanic if you apologize. So if you want to keep helping your folks, you'd best eat humble pie."

My jaw drops at the words flying from his tongue. Words that point to one thing. "You think I'll lose."

Frank folds his arms. "I never hold back in a contest. You'd be a fool to underestimate me."

I was fool enough to imagine he'd throw the competition for me. Yet I'm grateful for his declaration. Because it makes clear where we both stand.

"So," says Frank, "end this now or fight me. Your choice."

My mouth twists. "Then consider this war."

I start to flounce off, but halt for a final gauntlet. "One more thing," I hurl at Frank's stunned face. "I'll raise the ante. Beat me, and I'll not only give up being a mechanic, I'll bring you coffee. Every morning."

Chapter 8

UNCLE THOMAS'S PORTLY FIGURE FILLS THE CELLAR DOOR AS he peers down at us. "What are you girls doing in there?" he calls, suspicious as a fattened goose on Christmas Eve. "It's the Sabbath, you know."

I grimace amid the musty shelves. Uncle Thomas's interpretation of keeping the Sabbath is rather strict. No work, no chores, and no matter how much I insist that whittling is a pleasant pastime, he contends that it violates the Lord's command to rest. Interestingly, his standards do not categorize knitting or embroidery as labor.

Because I live under his roof, I must respect his rules. However, Uncle Thomas is leery of stairs. His leg did not heal perfectly after his fall, and his girth has swelled from Eliza's cooking. Thus, he permanently turned the sitting room into his bedroom to avoid going upstairs, and he'd never risk descending the rickety cellar steps.

So I pluck a spiderweb off a box in a manner he would certainly consider "cleaning" and reply innocently, "We're only trying to find some things. That's all."

He snorts. "If you ask me, your time would be better spent endeavoring to find a good husband."

My face burns as he shambles away. For the hundredth time, I berate myself for my lack of discretion this morning. Apparently, the entire congregation witnessed my argument with Frank from the Fellowship Hall windows. Suffice to say, I drew an inordinate number of glances during the young ladies' Sunday school as the reverend's wife taught the gospel verse "Blessed are the meek."

Eliza touches my arm. "Mattie, are you all right?"

"I'm fine," I say, straightening up. Reminding myself I have a contest to win, I resume taking stock of materials in the cellar. "Looks like there's a three-foot rod and another box of nails, so please add them to the list."

While Eliza tallies the items on the memoranda pages of my diary, I lift the lantern for a final scan. Amid the gardening tools, old furniture, and laundry supplies are an assortment of wood pieces and fasteners, odds and ends left from when I built a ramp to the porch for Uncle Thomas last summer. It took weeks because of his prohibition against Sabbath labor, but once complete, I had his begrudging respect for my skills as well as permission to use the remaining material and his tools as I liked.

I didn't think I'd have use for it at the time, but now I'm grateful. Heaven knows I haven't much money for this machine I've got to build.

Eliza looks up from her list. "What do you think? Will this be enough?"

"I'll have to purchase some hardware," I reply, "but this should suffice for most of it."

We leave the cellar for the kitchen. I head to the stove to warm myself, but Eliza sits at the table to stare into my diary with a perplexed expression. "Mattie, whatever is this?" she finally asks, holding it up.

On one page is a penciled list of materials in Eliza's neat print. On the page opposite is a sketch of parts with arrows pointing out their motions.

"That's the mechanism for my bag machine," I reply. "I was working it out last night. The details are here."

I flip to the journaling section, and Eliza's eyebrows go up at the rough drawings and notes scrawled beneath the preprinted dates heading the pages. "My," she says, "I daresay Uncle Thomas didn't envision this when he gave you your diary for Christmas."

I shrug. "I don't have a notebook to write in, and it's more practical than filling it with drivel about the weather no one will read."

She giggles and leans to whisper into my ear. "Truth be told, I've been using the one he gave me to keep track of my sewing jobs."

"In that case," I say with mock seriousness, "if he asks about our diaries, we shall say they contain the deepest secrets of the maiden heart, and he should leave us well enough alone."

"Then your heart is far more complex than mine." Eliza cocks her head, studying the sketches from different angles. "I've tried my hardest, but they might as well be Egyptian hieroglyphics to me."

I laugh. "My drawings are a mess. Here, it'll be easier to show you."

I leave the kitchen and return with a paper tube and a tin rectangle cut from a fish can. "You're folding a square-bottom bag with that?" Eliza asks as I place them on the table.

"This, too," I say, taking her pencil.

Intrigued, she leans in as I explain. "Right now, the machines only get us this far." My fingers tap the paper tube. "The factory hands finish the bag bottoms using a folding plate and their fingers."

I hold up the pencil. "Instead of an actual finger, I'll use this. And that"—I nod at the tin rectangle—"will serve as our folding plate."

I point the pencil's blunt end toward one end of the tube. "Imagine the tube going through the machine," I say, moving the tube forward until the pencil goes in. "Once our 'finger' inserts, our 'folding plate' will swing into place."

I place the tin rectangle flat upon the tube, two inches from the opening. With the pencil pushing the tube's upper lip against the tin's edge, the paper creases into a diamond fold. "And there we have the first fold of our square-bottom bag."

Eliza's mouth and eyes form O's of amazement. "Mattie,

you're brilliant."

Satisfaction brims up, but I shake my head. "I haven't made the parts, and I've still to work out two more folds. Although I suspect I can use a variation of the flat bag paster to—"

"Mattie, the fact that you've already gotten this far is astounding." Eliza chuckles. "This is why you were up late last night. You looked so serious, I was afraid to ask why."

I drop into the chair beside her. "Well, now you know about the contest," I say, slumping against the backrest. "As does half of Springfield."

The cheery mood vanishes. "M-Mattie," says Eliza, fidgeting, "I'm sorry about F-Frank."

"It doesn't matter." I tip my chair back onto two legs and stare at the ceiling beams. "Actually, it's for the best. If I realized from the start he was such an uncharitable . . . anyway, I'm glad I found out before I did something truly addlebrained like letting him court me."

"He was terribly a-angry when he left. You don't suppose he'd try something u-underhanded?"

"He won't. Frank may be a pigheaded fool, but he's too proud to win by anything but his own efforts. And if it's a fair fight, it'll be an even fight." I shift my weight to right my chair and find my friend gaping as if I've sprouted another nose. "Er, did I say something strange?"

"No, it's just . . ." Eliza pauses, grasping for words. "I've never seen you like this, Mattie. I always knew you were clever, but I never realized you were so . . . fierce."

The stares during Mrs. Parsons's Sunday school lesson rush back to mind. "Do you not like that part of me?" I ask, self-conscious.

"No, I do! I think you're brave, and I admire you for it." Eliza hesitates again before saying, "Is that how your other invention came about? The one Ida mentioned? Was it also your response to a challenge?"

I exhale a nervous laugh. "Heavens, no. Those were entirely different circumstances."

"Will you tell me about it?"

There's an unusual urgency in Eliza's voice that makes me blink, and she lowers her head sheepishly. "I must confess I was embarrassed and . . . jealous Ida knew of your achievement when I did not."

I throw an arm around her. "I'll have you know, I consider you the dearest of friends, and the only reason Ida knew was because her cousin and I worked together in Manchester. However," I add when she gives me an unconvinced look, "I will tell the tale if you wish."

Eliza nods emphatically. Heaving a sigh, I begin. "As you know, I went to the cotton mills when Charlie enlisted. I was only eleven, so I doffed bobbins in the spinning room and swept floors. Six months after I started, I was sweeping the weavers' room when there was a terrible accident. A shuttle became dislodged, and it shot out and struck its operator in the leg."

Eliza gasps. "That's dreadful."

"It was." I suppress a shudder as I recall the bloodcurdling shriek and the girl writhing beside her loom, the sharp-tipped shuttle stabbing her thigh. "For the factory, though, time is money. Even as the manager carried her, screaming, to the doctor, the foremen ordered everyone back to their tasks—except me. I was told to clean up the mess. Until then, I'd only thought of the factory as a fascinating place. Certainly, I knew I'd lose a finger or get my hair ripped out if I was careless, but so long as I respected the machines, I thought I would be fine. Louisa's blood on the floor told me otherwise. As I wiped it up, for the first time, I was afraid—quite afraid—of the machines surrounding me."

"You, afraid of machines?" Eliza's eyes go wide. "I can't imagine that."

"It's no exaggeration," I say softly. "I was so shaken, I couldn't eat at lunch break. And hearing everyone talk about the accident made me feel sicker. But as I listened, I learned the accident wasn't a singular happenstance. According to the older operators, weft threads occasionally snap. If the loose thread chances to fall into the shuttle race, it can snag the shuttle and send it flying. That's what caused the accident. And what caused such accidents to happen every few months throughout Manchester."

"Every few months?" Eliza sputters. "If the machines regularly hurt people, why didn't anyone do something to fix it?"

"My thought exactly," I say. "The more I thought about it, the angrier I got, until I made up my mind. If these accidents had a pattern, there had to be a way to break it. And I felt certain I could discover it if I paid attention. So that's what I did. I'd watched the machines before, but now I deliberately studied their motions. And by the following week, I contrived a fix."

Eliza starts, as if I had proclaimed Christ's second coming. "That quickly? Wasn't it complicated?"

"Not as complicated as one might think. In fact, once I figured it out, everyone was astounded no one thought to do it sooner. All we needed was a small modification to disengage power to the shuttle when a weft thread broke. When I told the factory mechanics my idea, they immediately agreed to help. Two weeks later, we had a working restraining device. We demonstrated it to the manager, and he ordered them on all the looms. By year's end, all the Manchester mills had them."

"Bravo," exclaims Eliza, clapping her hands. "So did they write about you in the newspaper? Make you the town celebrity?"

I laugh. "I believe the manager gave me a piece of cake and said, 'Good job, kid.'" Seeing Eliza's face fall, I assure her, "It's all right. I didn't do it for money or attention. I did it to protect myself and the other workers."

"Speaking of whom, what happened to that injured operator?"

asks Eliza. "Did she ever return?"

"That was the best reward," I say, beaming. "Poor Louisa took a while to recover, but she did return. Not surprisingly, she was terrified of returning to the weavers' room. However, when we showed her the restraining device, she told me I'd wiped all the fears from her mind."

"My." Eliza rests her chin in her hands, regarding me with awe. "Mattie, you say the circumstances behind your loom invention and your proposal with Mr. Yates are different, but they are very much alike."

I frown. "I made the shuttle restraint to protect people. With Mr. Yates, I'm merely proving him wrong—"

"Because he's using a fallacy to justify iniquity," interjects Eliza. "Don't you see, Mattie? When you see something wrong, you act. You built that loom device because people were needlessly harmed. You spoke against Mr. Yates because he's cheating employees."

"You're getting carried away, Eliza," I say with a sigh. "My goals aren't so lofty, considering my personal wages are at stake."

"Even so, you are still acting out of conviction." She taps the partially folded bag on the table. "Most people wouldn't go to this extent to prove a point. If you ask me, I'd call you an angel of justice."

Her declaration sounds so far-fetched, I would have laughed aloud were it not for the utter certainty in her eyes. She believes in me, without a doubt, and with so many others scorning my abilities, perhaps I should let her faith buoy me up.

"An angel, eh?" I reply with a grin. "Well, I never heard of angels manufacturing bags, but if Providence is on my side, this contest is good as won."

Chapter 9

WHEN EXAMINED OBJECTIVELY, THE PRINCIPLE BEHIND MY loom shuttle restraint was stopping motion. Once triggered, its only action was to disengage power, thereby bringing everything to a halt. Creating precise, productive motion, on the other hand, is a more difficult feat.

I knew this when I challenged Mr. Yates, but I didn't anticipate how much more difficult it would be.

With a sigh, I shut off Machine 6 and unscrew the wooden finger from the miniature scaffold I've attached at the machine's delivery end. I place it beside the two other finger models I tested earlier and record today's results in my diary. A month of trial and error has taught me that almost any flat piece of sufficient width will serve for a folding plate. However, the substitute finger . . . generally speaking, it's more liable to tear the tube rather than fold it back.

I study the most promising of the designs. Although my results are improving, even this latest model ripped the paper two times out of ten. Poking its tip with my fingernail, I muse, *Perhaps a roller at the end might help?*

As I jot that idea down, the workroom door opens. "You're still here, Mattie?"

Mr. Mowe stands in the entryway, keys in hand. I jump, aghast to see the clock pointing to half past six. "I'm sorry," I say, scooping up my belongings. "I'll leave at once."

"Please don't rush on my account," says Mr. Mowe. He clears his throat. "In fact, if you're not quite done, I don't mind waiting until you've finished."

I nearly drop my handbag. Ever since word of the bet got out, Columbia Paper's men have given me the cold shoulder. After all,

I'm the fool girl out to prove the boss wrong. Their collective antagonism is a natural consequence.

The one exception is Mr. Mowe. While his male cohorts refuse to spare breath for a civil hello, the junior bookkeeper continues to greet me with his usual smile whenever our paths cross. I thought he was merely maintaining some middle-class sense of decorum, but this offer goes beyond a show of manners. Indeed, it goes beyond my comprehension. "Won't that get you in trouble?" I stammer.

He shrugs. "My job is to lock up after quitting bell. As long as I complete the task satisfactorily, there are no grounds for complaint." As I gape, he leans over and whispers, "And just so you know, not every man here wants you to lose, Mattie."

Shock thunders through me. I search his expression for ridicule and contempt, but only a warm smile beams back. "Why?" I ask, finally regaining my tongue. "Are you wagering for me to win?"

He chuckles. "I'm hardly the betting sort. No, I'd like to see you win because, unlike our Marylanders, New Englanders are capable of more progressive concepts, such as women's rights."

I blink. "You're a suffragist?"

"I don't campaign actively, but my mother and sisters belong to the Suffragist Association, and I applaud their efforts."

As I struggle to absorb everything he's told me, he turns toward the door. "I imagine my presence is distracting, so I'll wait outside."

"No! I mean, I'll leave." As tempting as his offer is, I shouldn't inconvenience the one man sympathetic to my crusade for equal pay. "It's late, and it wouldn't be right for me to stay any later."

Mr. Mowe glances out the window toward the East Workroom. "Frank Niebuhr's still tinkering away," he says. "In fact, Mr. Yates gave him his own key."

"He and the boss have an agreement. One I don't have." Although Frank and I haven't spoken since our argument at church,

I'm well aware he's spending all his spare time on his machine. It's galling that he has full use of the factory and everything in it, but I can't complain. This competition was my doing, not his, and Mrs. Parish certainly won't allow him to clutter her boarding house with machine parts.

Lifting my chin, I declare, "When I told Mr. Yates I could build a machine, I meant I could build it without his help. I'm not taking more than I'm due now."

Mr. Mowe regards me a moment, then shakes his head. "Far be it from me to dissuade a woman from her principles."

I smile back. "I'll be but a minute."

I whisk my diary and finger models into my handbag, then hasten to remove the scaffold from Machine 6. As I loosen the thumbscrews clamping the framework in place, Mr. Mowe goes to the side opposite. "Let me help," he says.

I begin to protest, but he interjects, "The more hands, the sooner the task's done. You did wish to leave at once, correct?"

He winks, and I'm struck by how boyish his expression is. His wire spectacles and office attire always lent him an air of maturity, but now that I'm close, I realize he's not much older than me.

Somehow, that makes it easier to accept his help. With a laugh, I say, "Yes, you're correct. I appreciate your assistance."

In a twinkling, the scaffold is removed. As I unfold the flour sack I use to carry it, he squints at the framework of adjustable crossbars and screws. "I'm surprised your contrivance has no moving parts."

"That's because this is a scaffold, not a contrivance." When he returns a puzzled look, I gesture toward Machine 6. "This gets us halfway to a square-bottom bag. Finishing the process is a matter of adding to the existing machinery. The tricky thing is, I can't tell if the new pieces I make will harmonize with it."

"So your scaffold allows you to test them on an actual machine," he says, regarding the frame with new appreciation. "Very clever."

"It lets me experiment while I'm still making the parts for my own tube-forming mechanism," I explain, sliding the scaffold into its sack.

Mr. Mowe frowns. "You're building everything from scratch?"

I smile wearily. "I haven't the money for manufactured parts, and I can't in good conscience use company stock." Taking my bags, I say, "Well, I've delayed you long enough. Good night."

"Would you like help? With your machine?"

I stop short. Mr. Mowe runs a hand through his flaxen hair, seemingly embarrassed. "To be sure, I'm no good with mechanical things. However"—he throws his shoulders back—"I can cut and smooth wood, and I can use a gimlet."

"That's generous of you," I stammer, touched. "But I shouldn't. This wager is between me and Mr. Yates."

"And Mr. Yates is my employer, but his will does not dictate what I do in my spare time."

This staunch declaration gives me pause. "I realize you are to build your machine without Mr. Yates's assistance," he presses, "but must you refuse all help? Frank Niebuhr has the advantage of Mr. Yates's workroom, equipment, and stock. If your opponent has such support, surely you can accept my paltry assistance."

For a moment, I can only stare at Mr. Mowe, his normally pale cheeks flushed with emotion. Then a giggle escapes my lips. "Mr. Mowe, I'm positive your assistance will be anything but paltry."

His gray eyes light up. "Does that mean . . ."

I gesture for him to follow. "It means it's time for you to lock up here and start working for me."

Eliza is upstairs when I arrive home with my new assistant. As Mr.

Mowe and I hang our coats, she calls, "I'll be downstairs in a few minutes, Mattie. Just two more buttonholes!"

"Take your time," I shout back. To Mr. Mowe, I say, "Eliza's helping with a wedding dress for a girl from church. It's her first time sewing something so fancy."

I lead the way to the kitchen. It's dim and redolent with the aroma of simmering beans and bacon. I light the oil lamp with a taper, and when brightness floods the room, Mr. Mowe lets out a low whistle. "You've been productive."

Next to Eliza's tidy shelves of bowls and pots are an equally tidy stack of half-inch-thick boards, a pail holding rods of various lengths and diameters, and a crate brimming with hand-carved boxwood parts. "Unfortunately," I say, setting the scaffold beside the box, "I'm not as productive as I wish."

Having to make so many pieces by hand has taken longer than I expected. Uncle Thomas's prohibition against Sabbath labor is an additional handicap, and I've grown increasingly anxious about whether I'll finish by September. However, Mr. Mowe's help might just keep me on schedule.

I place the boards on the table, where the lamplight illuminates lines and curves penciled on the wood. "I'd be much obliged if you could start with these."

Mr. Mowe traces the markings with a finger. "These are the shapes you want them to take?"

"Yes. I've also written the dimensions." I point to numbers printed around the shapes. "Once they're cut and smoothed, they'll form the machine frame."

"I see."

As Mr. Mowe examines the boards, guilt pricks me. "Is it troublesome to do so many?"

He looks up with a smile. "It's no trouble at all. In fact, since tomorrow is Sunday, I should be able to finish by Monday, and if my work passes muster, I demand you reward me with another task."

My heart warms. I'm grasping for words to express my gratitude when the bang of the front door resounds, followed by a gruff, "Eliza! Margaret!"

"That's Uncle Thomas," I tell Mr. Mowe, as Eliza shouts that she'll be down in half a buttonhole. "We had better greet him."

We find Uncle Thomas leaning on his cane, frowning at Mr. Mowe's hat and coat in the entryway. His gaze darts to me, then to Mr. Mowe.

"Uncle Thomas, "I say, "welcome home—"

"So he's *your* guest, Margaret," says Uncle Thomas, stern. "What are you thinking, putting a visitor in the kitchen?"

"Well, you see . . ." I trail off in bewilderment as Uncle Thomas stomps past me. Planting himself before Mr. Mowe, he barks, "What's your name, son?"

The younger man snaps to attention like a soldier. "Daniel Mowe. Pleased to make your acquaintance, sir."

Instead of offering a handshake, Uncle Thomas scrutinizes Mr. Mowe's lanky frame like a slaver evaluating merchandise. "What's your occupation?"

"Junior bookkeeper. I'm a coworker of Miss Knight's at Columbia Paper."

"Age?"

"I'll be twenty-one in May."

"Uncle Thomas," I interject, appalled by his rudeness, "what are you doing?"

He ignores me, continuing his inquisition. "Residence?"

"I board with the Morris family on Salem Street. I attend Christ Church with them."

"Family?"

"My parents and two younger sisters. They reside in Newton Lower Falls outside Boston. My father is a manager at the Boston and Worcester Railroad."

Uncle Thomas grunts, seemingly satisfied. "Margaret may not be my blood relation, but while she lives under my roof, I am her moral guardian. Daniel Mowe, you have my permission to court her."

As my dismay flares to searing mortification, Uncle Thomas whirls on me. "And you, Margaret, take your young man to the parlor and entertain him properly. A girl like you can't do better than to be situated with someone sensible." Turning back to Mr. Mowe, he says, "You seem the sort who understands proper conduct, so I will only say this: I will not frown upon meetings out of home, but I insist you return Margaret by nine o'clock. Am I clear?"

"Wait," I sputter, "it's not—"

"Yes, sir," replies Mr. Mowe crisply. "Quite clear, sir."

"Good," says Uncle Thomas. "If you wish, you may join us for supper. Until then, please sit with Margaret." With that, he shoves us into the parlor and hobbles off to his room.

As I gape after Uncle Thomas's disappearing back, Mr. Mowe drops onto the horsehair couch with a chuckle. "Quite the character, isn't he?"

My consternation redoubles. "Mr. Mowe . . . surely you don't . . ."

"Mattie." Mr. Mowe looks up with a droll twinkle in his gray eyes. "My intent hasn't changed. I'm here merely to assist with your machine."

"Then . . . why?" I stammer.

"I doubt your landlord can conceive of a man visiting a girl for any purpose other than courtship," he says, leaning against the armrest. "If I'm to come as frequently as I imagine, it's far simpler to call me a suitor rather than explain that I'm your assistant."

I clap a hand over my mouth to stifle a snicker. He's right. My bag machine project already has Uncle Thomas perplexed. A male helper would befuddle the poor soul a hundredfold more. "True, but won't that inconvenience you? Pretending to court me?"

He cocks his head. "And what is courtship? Nothing more than an unengaged man and woman spending time in one another's company. We'll just do it in a more productive manner. No doubt, the old fellow will find our choice of activities peculiar, but so long as we follow his rules, I doubt he will object."

I laugh in earnest. "Well, shall we return to the kitchen to resume our 'courtship'?"

"By all means," he says, getting to his feet. "And Mattie?"

"Yes?"

He takes my arm and winks. "Call me Daniel."

Chapter 10

I yawn repeatedly as Ida and I trot down Market Street to work. When my mouth stretches wide for the twelfth time, Ida's face crinkles with worry. "Are you well, Mattie?"

"Just had a late night," I mumble. "I got an idea for doing the second fold of the bag bottoms and wanted to jot down the details while inspiration was fresh."

Ida clucks like an anxious hen. "You look anything but fresh with those bags under your eyes. I realize you've a contest to win, but at this rate, you'll ruin your constitution."

I wave away her concern. "I'm fine. Like you always say, I've got the vitality of youth." I pump my arms to demonstrate. "And tomorrow's Sunday, so I'll sleep then."

"So long as it's not during Reverend Parsons's sermon," she mutters as we join the ranks of workers entering the Columbia Paper gate.

"Mattie!"

Our heads snap up at Daniel's voice. He's a few yards back, his bespectacled face bobbing above the crowd. His lanky form sidles through the press to fall in beside us. "Good morning, Ida, Mattie."

As he greets us, several factory men grumble. Ida counters their scowls with a glare that could incinerate a forest. Daniel and I pretend not to notice.

Word of his support spread as quickly as my bet with the boss. Most think Daniel's besotted with me. Some speculate that he's a subversive. A few murmur that we've struck a lurid bargain. But no matter what they believe, everyone was surprised by his stance.

Fortunately, the boss and office staff haven't treated him

differently. So long as he keeps his books in proper order, he can associate with me as he likes. The East Workroom workers, however, deem him a traitor.

I felt terrible when the black looks started going his way. Daniel shrugged them off. According to him, focusing on a winning invention was more important than confronting naysayers.

Reminding myself of that, I leave the glowering to Ida and pay full attention to Daniel as he hands me a gunnysack. "I finished the crank pieces last night. If you approve of them, we can complete the tube-former after work."

I accept the parts with gratitude. Daniel has been a godsend. Although his skill with tools doesn't compare with Frank's, he can tackle a range of simple tasks with guidance. With him shouldering the lion's share of mundane work, I'm free to concentrate on designing the bag folders, and if we finish the tube-former mechanism tonight, I'll have the luxury of testing new parts at home rather than running them on Machine 6.

"That's wonderful," I say, clutching the sack to my chest, "and quite timely, I might add."

A knowing look sparks in his gray eyes. "You've figured something out."

I open my mouth to share my late-night folder idea when I glimpse Frank glowering from the East Workroom entrance. My sunny mood instantly clouds, and I recall with bitterness how he once listened to me as attentively as Daniel does now.

"I have figured something out," I say, my tone clipped, "but this isn't the place to share."

"You're right," says Daniel, tracking my gaze to Frank's frown. "It's better if you tell me after work."

"Yes," I say, turning my back on my former friend as the factory bell rings.

I attach the crank to the main shaft, insert the paper roll, and look up at Eliza and Daniel. "Here goes."

Eliza crosses her fingers at the kitchen table. Daniel grins and says, "Let her rip!"

With bated breath, I grasp the crank handle and begin turning. Wooden shafts and cogs whirl within the hatbox-sized frame, and my spirits soar to see paper going into the machine and uniform tubes coming out.

As Eliza and Daniel's hurrahs resound in the kitchen, I dip into a curtsy. "Lady and gentleman, we have a functioning tube-maker in the house."

"And it won't stay a mere tube-maker for long, right, Mattie?" says Eliza.

"Right." I pick up the scaffold, which Daniel has resized for my wooden machine, and start attaching it to the delivery end. "Once I finish the gears, I'll install a folding mechanism here."

"Speaking of which," says Daniel, "you've kept me in suspense all day. Care to share your new idea?"

I grin. "With pleasure."

My friends lean in as I place a freshly made tube and my latest finger and folding plate models on the table. Curiosity lights their faces when I add two matchsticks beside them.

"As you know, these make our first fold." I use the model finger and folding plate to make a diamond fold on the tube. "Next we must fold down the top point of the diamond. To do that, the folding plate and finger will withdraw," I say, sliding the parts away, "and two side folders will come down where I want my next fold."

I place the matchsticks end to end upon the diamond so that they form a line beneath the top point. While I hold the matchsticks in place with one hand, my free hand retakes the folding plate. "Then the plate will swing a second time." As I bring it back toward the diamond, the plate catches the tip of the top point, causing it to crease backwards against the matchstick line. "And there, we have our second fold."

"Clever," says Daniel, rubbing his chin. "This way, the folding plate makes two folds, not just one."

"But why use two matchsticks, Mattie?" asks Eliza. "Wouldn't a single stick be simpler?"

"It would. Except I need to remove it. If I used a single piece, it must exit through the fold it just made and ruin its own work. However, with two pieces, they can come out like so." Taking the matchsticks by the ends, I pull them apart, sliding them out the sides of the crease to keep the fold intact.

Eliza's eyes go wide. "You can do that, Mattie? Have the matchsticks—I mean, have the folders come down, then apart like that?"

"I'll have to get some springs and experiment," I say, massaging my temples. "But I know that motion is possible."

Daniel's eyebrows draw down. "Does your head hurt, Mattie?"

"It's not serious," I say airily. "Nothing that'll slow me down."

He studies me a moment, then says, "Not to gum the wheels of ingenuity, but if you've a headache, perhaps you should call it a night. After all, maintaining your health is as important as making progress."

I shake my head. "It's only eight o'clock, and tomorrow's Sunday, so—"

"I agree with Daniel," Eliza says, laying a hand on mine. "You've been working so hard the last three months, I expect gears to tumble out your ears. Even on Sundays, I know you're making designs in your head. Why don't you take it easy for once?"

The concern in her gaze gives me pause. Clearing his throat, Daniel adds, "If you're worried about falling behind, I'll be your errand boy and fetch those springs and whatever else on Monday."

"Daniel, you shouldn't—"

"Stop already, Margaret." Uncle Thomas's voice comes

thundering from the sitting room, startling us. "Industriousness is well and good, but it's unnatural for you and your beau to spend all hours making machine parts in my kitchen. The high school's having a fundraiser fair tonight, so get out and have a candy stick there."

For a moment, shocked silence hangs in the kitchen. Then we three burst into laughter. Uncle Thomas is forever extolling the Puritan virtues of morality and hard work, but if even he is telling me to go to a fair, a break is in order.

"Well," I say, wiping away tears of mirth, "I can't disobey my elders, can I?"

Daniel rises from his seat. "Eliza, you'll come, too?"

As we head to the entryway, Uncle Thomas adds gruffly, "And be sure to return those girls by nine o'clock, son!"

Springfield's Classical High School has utterly transformed. Festive lanterns and garlands lend an air of gaiety to the solemn brick walls. In one classroom, matrons hawk sausages and pies; in another, a wattle-necked schoolmaster recites poetry amid an art exhibit. Tables display cigars and fancy work for sale, and students holler for fairgoers to try their skills at game booths. The stalls are so numerous, they've sprawled beyond the school grounds into the adjacent Court Square, where the school band plays upon the bandstand. Their strains are enthusiastic, if not entirely harmonious, and a crowd dances to the lively sound.

Daniel and I sit on a bench at the edge of that cavorting chaos. While we nibble on popcorn, Eliza dances with Albert Lamb, a young church acquaintance whose beard is as woolly as his name. As she whirls with her partner, Daniel remarks, "I'm surprised Eliza's such a good dancer. Actually, I was surprised she was willing to dance at all. I thought she'd be too shy."

I laugh. "Eliza only gets nervous if she's required to talk. With a reel, all she has to do is nod yes and off they go without a word. So even though socials are usually difficult for her, if there's dancing, she can enjoy herself."

"What about you, Mattie?" Daniel asks as the reel ends and the sweating conductor announces an intermission. "Are you enjoying yourself?"

"Yes." The dull throb that had plagued my skull relented the instant I stepped into the spring evening air, and the fatigue that had weighed on my bones dissipated in the midst of the fair's sights, sounds, and aromas. "I thank the Good Lord for friends who would not abandon me to my grindstone."

As Daniel chuckles, Albert returns Eliza to our bench. With a tip of his hat, the bearded gallant says, "Thank you for the dance, Miss Eliza. Please allow me to treat you to lemonade."

Daniel jumps up. "Lemonade sounds like a capital idea. I'll get some for us, too, Mattie."

"Wait—" I start to protest, but Daniel has already bustled off with Albert.

I rise to my feet. Daniel paid the three-cent entrance fee for me and Eliza, and he insisted on buying our popcorn; I couldn't possibly let him buy another thing for us.

But before I can give chase, Eliza grabs my sleeve. "Mattie, if they want to, let them." Her soft gaze hardens as she watches Daniel and Albert disappear into the crowd. "Being treated is one of the few advantages of being a girl, so we may as well enjoy it."

Eliza's bitter tone jolts my concern from Daniel's wallet to her uncharacteristically stony expression. "Eliza, is something wrong?"

"No. Yes." Her expression cracks, and she buries her face in her hands. "I got a letter from F-Father. The next t-teachers' examination is in June, and he wants me to return to B-Boston for it."

Her news catches me off guard. I've grown used to living

with Eliza, and have taken her presence in Springfield for granted. However, I'm harshly reminded that her sojourn at Uncle Thomas's was always intended to be temporary. "What will you write him?" I ask.

"The same thing I wrote last time there was an e-examination," she replies, dabbing her eyes with a lace-edged handkerchief. "That Uncle Thomas hasn't yet engaged a housekeeper, and I can't in good conscience leave him. But that excuse won't work forever, and . . ." Her voice hitches. "I don't want to be a t-teacher. I don't want to ever take that h-horrible exam again!"

She sobs in earnest, and I rub her back awkwardly. "Can't you tell your father that? There are other paths besides teaching."

Eliza shakes her head. "The d-duty of a well-bred daughter is obedience to her family. You know that."

I do. A factory girl has it hard, but middle-class girls don't have it much better. Certainly, they have more material comforts, but the social constraints binding them are as tight as the corsets crushing their ribs.

"If Father insists I take the e-examination, I must. But even if I stay in Springfield, I remain under Uncle Thomas's thumb. Seems like the only ones who care about a maiden woman's opinion are young men on occasions like this." She gestures toward the mass of fairgoers with a sniffle. "But like my cousins say, once you catch a man, it's back to o-obedience, this time to your husband."

She sags, the vitality seeping from her frame. I can't stand to see her so miserable.

"It doesn't have to be like that, Eliza," I say, grabbing her hands in mine. "You've heard Daniel talk about suffragists. Slavery's abolished; things will change for women, too." When she doesn't respond, I press, "Say what you will about obedience, but it's not a sin to dream. If you had your choice, what would you do?"

"I . . ." Her cheeks flush, and she lowers her head. "It's outlandish."

"Isn't that the point of a dream?" I nudge her gently. "I won't laugh. I promise."

Eliza hesitates. Then, in a surprisingly steady voice, she declares, "I want to be a dressmaker. Not just the girl who mends shirts for quarters, but a real Boston modiste making the latest fashions in my own Washington Street shop."

I blink. I hadn't expected her dream to be so specific, down to the very address. However, outlandish it is not.

"If you ask me, that's a fine dream. It's also a distinctly possible one. It's certainly not as far-fetched as inventing a bag machine. I say you pursue it, Eliza. A dressmaker is a perfectly respectable profession."

"Not as respectable as a s-schoolteacher." Eliza wilts once more. "No, my parents won't agree, and I can't stand against them."

"Eliza—"

"All my life, I've obeyed them, Mattie. I don't have the courage to change that. That's why I admire you so." Her gaze snaps up, locking on mine. "You're brave. You're smart. That's why you'll succeed against Frank and Mr. Yates."

I protest that she too can succeed, but Eliza interrupts me again. "This is my cross to bear," she says, blowing her nose and putting her handkerchief away. "It's enough that you care. So let's change the subject."

When I pout, she digs her elbow into my side. "Tonight's supposed to be a pleasant diversion for you, and I refuse to ruin it further. Otherwise, we will have wasted Daniel's generosity. Speaking of whom, I'm surprised he didn't ask you to dance." She tilts her head. "Perhaps he doesn't know how?"

"Actually," I mumble, fidgeting with my cuffs, "he did ask. I declined."

Eliza's jaw drops. "Declined? Why? Daniel escorted us here. He paid our way."

Moreover, Daniel's taller than me. Eliza's too kind to mention it, but I never get asked because men don't choose partners who outstrip their height. By turning Daniel down, I might've lost the opportunity of a lifetime.

Yet I made my choice and remain resigned to it. "I begged off, claiming a headache, but that was an excuse. The truth is, I declined because it didn't feel right to have so much fun."

Eliza's shock turns to confusion. "Why shouldn't you have fun, Mattie?"

"Because Mother's not. Neither is Charlie." The thought of my mother trapped at home and my brother trapped in nightmares sends a fresh barrage of guilt pelting my soul.

"Mattie," says Eliza, "I know how devoted you are to your family. You work your fingers to the bone and ask nothing in return. I am positive they won't begrudge you a dance."

I regard the merriment surrounding us, and my conscience pangs. Shaking my head, I say, "I begrudge it."

"Enough." Eliza seizes my shoulders with such force that I gasp. "Misery may love company, but that's no reason to fling yourself into the abyss." She jerks her chin toward the bandstand, where musicians are reassembling with their horns and pipes. "Once that music starts, I want you dancing and having a good time. Do you understand?"

Of all things, I never expected Eliza to insist on this. As my discombobulated brain grasps for a response, I glimpse a familiar stocky figure near the bandstand.

It's Frank, enjoying drinks with his Maryland pals. My stomach twists as the men sneer my way. Then Frank says something to the others, and the group bursts into laughter.

My hackles rise. From this distance it's impossible to hear what Frank said, but I can imagine: *Look at the giant wallflower there. Who'd dance with her?*

"Mattie," says Eliza, oblivious to their mocking, "are you

listening to me?"

Just then, our male companions return with empty hands and apologetic expressions. "It is with utmost regret that we inform you—the wellspring of refreshment has run dry," says Albert with an exaggerated bow. "Youthful horseplay erupted near the casks, and now the floors are awash in lemonade."

"However," Daniel chimes in, "if we can in any way make up for this disappointment, just say the word."

I leap to my feet. "Then make it up to me with a dance, Daniel," I say brightly. "That is, if your earlier invitation still stands."

Albert's bushy brows go up. Eliza giggles behind her hand. Daniel, however, smiles broadly and says, "It does still stand and would be my honor."

We stride arm in arm to the dancing ground. As we take our places, I catch Frank's eye. His expression sours as if his drink's turned to vinegar in his mouth. I toss a smirk back.

The band strikes up. Shifting my attention from my scowling rival to my chivalrous partner, I dance away, triumph lightening my steps.

Chapter II

June has arrived, bringing warm weather and long days. With temperatures climbing, Springfielders take to lingering outside, and this Friday evening, all members of our household are out on the porch. Uncle Thomas dozes in his rocker, the *Springfield Gazette* half-crumpled in his lap. Eliza sits on the steps with her needle and a basket of mending. As for me . . .

"Please work, please work . . . drat."

I release the crank with a groan. As I pry mangled paper from the folding platform now attached to the end of my machine, Eliza makes a sympathetic noise. "Are the gears not meshing, Mattie?"

"These mesh fine," I say, squinting at the paper bits caught in the machine's innards. "Unfortunately, the timing is off, which means they're still not sized right."

I've created the parts needed to fold bag bottoms. Now I must incorporate those parts into the rest of the machine. Suffice to say, controlling the plate folder and wooden finger with my hands is one thing, and replicating that motion with a mechanical assembly is entirely another. To make the power from the crank do my bidding, I need an army of shafts, cams, and gears, all of which must be the correct size and shape.

And all of which must be completed in time for September's contest.

After some tinkering, I remove a gear from the gear train. I make measurements and notes, then toss it into a box holding a hundred other rejects.

As parts go, shafts and lever arms are simple to make; they're merely modified wood rods. Cams are more complicated but come with a degree of forgiveness, as an incorrect curvature can be fixed with a few snicks of the knife. Gears, though . . . carving teeth is time consuming, and getting them to mesh has been un-expectedly difficult. The worst part is that I can't simply adjust them to fit. If the diameter isn't perfect or the number of teeth is wrong, I'm obliged to carve yet another gear.

Gears have been a headache—literally. My skull pounds as I pencil the outline for a new gear onto a piece of boxwood with cross-eyed concentration. Things would go smoother if I knew how to draft, but I don't, so I am ensnared in this cycle of trial and error. I don't believe in Purgatory, but if such a place existed, I imagine the inhabitants would be carving away at some prodigious quota of gears.

As I flick open my jackknife, I hope Frank's encountering the same problems. I'm wishing a mountain of ill-fitting gears upon his head when Eliza starts and says, "Daniel, what a pleasant surprise!"

My eyes snap up. Sure enough, entering the front gate is Daniel. "Good evening, ladies, Mr. MacFarland." Uncle Thomas responds with a snore.

I set down my knife and meet him at the bottom of the porch steps. "Daniel, what brings you here?"

Although he has visited almost every evening this spring, it's been a week since his last drop-in. That's partly because all the simple tasks he's capable of have been completed. And partly because, during his last visit, he made an attempt to carve a gear and slashed his left palm instead.

Fortunately, the injury doesn't hinder him much. But the cut was deep, and the sight of the bandage around his palm pricks my conscience.

Oblivious to my guilt, Daniel cheerfully holds up a basket of strawberries. "I've felt badly that I haven't contributed to the cause lately. I figured I'd come to offer encouragement."

"How thoughtful," says Eliza, taking the basket. "There's cake in the kitchen that would go perfectly with them. I'll be right back."

As she disappears into the house, I say, "You shouldn't have.

You've already done so much."

"And I would do more if I could, Mattie. Truly."

My brain jams at Daniel's words. Before I can form a reply, he marches me up the steps. "Now, my purpose is not to distract but to speed you forward," he says, steering me to my machine. "I realize I'm not at full capacity, but if there is anything I can do— anything at all—name it."

Daniel has literally shed blood on my behalf, yet his enthu- siasm has not waned a whit. To decline his offer seems cruel, so I consider a moment and say, "Then I'd be grateful if you'd clear this paper from the machine. I haven't yet managed to teach the new parts that they're meant to fold and not shred."

He grins. "It would be my pleasure."

Daniel folds his long legs beneath him and begins plucking paper from the machine. I settle on the floorboards beside him. As I retake my knife, I realize I'm relaxed, my earlier frustration vanished. *Perhaps I've missed Daniel's encouragement more than I realized.*

The parts he made and the errands he ran eased my work. On days where failure seemed the rule, his unswerving confidence in me bolstered my resolve. And as we sit silently at our respective tasks, his mere presence brings me peace.

But though my agitation has dissipated, my headache has not. Within a dozen snicks of the knife, the pounding crescendos into something fierce, forcing me to put my whittling down. Clos- ing my eyes, I pinch the bridge of my nose. After several breaths, the pressure relents somewhat, and I open my eyes to find Daniel staring at me.

I freeze. His gaze is intense, serious. The companionable at- mosphere has disappeared, and in its place is something dizzying- ly foreign. I'd always dismissed the talk about Daniel fancying me as balderdash, but those rumors suddenly seem like God's truth.

His hand lifts to my face, and panic seizes me. *Is he going to . . .*

but out here? Now? In front of Uncle Thomas?

My thoughts fly at the touch of his fingers against my forehead. I can't draw breath, let alone speak, as he sweeps an errant lock from my eyes. His gaze bores into mine, and he says:

"Mattie, have you considered spectacles?"

At a quarter to one the following day, I exit Mr. Bennett's optician office with a shiny pair of steel-framed glasses on my nose and a new perspective on everything. As I marvel at how much crisper Main Street's storefronts and signposts appear, Ida chuckles. "I daresay that was money well spent."

Shame rises up at her words. When Daniel suggested that perhaps poor eyesight was hindering my progress, I dismissed it. Partly because I thought my eyes were fine, but mostly because of the expense. Between sending money home and purchasing hardware for the machine, I have nothing left.

Aware of my circumstances, Daniel gallantly offered to cover the cost. That made me feel more wretched, and I refused. But he would not take no for an answer. So we argued, raising a row that woke Uncle Thomas and brought Eliza and Ida scurrying from their kitchens.

We were obliged to explain ourselves. Once we'd finished, Uncle Thomas tugged on his beard and said, "Margaret's right. A basket of berries is one thing, but a gift of that cost is improper for anyone but a fiancée. However, my Christian sensibilities will not allow anyone under my roof to suffer needlessly. If Margaret requires spectacles, I will pay—"

"Uncle Thomas," Eliza cut in, "Mattie's my friend. I should help."

"I can, too," said Ida. "We should shoulder the burden together."

That's how my four friends contrived to contribute a dollar each to fit me with glasses.

I'm exceedingly grateful; I can already tell the new spectacles will make a tremendous difference. But I'm also embarrassed. I don't like to owe anyone. Moreover, my friends are not wealthy. So I tell Ida, "I'll repay every penny, I promise. I just need some time—"

"Mattie," says Ida, without a break in stride, "how much do you suppose the toys you made Clara and Sam are worth?"

"What?" My brain stumbles at her sudden question, then stops short when I realize what she's getting at. "No, Ida! You don't owe me anything. I wanted to do that for the kids."

"And I want to do this for you." She gives me a sidelong glance. "Even a widow can put money toward what's important."

My tongue falters. Ida has her pride as much as anyone. To help her but insist she can't help me is a form of arrogance.

Seeing that her words have sunk in, Ida loops her arm through mine. "Mattie, you're a good, reliable person," she says, as we continue through the lunch hour crowd. "You take care of your own, and you got a big heart. But you don't have to bear the weight of the world alone."

"I don't."

"You do," says Ida, firm. "This bet of yours, every woman in the factory stands to gain from it. But what are we risking? Nothing. You're the only one with something to lose."

I shake my head. "I was the one who stormed into the boss's office. Why should I drag the rest of you into it?"

"Why assume we want nothing to do with it?"

Ida's words give me pause. "It's true none of us has spoken up for you," she goes on. "Even I don't dare contradict Mr. Yates, I'm ashamed to say. But that doesn't mean I don't want to support you, and if I can help pay for these glasses, let me. Please."

I'm touched. As the object of Mr. Yates's ire, I expected the other women to avoid me like the plague. Mr. Yates might be beholden to that promise to his grandfather, but a factory boss has other ways of retaliating against employees whose sympathies don't match his. To know that Ida believes in me enough to part with her hard-earned cash leaves me speechless.

Ida pats my forearm. "It's no sin to lean on others, Mattie. It's why the Good Lord gave us friends."

Just then, snickering rankles our ears. Up ahead, two East Workroom men loiter by the factory gate. Through my new glasses, I can tell they're sneering at me. As we get closer, I hear:

". . . Bet she got them 'cause she thinks glasses'll make her smarter."

"Smarter? Homelier, more like."

Their gibes hit like a punch to the face. I'm not pretty like Fannie, and my height already makes folks look askance. I'd hoped these spectacles wouldn't attract additional scorn, but the world is a harsh place.

My insides are shriveling when Ida drops my arm. "Excuse me, Mattie, I need to school some fools."

She storms off like an enraged bear. As the mouthy pair retreat before her, my embarrassment gives way to awe. Maybe Ida can't gainsay the boss, but she sticks up for me in other ways.

It's no sin to rely on others, Mattie. It's why the Good Lord gave us friends.

I'd kept the other women uninvolved out of consideration for them. But if Ida is determined to help, relying on her might be another form of consideration.

Confidence renewed, I adjust the glasses on my nose and enter the factory with my head high.

Chapter 12

SPRINGFIELD IS A PATRIOTIC TOWN, AND NEVER IS THAT MORE apparent than on the Fourth of July. Every year, it honors the founding of our nation with orations, gunfire salutes, regattas, and the ringing of church bells. Festivities begin at dawn and last well after dark, and for Springfield's working class, it is a merry respite from the grind of industry.

I, however, remain hard at work at my own enterprise.

The only sound is the clack of gears as I tinker with my machine at the kitchen table. Not only are Eliza and Uncle Thomas gone, but the entire neighborhood has left for the Independence Day harness races at Hampden Park.

Eliza was visibly disappointed when I declined to join. After all, I've made remarkable progress, thanks to my new glasses. At present, not only are the wooden finger and plate folder synchronized with the rest of the machine, but I've also added the mechanisms for the second and the third bag folds. I even devised a tiny roller for my wooden finger that prevents the paper from ripping. In short, my machine is capable of folding a square-bottom bag from start to finish.

The problem is that it does not do so consistently.

After a final adjustment, I turn the crank slowly, one revolution every ten seconds. The myriad parts at the folding platform do their tasks harmoniously, and with every revolution, a square-bottom bag comes out of the end. *So far, so good.*

I double the pace. The machine rattles at the faster speed but continues folding. With bated breath, I silently count as the bags drop out. *One . . . two . . . three . . . four . . . five . . . six . . .*

CRUNCH.

The feed goes awry, the paper snarling upon the folding

platform, and I let go of the crank with a groan. *Not again.*

I don't need a closer look to know what's gone wrong. This scene has repeated so many times, it's starting to haunt my dreams.

For the mechanisms to do their job, the wooden finger must insert into the paper tube for that crucial first fold. At slow speeds, it goes into the opening easily. But when the speed increases, the paper distorts, collapsing the tube opening. The finger goes *over* rather than *into* the tube, and the whole process gets derailed.

I don't know whether to weep or tear my hair. I'm so close I can practically taste success, but I can't seem to clear this final obstacle. And clear it I must. After all, a machine that can only reliably fold one bag every ten seconds is useless when a worker produces double that rate.

I smack my cheeks with my palms to rouse myself. I can't afford to wallow in despair. Today is a rare Saturday off; I need to make the most of it and perfect my machine. Scanning the folding platform, the wooden finger, the snarled feed, I rack my wits for that missing detail that will fix everything.

And I come up with . . . nothing.

I slump over the tabletop. My reservoir of ideas has dried up. After days of pondering and hundreds of readjustments, my brain's exhausted.

My body, too, feels tuckered out in the late afternoon heat. Although I'm in my thinnest blouse, the cotton clings uncomfortably, and my bun feels like a sweaty squirrel curling into my neck. I reach for the lemonade Eliza left me this morning and find it warm, the ice long since melted.

Perhaps it's time for a break.

I stand on the dirt footpath alongside the Connecticut River. A stiff breeze whips the Stars and Stripes streaming from passing boats and riffles the riverbank's knee-high grass. After the stuffiness of the kitchen, the rising wind is literally a breath of fresh air. And carried upon it is the jaunty beat of a polka.

The dancing's started. According to the newspaper, a 300-piece brass and reed band is providing dance music at Hampden Park after the harness races. Then, at nightfall, the festivities will conclude with a grand finale of fireworks.

All of Springfield must be gathered at the park by now. Eliza's probably dancing with some gentleman under Uncle Thomas's watchful eye. Yet I cannot summon the wherewithal to join them.

The polka on the breeze concludes, and a reel begins. The same tune Daniel and I danced to at the fair. My stomach flips at the memory, and I wonder if I'd feel differently about going to Hampden Park if Daniel was there.

However, I know he's not even in town because I saw him off at the depot yesterday. For him, the Fourth was a chance to go home, so he joined the swarms of holiday travelers taking the evening train to see family.

I, on the other hand, would rather pretend I don't have a family right now. I owe Mother a letter but have put it off for days. Partly because of the machine, but mostly because I don't know how to respond to her latest message.

Not only does Charlie remain unemployed, he also got into a scrap and was tossed into jail while Mother was at market. Fortunately, she had a bit of money saved from Charlie's enlistment bounty and used it to pay the fine for his release. But now Charlie's withdrawn further into himself. He's stopped talking, and Mother's at her wits' end.

I wish I could offer comfort, but I've none to give. I've done all I can, and things haven't gotten better.

Family needs to support each other, I believe that, but it's tiring when I never get to lean on them. Mother's letters only ever contain sad or bad news; I can't remember when one made me smile. For that reason, I haven't told her about my bet with Yates because I don't want to add to her worries.

But even if I can't unburden myself upon them, I do have friends to lean on.

I touch the bridge of my glasses, recalling what Ida said about the Good Lord giving us friends. Certainly, Ida and Eliza have been a support. Although Uncle Thomas clearly thinks my time would be better spent otherwise, he's never once complained about the extra noise and clutter from my machine building. And Daniel . . . I couldn't have gotten this far without him.

I'm wondering what he's doing in Newton Lower Falls when a motion flashes at the edge of my vision.

It's a straw hat, soaring on the wind. It sails towards the river and, instinctively, I chase after it. Hiking up my skirts, I race down the bank and leap, snatching the hat at the water's edge.

"Nice catch," hollers a familiar voice.

My stomach clenches. I turn slowly, hoping I'm wrong, but one glance tells me I'm unfortunately right.

Hobbling down the otherwise deserted footpath is Frank. He waves and smiles, but then recognition stops him short. Time freezes as we stare across the grassy slope separating us.

My fingers tighten around the hat brim. The temptation to fling it into the river is overwhelming. However, I am not so uncharitable to do that to a lame man. Telling myself I am the more high-minded person, I march up to Frank.

"Here." I shove his hat into his hands and flounce off.

"Wait," he shouts after me. "Aren't you going to let me thank you?"

I halt. Biting back irritation, I whirl and return to make a show of manners.

The thanks don't come. He just stares at the hat in his hands, his mouth pressed in a firm line. Impatient, I snap, "If you're only going to waste my time—"

"Can't we go back to the way we were?"

The abrupt question takes me aback. Frank looks up, his expression pained. "I hate how it is between us, Mattie. I miss talking with you. I miss being friends."

I miss it, too. The sudden thought strikes me as traitorous, but it's true. Daniel and the others are wonderful, but they don't see machines the way I do. The way Frank and I both do. We shared something special, and if I were honest, I do want it back.

I don't say that, though. Squelching the yearning in my chest, I cross my arms and frown. "In case you've forgotten, we're on the opposite sides of a fight."

"I know that," he says quietly. "And I know you have your reasons for fighting. I do, too. But that doesn't mean I want to be enemies forever. You might not believe this, Mattie, but I don't want you to hate me. I never have."

The sincerity in his voice strikes a chord within me. Yet even if we both wanted things the way they once were, we're too far deep in this war to back out now. As my emotions twist into a complicated knot, I notice a blood-stained bandage around his right palm. "What happened to you?"

"You mean this?" He holds up his hand, and his sleeve falls to reveal that the sloppy wrap goes past his wrist. Smiling wryly, he says, "Let's just say the only thing worse than a machine that doesn't work like it's supposed to is one that bites the hand building it."

"Amen to that." The words pop out of their own accord, and the next instant we're both laughing. As I hold my sides, I realize how wrong it is to be fraternizing, but I can't help it. The bitter humor underlying Frank's joke resonates more deeply than Daniel's cheery encouragement, and I'm again reminded that Frank understands me in a way others can't.

Our laughter ebbs, and I make up my mind. "Truce?" I say, offering a handshake. "But only for today. And if I smell anything rotten, I'll throw you and your hat in the river."

"Done." Frank plunks his hat on his head and reaches to shake with his left. "Sorry, my right's a mess."

"Give me that." I snatch his bandaged hand, undo the linen strip, and wrap it properly. "It won't do any good unless it's done up tight."

He grunts as I tug the bandage. "Kind of hard to wrap things one-handed."

It dawns on me that he's alone this holiday, too. No doubt his friends went to enjoy the festivities while he wrangled with his machine. Like me. As I consider this, he heaves a wistful sigh. "You know, Mattie, if we were working together, that bag machine would be done—"

"Stop." My tone is sharp. Not because I think he's wrong, but because I agree. So much so, my heart aches. I recall the evenings making toys in Ida's kitchen, our conversations about boilers and engines. Under different circumstances, this machine could've been a shared joy and success.

But I cannot allow myself to dwell on what could've been.

"If you want to keep this truce," I say, tying the bandage and releasing his hand, "no more talk about the contest."

Frank regards me a moment, then huffs. "Fine. So tell me why you're gawking at the river instead of having fun with the crowd." He jerks his head in the direction of Hampden Park.

His question is blunt, and so is my reply. "Because the crowd wouldn't be fun for me. Not right now. My brain's so frazzled, I want to let it be empty for a spell."

I half expect Frank to tease me for my answer. Instead, his gaze softens. "I can see that."

"What about you?" I ask, curious now. Hampden Park is only a fifteen-minute walk west of Columbia Paper. But this riverside spot is a long detour south of both the factory and the park.

Shame flits across Frank's features, and he drops his gaze.

Long seconds drag with only the faint strains of the Hampden Park band in our ears. Just as I'm about to give up on an answer, he murmurs, "It's the fireworks. They're supposed to be pretty and all, but the war gave me enough explosions to last a lifetime."

His strained reply is completely unexpected. I've only ever thought of fireworks as brilliant displays of beauty. But then I think about poor Charlie and what the flashes and noise might do to his nerves, and I grasp a sense of how Frank feels.

I doubt he wants to dwell on the matter, so I say, "No sense going to something you won't enjoy, but the fireworks won't start till dark. You can still dance a couple hours and leave before sundown. "

His mouth twists. "Now you're just being mean."

My brow furrows at his rueful tone. "Mean? What are you talking about?"

He turns away, his shoulders hunching. "No girl wants to dance with a cripple."

The barely audible words leave me thunderstruck. I've only ever seen Frank as overflowing with confidence. He hadn't let his leg or lack of schooling get in the way in the Army or at Columbia Paper, and his wits and spirit have always made up for any shortfalls. As such, it's perplexing to see Frank perceive himself as afflicted. Because I never have.

"Well, I think you're wrong," I say, smacking him on the back.

He starts, but I ignore his aggrieved look and add, "I mean, have you ever even tried asking?"

His face screws up, but then he sheepishly shakes his head.

I blow out my breath in exasperation. Although I recall Frank skulking near the dancing ground at the fair, I never saw him actually dancing. I realize now he lacked the nerve to seek a partner.

"The entirety of womankind isn't as small-minded as you think, Frank Niebuhr," I declare. "And if you're still too much of a coward to ask for a dance, you've only yourself to blame for being alone."

Frank gawks at me. Then his jaw sets. "So would you dance with me if I asked?"

My heart stops, then pounds hard enough to burst. "Why would you ask me?" I blurt.

"Because," he replies, eyes burning, "I meant it when I said I don't want you to hate me."

In the distance, the sprightly jig concludes, and the band strikes up a waltz. As the slow melody swells, Frank bows and extends a hand. "May I have this dance, Miss Mattie Knight?"

I can't. This was not my intention when I said he shouldn't hesitate to ask for a dance. But Frank's dark gaze compels me like a magnet, and before I know it, my hand's in his.

"Just this once," I say, struggling to keep a steady tone. "And only because we have a truce."

He smiles. "Understood."

Placing his right hand at my waist, he draws me close, and we rock gently in time with the melancholy tune.

Not daring to trust my self-composure, I look fixedly away from him. Yet I'm more aware of Frank than I've ever been. The roughness of his calloused fingers, the pressure of his hand on my waist, the firm muscles beneath his linen shirt.

A lump forms in my throat. My dance with Daniel was all joyous exhilaration, but this standing sway with Frank is like lingering in the embrace of a lost dream. Here on the riverbank, away from prying eyes, all our differences seem to fall away. Mr. Yates, our wages, the bet—none of that exists. The only ones left in the world are him and me.

"Mattie." Frank's rich baritone murmurs in my ear, sending shivers down my spine. "Thanks for giving my hat back."

"You're welcome." And in that instant, I sincerely mean it.

Chapter 13

HEART IN MY MOUTH, I YANK ON MY SHOES, GRAB MY WORK apron, and bolt for the front door. I'm vaguely aware of Uncle Thomas scolding me, and as I burst into the cloudless August morning, Eliza shouts, "Mattie, you forgot your hat!"

I don't stop. I can't stop.

I'm late. God in Heaven, I won't get to the factory on time. Just then, a church bell tolls seven o'clock, a resounding confirmation that rattles my core.

I am typically an early riser, up before six and off to the factory by a quarter to seven. But long hours with the machine have interfered with my waking habits. So Eliza, who's perpetually up with the lark, has been rousing me in the morning.

Except she didn't today.

A neighbor came with a rush order yesterday. Her Baltimore niece had died of childbed fever, and she needed mourning clothes altered before she left for the funeral. So last night Eliza and I both burned the midnight oil, her plying her needle, me struggling to perfect my machine—and nodded off over our tasks. If not for Uncle Thomas shouting us awake from downstairs, I'd still be asleep.

Market Street seems the span of a continent as I hustle through the morning crowd. I'm late, there's no escaping that now, but it is a known fact that Mr. Yates's ire worsens with every minute past the start bell. Dodging people and pushcarts, I race to the Columbia Paper gate.

The gate is empty.

Confusion ripples through me. Mr. Yates makes a point to confront latecomers the instant they arrive. But there's no sign of anyone at the entrance.

Maybe he's sick. Or perhaps he's at the paper mill? According to Daniel, the contractors for the mill addition are behind schedule, and the boss has been preoccupied with ensuring they finish in time for Columbia Paper's anniversary celebration.

Even if Mr. Yates is elsewhere, I can't relax. While a late factory hand might succeed in slipping in without notice, the entire West Workroom already knows I'm late. Because machines can't run without the engine on, and the one who turns on the West Engine every morning is me.

Wondering how I might convince the others to keep mum about my tardy arrival, I dart inside the West Workroom.

My heart stops. The line shaft whizzes merrily overhead. Operators are already connecting their machines to power. Bag folders cast pitying looks my way, and my stomach drops when I grasp my predicament.

"Miss Knight."

Mr. Yates's voice booms over the workroom whir, giving me a start. I turn to see him and Frank emerging from the West Engine Room. Frank's expression is an unreadable blank, but the boss is plainly fit to be tied. He stalks over, his black frock coat flapping like a descending bird of prey.

My mind races. I've never given an employer cause for reprimand before, but any excuse short of the Specter of Death will only make Mr. Yates more furious. Tears won't help either. When he caught Fannie returning late from lunch last January, she made a show of crying only to be sent home with a half-day's wage taken away.

Nothing to be done but take it. So I brace myself as Mr. Yates plants himself before me and says, "How kind of you to grace us with your presence this morning."

His words are a scalding mix of acid and sarcasm, and I wince like a child admonished by a teacher. Unfortunately, my mistake is more serious than a misspelled word, and the repercussions far greater than a slap on the wrist.

The boss looks deliberately to the workroom clock. "Twelve minutes past seven," he reads. "That's twelve minutes of lost production, twelve minutes my machines and my employees stood idle because you failed your duty as a mechanic."

He spits that last word like a curse, and I bite my lip. I want desperately to defend myself, but what justification can I offer? That I overslept working on a machine intended to prove him wrong?

"Well," says Mr. Yates, nostrils flaring, "what do you have to say for yourself?"

Lowering my head, I give the only reply I can. "I'm sorry, Mr. Yates. It won't happen again."

"Won't happen again?" Mr. Yates scoffs. "Fine words from a girl who was so certain she deserved her job. Perhaps you aren't as entitled to your position as you fancy yourself to be. At any rate, since you failed your duty, I'm entitled to remove you from being mechanic for the day."

Shock thunders through me. As the women exchange astonished looks, I stammer, "But sir, you need me to—"

"Frank," says Mr. Yates, turning to face him. "I realize I've already imposed on you, but could you mind both workrooms while Miss Knight joins the bag folders today?"

Frank nods. "You can count on me, Captain."

"Good. Now that that's settled, everyone get to work. We've wasted enough time on account of Miss Knight."

Mr. Yates claps his hands, and the workers instantly shift their attention to bag making. However, Fannie's sympathetic gaze lingers on me. "Here, Mattie," she says, pointing to the worktable beside hers. "Sit next to me."

Half-dazed, I start toward her when the boss stops me. "One more thing," he says with a sniff. "With all this fuss, I haven't had my coffee. Fetch me a cup. I'll be in the East Workroom."

Mr. Yates is clearly delighted to pour salt into my stinging wounds. Bad enough to be humiliated here, but he's out to make me a fool before the men, too. Unfortunately, he's won this battle, and we both know it.

"Yes, sir," I reply meekly. "Right away, sir."

"Oh," adds Mr. Yates idly, "and bring a cup for Frank, too."

My head jerks up in surprise. Beside the boss, Frank looks equally startled. But then he meets my gaze and shrugs. "I'll take mine with extra sugar," he says, lips twitching into a smile.

Fury sears my veins. It takes all my self-restraint not to throw a fist through Frank's teeth. Biting back the scream building in my throat, I duck my head and retreat out the door.

So much for being friends. Angry tears burn my eyes as I stalk to the office. Following the boss's orders is one thing, but this . . . I don't know if Frank told Mr. Yates about our private bet, but even if he didn't, he was all too willing to join the boss in humiliating me.

And the worst part is, there's nothing I can do about it.

The office staff give a collective start when I flounce inside. The older men shrink back, as if fearful I've come to cause trouble, but Daniel jumps up. "Mattie," he says, eyes wide with alarm, "what—"

I cut him off with a warning look and a shake of my head. If I hear a kind word now, I'll surely fall to pieces. Turning my back on his worried face, I march to the coffee pot. Stares bore into my back as I fill two of the tin cups on the office sideboard. None of these men could forget how I refused to fetch coffee for Mr. Yates last February. Now here I am, doing exactly that. Mortification fills my mouth, and my façade threatens to crack.

Get a hold of yourself. If you show weakness, the boss gets exactly what he wants. Even so, I feel my composure fraying, and my hands shake.

Somehow, I fill the cups without spilling coffee all over the sideboard. As I set the pot down, my gaze lands on the sugar bowl. Squelching the temptation to dump salt into Frank's coffee, I turn my attention to locating a spoon and yank a drawer open.

The drawer flies clean out the sideboard. Its contents arc through the air, and a metallic crash shatters the office silence.

For a slack-jawed moment, I stare at the scattered flatware, the extricated drawer hanging in my grip. Then snickering fills the room, and I want nothing more than to disappear through the floor.

Don't cry. Do not cry. My throat tightens to the point of choking, but I swallow the tears back. Shutting out the laughter rankling my ears, I hasten to put the sideboard back to rights.

But the drawer is uncooperative. The tight opening makes it difficult to insert behind the drawer stop and onto its runners. As I struggle to wedge it in, I realize the drawer was never installed properly to begin with.

My blood boils, irked that my embarrassment is the result of someone else's shoddy work. I, however, am the daughter of a woodworker. Refusing to let a piece of cabinetry get the better of me, I keep at it, and after a couple minutes, it slips in. I open the drawer to test it, and it bumps against the drawer stop with a satisfying thud. Feeling vindicated, I push it shut, the drawer gliding smoothly over the runners on either side.

Runners on either side?

An idea flickers in my brain. Grasping the handle, I slide the drawer open and shut, open and shut. The back-and-forth motion fans the spark in my mind, and it suddenly explodes into full-blown inspiration. *This is it. This can work!*

The next instant, I'm laughing. I clap a hand over my mouth, but I can't contain the peals doubling me over. Through watering eyes, I see Daniel pale with worry, the other men slack-jawed, but I don't care.

I know how to make my machine work.

Chapter 14

BLAZING SUMMER MELLOWS INTO AUTUMN, AND BEFORE I know it, it's the eve of the company anniversary. With the grand event drawing close, quitting time is livelier than usual. Donning her hat, Fannie chants a singsong "Tomorrow's a party, so tomorrow's a half-day—"

Ida smacks Fannie's side with her handbag. "Just because we're getting the afternoon off for the anniversary party doesn't mean we can slack in the morning." She jerks her chin toward the far wall, where towering stacks of paper tubes await folding.

As Daniel predicted, the square-bottom bags were a hit with Jordan Marsh's Department Store, and at the end of August, a rival store placed an order for them, too. Which means the bag workers have been in a square-bottom folding frenzy to keep up. "If we want to drink lemonade at the party," says Ida, her tone stern, "we need to finish those bags first."

Fannie gives a careless wave. "Don't you fret. I'll work so hard, they'll be done in a twinkling. After all, I can't possibly miss the big contest." She throws an arm over my shoulder. "So, Mattie," she says, "is your machine ready to beat Frank's?"

Her question propels my stomach into somersaults, but I muster a smile. "It is."

And just in the nick of time. Although inspiration for the final critical piece came to me in a flash, parts don't materialize through mere thought. The last six weeks have been a mad race to create and fit that last mechanism, but God be praised, two nights ago my efforts finally coalesced into a fully functional bag machine.

It is a feat I'd otherwise be proud of, but with the contest looming, I can only wonder: *Is it enough to win?*

"You sure you don't need help tomorrow, Mattie?" Ida asks as we exit the workroom.

"I'm fine." While Ida and the other factory hands fold square-bottom bags at the Market Street factory, Frank and I have the morning to set up our machines at the new paper mill addition where the anniversary party is taking place. "One of the East hands is helping Frank transport his machine to the mill, so Daniel's helping me do the same."

"Speaking of our gallant bookkeeper," says Fannie, pointing toward the gate, "isn't that him?"

Sure enough, coming down Market Street is Daniel, accompanied by another young man in traveling garb. "Mattie," says Ida, "who's that with him?"

I tilt my head, my own curiosity piqued. "I haven't the faintest idea."

This is the first I've seen of Daniel all week; he's been at the paper mill, boss's orders. Or, more accurately, the boss's missus's orders. Apparently, Mrs. Yates got wind of the anniversary party two weeks ago and insisted on organizing the festivities. As a result, Daniel was assigned as her assistant, partly to do her bidding and partly to ensure that her expenditures wouldn't bankrupt her husband.

Excusing myself from my friends, I hurry to meet Daniel at the factory entrance. "What are you doing here? I thought you were slaving day and night for Mrs. Yates."

"I was. But by God's grace and mercy, she approved the bunting placement after only fifteen rearrangements, rather than the fifty I anticipated. So I was dismissed early for once, and as luck would have it, I chanced upon an old pal by the train depot."

Daniel's friend holds out his hand. "Name's Charles Annan," he says. The wiry fellow is even taller than Daniel, and his thick, rust-colored eyebrows resemble woolly caterpillars. "Dan and I grew up together in Newton Lower Falls."

"My brother's name is Charles, too," I say, accepting the

handshake. "I'm Mattie Knight. What brings you to Springfield?"

"I came to tour the Armory. I'm a bookkeeper like Dan, but mechanical things are my hobby. Which is why I was so intrigued when he told me about your contest."

"That's why we came to find you," says Daniel. "Unfortunately, Charles can't tarry for your grand debut. He's got to take the first train tomorrow morning. We were hoping you might show him your machine tonight."

Charles's blue eyes turn sheepish. "I realize I'm being awful forward for a new acquaintance, but this is the first I've heard of a lady inventor. I'd be terribly obliged if you'd do me the favor of showing me your work."

Pride swells in my chest. Most people would scoff at the phrase "lady inventor," but Charles's interest is so keen, it emanates off him in waves. I can't help grinning from ear to ear as I reply, "I'd be happy to. After all, any friend of Daniel's is a friend of mine."

❄ ❄ ❄

"It's smaller than I thought," says Charles when I place the machine on the kitchen table. "I thought an industrial machine would be big as a pushcart."

"Don't let the size deceive you," Daniel warns. "It'll bury you beneath a mountain of bags if you're not careful."

I shake my head at Daniel's exaggeration before addressing Charles seriously. "You are correct that it's smallish. Two and a half feet by one foot by one foot high, to be exact. But in a factory, this basic mechanism would be incorporated into a heavy frame to accommodate mechanical power, which would bring it closer to the size you imagined. However, because Uncle Thomas's house lacks a power shaft, we power it like this."

I turn the crank as fast as I can. Paper whisks off the feed roll, flows through the machine, and exits as uniform bags. "It's a bit of a rattletrap," I say over the machine's clattering, "but the bags are perfect, as you can see."

"Astounding," remarks Charles once I stop. "How did you come up with it?"

"It's actually an improvement of another machine. What I did was modify the existing tube-former and add a folding platform and folders at the delivery end."

"Tube-former?" Charles's caterpillar brows knit. "Which and what is that?"

"This is the tube-former." I point to the oblong part mounted between the paper feed roll and the folding platform. "On a standard factory machine, it's just a piece of wood the paper wraps around to go from a flat sheet to a tube. However, I've incorporated an additional part."

I remove the tube-former from the machine to show Charles a wire rectangle on top of the oblong wood. The rectangle is longer and slightly narrower than the tube-former, and its lengthwise sides rest in parallel grooves carved into the wood. When I tug the rectangle forward, the wires glide smoothly in their tracks.

Like a drawer sliding open, I muse, recalling the sideboard drawer that inspired it.

"I call this metal rectangle the follower. As the paper tube exits the tube-former, the follower moves forward with it to keep the mouth of the tube open. Once the tube reaches the folders, the follower retracts to get out of the way," I say, demonstrating the motion.

"Is it necessary to have this follower move continuously back and forth?" Charles points at the mechanism that controls the follower. "Seems like a lot of extra parts for something that doesn't actually fold."

"Believe me, it is quite necessary. Without it, the bag making rate drops to—"

Just then, Eliza opens the rear door and jumps to see so many in her kitchen. "I'm s-sorry," she squeaks, nearly dropping her shopping basket. "Am I i-intruding?"

"Not at all," I say, rising. I quickly make introductions, and when I explain the reason for Charles's visit, Eliza's eyes gleam.

"You came for a demonstration?" she cries, pouncing upon Charles. "How marvelous! What did you think?"

He backs up a step, startled by her enthusiasm. "I . . . I'm impressed. Your friend's done fine work."

"Hasn't she? I mean, just look at this." Eliza lifts her basket lid to reveal several filled square-bottom bags. "I brought them to market, and they work so well. This one has cheese, and I have apples in this one—you can't fit apples in those flat bags."

With so many bags from my test runs, Eliza's been using them everywhere. And after I finally completed the machine two days ago, she started bragging about it to any who would listen.

Plucking a freshly made bag off the table, she holds it up to Charles. "See how nicely it's pasted? How perfect the folds are?"

My face warms at her unbridled praise. "Eliza, it's just a bag."

She waggles a finger. "It's not just a bag. It is a marketable square-bottom bag people would pay money for. Speaking of which, Charles, let me show you what I've done with her bags in the parlor . . ."

As she whisks Charles from the kitchen, I shake my head and say to Daniel, "You'd think she was practicing to be a saleswoman."

I expect a laugh, but he returns a serious look. "Why not? To tell the truth, I've wanted to propose that to you. For me to be your salesman, that is."

My jaw drops. The proposition sounds so preposterous I can only stammer, "You're joking."

"I'm not." Directing his gaze to the machine, he remarks, "Like Eliza says, people will pay money for those bags, which means your machine has the potential for profit. Given the choice of staying at Columbia or leaving to promote your invention into a commercial success, I'd choose the latter in a heartbeat."

"Wait. Stop." For a junior bookkeeper, Daniel has a dizzying imagination, and his vision is so high in the clouds it makes my head spin. "First things first. I have to beat Frank first."

"But victory is certain, is it not?"

I hesitate, and that is a response in itself. "Mattie," says Daniel, his expression clouding, "what's wrong?"

I drop into a chair with a sigh. "To win, I need to make more bags than Frank in the span of two minutes. That partly depends on how fast our machines run. Frank's been building his at the factory, so I'm near certain it's powered by line shaft. The thing is, I don't know if I can do the same."

Daniel's brow puckers. "I don't understand."

My finger taps the machine frame. "This is a wood machine. It's only ever run on hand power. Even then, it shakes something fierce. You heard it rattling when I demonstrated earlier. So I don't know if the parts will break under the higher speed of a mechanical shaft."

"Break?" Daniel inhales sharply. "I didn't realize . . . wait. Is it even possible to connect your machine to the line shaft?"

I nod. "It's possible if I replace the crank with a pulley adapter. I'd have to make one tonight, then adjust it tomorrow morning at the mill, but I can do it. The question is, should I?"

My gaze skims over the wooden frame and components. Could they bear up? Or would they splinter? I'm especially uncertain about my newly perfected follower mechanism. If I had another month or even another week, I could experiment and devise ways to accommodate the strain, but time has run out.

"It would be different if the parts were metal," I say glumly. "But they're not, so I have to choose whether to play it safe with the hand crank or risk destroying my machine."

"Don't hold back, Mattie."

The forceful words stop me cold. Daniel averts his eyes, as if embarrassed by his interjection. "It's not my place," he goes on, "but I speak with your best interest in mind when I say you've got to fight Frank with everything you got, even if it means taking a risk."

For the second time tonight, Daniel leaves me speechless. When I regain my tongue, all I can manage is, "I never expected to hear that from you."

He returns a wry smile. "Sound too reckless for a bookkeeper? I assure you, I'm looking at this realistically."

"How so?"

"By accounting for the fact that this contest is about more than bag-making. Mattie, you've been so deep in the cogs that you may have lost sight of this, but you are attempting to overthrow a deeply entrenched belief. The belief that men are better with machines. The world won't change its mind unless you beat Frank, and beat him by a decisive margin. Which means you must do everything to increase that margin, no matter what."

He's right. I've been too preoccupied with finishing my machine to think about it, but true victory will require more than a higher bag count.

"Say your hand-cranked machine makes more bags than Frank's," Daniel goes on. "Per the rules, you win. However, quibblers will argue that Frank's line-driven invention is more mechanized and therefore the product of a better mechanic."

I grimace. Such criticism would sour victory as effectively as an ocean of vinegar. Unfortunately, I can count on Mr. Yates and the factory men to use that argument—and any others they can devise—to discredit my skill. "I suppose I have no choice but to gamble everything, then," I say, slumping over the tabletop.

"I'd agree, Mattie, except for one thing." Daniel leans to whisper in my ear. "I don't see it as a gamble."

Confusion jolts through me. "But you—"

"You might consider this splitting hairs, but there's a difference between a reckless wager and a calculated risk. Yes, you've never used the machine under mechanical power. Yes, it's uncertain if it can withstand the strain. However, you are a remarkable craftswoman." He tilts his head toward the machine. "Perhaps wood parts aren't meant for continuous high speed, but I believe your machine will hold for the duration of the contest. Because that's the kind of quality you create."

Butterflies whirl my stomach. Between Daniel's talk of commercial success and his assurance of victory, I'm floored. Confronted with such unswerving faith, my misgivings evaporate, and suddenly anything seems possible.

"Well, then," I say, getting to my feet, "if you'll pardon me, I've got a pulley adapter to make."

Chapter 15

THE PAPER MILL ADDITION IS ENORMOUS. ONCE OPERATIONAL, it will boost Columbia's paper production by fifty percent. But the equipment that will fill the cavernous brick structure won't arrive for two weeks, and for now, the place houses the trappings of a party.

Blue-and-white bunting adorns the high windows. At the center are long trestle tables and benches for the anniversary luncheon. Against one wall is a festooned platform—the stage for the boss's grand speech, no doubt—and above it hangs a banner that reads: COLUMBIA PAPER 10 YEARS.

Of course, Frank's machine and mine are present, albeit somewhat close for comfort. The partly finished factory only has two drive pulleys installed, and they're bolted to the floor twelve feet apart. So if Frank and I want mechanical power, we're obliged to remain within spitting distance. Fortunately, Mr. Yates had the decency to provide us with screens for privacy.

My machine is silent behind its screens. Once I finished connecting it to the drive pulley, I disengaged it. It folded bags without a hitch during three brief tests, but the wooden frame vibrated so intensely, I don't dare subject it to more before the contest.

Frank, on the other hand, continues testing his. Every few minutes, his machine engages, then halts for an interlude of squeaks and clinks. The sounds echo in the expanse, causing my emotions to alternate between burning curiosity and nail-biting nervousness.

I'm wishing my stare could penetrate Frank's screens when the mill foreman, Mr. Lovelace, enters carrying a bolt of blue cloth. "It's a quarter to noon," he barks. "You two done with the line shaft?"

Frank's frowning face pops out at the shout. His frown deepens when I answer, "Yes" to Mr. Lovelace. "I'm done, too," Frank says, but the irritable manner with which he retreats behind his screens indicates otherwise.

As I wonder what Frank could be doing with the contest less than an hour away, Mr. Lovelace heads to the power controls, located just to the side of the festooned platform, and throws the main switch.

The whiz of the main overhead shaft fades. The next time it starts, my machine will be contending against Frank's. Before that thought can unravel my nerves, two deliverymen appear at the door carrying a long, narrow plank. "Sir," one calls out, "where do you want this?"

Mr. Lovelace gestures for them to follow him up the platform's three steps. "Up here."

The men enter, and I realize their plank is actually a makeshift tray for a cake. The frosted white confection is an artful fantasy of piping and sugar roses, surrounded by a border of fresh flowers. Most impressively, it is a good ten feet long.

"A celebration wouldn't be a celebration without cake, don't you think?"

I whirl at the melodious voice to see a dainty woman in lavender silk so lustrous, it would make Eliza swoon. An ostrich-feather hat adorns her head, and beneath its plumes are lively eyes and an expressive mouth. As my brain flounders at the materialization of a fashion plate at a paper mill, she extends a lace-gloved hand. "You must be Margaret Knight. I'm Aurelia Yates."

Yates . . . "Mrs. Yates?" I squeak, somehow managing the wherewithal to accept her handshake.

"Yes. I'm so pleased to finally meet you, Miss Knight."

The warmth emanating from her leaves me at a loss. The boss's wife is nothing like I expected. That same instant, she chuckles and adds, "I imagine you're thinking how unlike my husband I am."

My face burns. "No! I—"

She waves away my sputtering. "We are different; that's a fact. But that only means I make up for his shortcomings and vice versa. In this case . . ." She trails off as she glances toward the platform, where Mr. Lovelace is spreading his blue cloth upon a table. "Mr. Lovelace," she calls out, "move the table forward. Otherwise, the cake won't make an impression in the photograph."

Photograph? Excitement thrills through my agitation. Although I've seen photographs, I've never seen one taken—a photographer's studio is beyond my pocketbook.

I'm hoping the photograph will include us employees when a thickset matron lugging two large cases and a folded tripod steps inside. "Aurelia, is this the place?" she asks.

"It is. And yonder stage shall frame our tableau." Mrs. Yates's arm sweeps toward the platform, where the men are lowering the python-length cake upon the table. "Set up your equipment however you think is best. Mr. Lovelace, would you please assist Mrs. Townsend?"

The foreman scurries over to take her cases, and I realize the lady photographer's skirt barely covers her knees. As I gawk at the scandalous length, Mrs. Yates says, "Martha Townsend is an extraordinary photographer. It takes technical ability and artistry to truly capture a moment, and she possesses both."

"I see," I say, watching the unusual woman survey the room, muttering about light and angles all the while.

"Anyway, Miss Knight, as I was saying about my dear husband . . ." Mrs. Yates heaves a sigh. "He's a clever businessman but lacks all sense of pageantry. Left to his own devices, he'd make a speech, toss the masses some roasted peanuts, and call it a grandiose event."

I laugh to myself. That sounds like the Mr. Yates I know.

"But a ten-year anniversary is a remarkable accomplishment

and should be hailed accordingly, especially with Grandfather Pope attending," Mrs. Yates declares, hands on her hips. "That means decorations, cake, and a commemorative photograph. Special occasions require special measures. And speaking of special measures . . ."

Her gaze slides toward the door, and I follow it to see Daniel entering with two cardboard boxes in his arms. He jogs over, huffing and puffing, and says, "Mission accomplished, ma'am. I didn't think they'd finish in time, but I've been happily proven wrong."

"I've told you all week, Mr. Mowe, anything is possible with the right encouragement."

While I wonder what sort of encouragement the boss's wife employs, she takes a box and says, "If you'd kindly bring Mr. Niebuhr his while I give Miss Knight hers."

As Daniel trots off, I notice that the box Mrs. Yates holds is marked "MK." "Today is the company anniversary," she says, turning to me. "But I imagine the day's special for you in another way. I don't know anything about inventing, but when I heard about your competition, I was utterly thrilled. So I thought, 'Why not give it extra flair?'"

She opens the lid, and my breath catches. Inside is a paper roll the same size and weight as the factory's bags. But instead of rough, tan manila, this stock is bright white. And printed continuously down the center of the roll in inch-high script are my initials: MK.

"It took some persuading to get my dear husband to agree. He couldn't fathom why ordinary paper wouldn't do. But a noteworthy moment requires something more . . . eye-catching. Not to mention that"—Mrs. Yates's finger taps the roll—"with your initials all over, there won't be any question as to whose machine made which bag."

My eyes go wide. Since my conversation with Daniel last night, I'd wondered whether I could count on an impartial evaluation, but I never expected the boss's wife of all people to address the matter so directly.

She presses the box into my hands and leans close. "Although I don't anticipate anything underhanded," she murmurs, her verbena perfume tickling my nostrils, "I promise I'll do everything in my ability to keep things fair."

Keep things fair? How? For someone of her social standing to publicly contradict her husband—especially one as prideful as Mr. Yates—is unthinkable. Yet instinct tells me this tiny woman has her ways of keeping him honest.

Awed, I stammer, "Mrs. Yates, I don't know what to say."

Her smile turns sly. "Say you'll deliver a scintillating performance. One worthy to have your initials all over it."

She winks, and my spirits soar. "Yes, ma'am!"

A half-hour later, it's patently clear why Mrs. Townsend dresses as she does. Capturing the hundred and twenty factory workers, plus office staff and management, that pose beneath the anniversary banner requires a lofty vantage. And so the photographer has perched her tripod upon a large crate and positioned a ladder behind it.

The stocky matron displays surprising agility as she scampers up and down the rungs. From what I can tell, photography requires painstaking placement. Mrs. Townsend spent the last three minutes adjusting the tall candles burning on the cake and is now repositioning the mill foremen in the front row. As she barks instructions, I wonder how Mr. Yates, who is frozen in a handshake with his grandfather behind the anniversary cake, feels taking orders from a woman.

Mrs. Townsend remounts her ladder for the tenth time and nods. "Perfect," she declares, taking out a pocket watch. "Nobody move until I say so."

As we hold still for the camera, I remember how we gathered similarly to watch Mr. Pope introduce Mr. Yates last autumn. Back then, all the factory hands were female; now twenty men stand in our ranks. Mr. Yates's arrival certainly brought change to Columbia Paper.

And if victory favors me today, he'll be obligated to change our pay to match the men's.

"Done!" Mrs. Townsend closes the camera lens. "Thank you for your patience."

Applause erupts, and our ordered rows relax into a muddle. Some watch Mrs. Townsend take down her camera. Others, like Fannie, gaze hungrily at the sandwiches and fried chicken occupying the tables. But what attracts the most stares are the two machines, their screens replaced by post-and-rope barriers. I myself am scrutinizing Frank's machine when Mr. Yates booms, "Attention, please."

All eyes leap to the boss, front and center upon the platform. Mouth stretched in a grin, he says, "Today is a day of celebration for Columbia Paper. Ten years is a proud milestone, and we appreciate your cooperation in immortalizing this moment for posterity."

As he speaks, Mrs. Yates beams from the sidelines, seemingly amused to see her husband claim credit for her photograph idea.

"Of course, Columbia Paper could not have attained its current success if not for the efforts of one man." With a sweep of his arm, Mr. Yates steps aside. "Everyone, please welcome our company founder and my grandfather, Alfred J. Pope."

Mr. Pope comes forward amid a rain of applause, and Ida murmurs, "The old man still got fight in him."

Indeed. Mr. Pope's build has shrunk further, and he leans heavily on his cane. Yet his steps are sure, if slow, and when his mouth opens, the voice that resounds sends nostalgia washing over me.

"Thank you, friends," says the old boss with unbridled enthusiasm. "Truly, it does my heart good to see you on this happy occasion. I've been asked to deliver a few words regarding the company's history, but I have decided to refrain from that subject. The war years were difficult, we all know that, and I feel no need to dwell on hard times. Rather, I wish to celebrate the future and what my grandson has achieved in one short year."

He gestures to the newly constructed walls. "This mill addition is a noteworthy accomplishment. I'm awed by his leadership, and I hope that you, his employees, also find it inspirational."

"Inspirational as a slaver's whip," Ida mutters.

"Speaking of inspiration . . ." Mr. Pope looks to his grandson. "It is my understanding that two employees have a contest of ingenuity today."

"Yes," says Mr. Yates, returning to the front of the platform. "Contestants, come forward."

All of a sudden, fear seizes me. The prospect of mounting that stage, of having all eyes upon me, puts me in a cold sweat. My heart palpitates so violently, I feel faint. But then Ida gives me a gentle nudge.

"Go on, Mattie," she whispers. "Let 'em have it." Beside her, Fannie surreptitiously pumps a fist.

Their quiet encouragement steadies my nerves. Squaring my shoulders, I stride up the platform steps. Frank hobbles close behind, thudding an uneven beat on the planks.

Mr. Yates welcomes us with showman grandeur, heralding us as Columbia Paper's finest, most devoted employees. "In fact, these two mechanics are so dedicated, they have engaged in a competition to build a better bag machine," he says, gesturing to the machines beside the stage. "As the Good Book says, 'Iron sharpens iron.' No doubt their congenial rivalry has brought out the best of their skill."

I stifle the urge to roll my eyes. Leave it to the boss to recast my rebellious challenge as an endeavor to improve his business.

"Now, the rules." Mr. Yates clears his throat. "The machine that produces the most half-pound-size, square-bottom bags of salable quality in the span of two minutes will be the winner. Both machines are running on mill power, so the contest begins when the factory line is turned on and ends when it is shut off. I will time the two minutes. Grandfather, would you do the honor of throwing the power switch?"

"I'd be delighted," replies Mr. Pope.

The boss nods his thanks and continues. "Competitors are allowed to monitor their machines and make adjustments or the like. However, no one may assist them, and once started, the clock will not stop. After the two minutes are over, the bags will be counted by my grandfather and me. As previously mentioned, only salable bags will count. If a bag's quality is in question, we shall submit it to a simple test."

He snaps his fingers. To my surprise, his wife approaches. Since the boss arrived at the party, the vivacious woman has melted into the background, the very picture of a demure matron. But at his cue, she steps into the limelight holding a pint tankard, and behind her is Daniel, hauling a pail of sand.

Mrs. Yates's twinkling gaze holds mine for an instant. Her promise reechoes in my mind, and I'm suddenly positive that the judging will be impartial.

She raises her tankard and Daniel his pail. "If a bag can hold a pint measure of sand, it passes," Mr. Yates says. "If not, it will be rejected." The boss then faces me and Frank. "Those are the rules. Any objections?"

"No, sir," we reply.

"Then shake hands, and let's begin."

As cheers fill the air, Frank regards me with an expression hard as a stone wall. For my part, I'd rather kiss an asp than shake his hand. But manners are important, especially before an audience, and we clasp hands.

"May the best machine win," he says gruffly.

I smile through gritted teeth. "You bet it will."

As we take our positions, I eye Frank's contraption. Unlike my gear-driven machine, his is driven by pulleys and belts. I can't see much beyond that, but with its large, freestanding metal frame, it closely resembles Columbia's standard bag machines. *Not surprising, considering he had free use of company stock.*

My machine, on the other hand . . . I strapped its little frame to a pine worktable to keep its position stable. From a distance, it looks like a crate of parts forgotten on the factory floor.

Appearances don't matter; results do. I silently repeat the phrase as I make a final inspection of the pulley adapter that has replaced the hand crank.

Alignment is critical in a pulley and belt system. If my pulley adapter is misaligned with the drive pulley, the belt connecting them will run aslant and off the pulleys. However, the two pulleys are straight and square across from each other.

Satisfied, I open the switch that connects the arrangement to the currently idle overhead line. Meanwhile, Mr. Pope is tapping his way to the controls. Once he throws the switch, my wooden machine will be plunged into the run of its life.

That thought turns my stomach, and I slip some tools into my apron pocket, placing the rest in a toolbox by my feet. If something goes wrong, I want them close by. Although repair will be nigh impossible if the parts get busted to smithereens. I notice Frank's also keeping his tools near.

Mr. Pope's voice punches through the chatter of the crowd. "Competitors, are you ready?" He stands with his hand on the main switch and excitement on his white-bearded face.

Shoving thoughts of doom aside, I shout, "Yes, sir." Frank also declares his readiness.

Mr. Pope looks to Mr. Yates on the platform. "At your signal, son."

Mr. Yates removes his pocket watch from his waistcoat. Members of the office staff, overseers, and even a few factory workers also take out timepieces. A hush falls as the boss positions his watch in one hand and raises the other high. "Without further ado," says Mr. Yates. "On your mark . . ."

At the front of the crowd, Fannie crosses her fingers while Ida clasps her hands prayerfully.

"Get set . . ."

Heart in my mouth, I murmur my own prayer for success.

"Go!"

Chapter 16

MR. YATES THROWS DOWN HIS ARM, AND MR. POPE YANKS THE switch. The overhead shaft whizzes, snatching pulleys and gears into motion.

The crowd roars, but I barely hear it through the blood pounding in my ears. My clattering machine drops snow-white bags into the delivery bin at double its usual rate, but Frank's flies at an even faster clip. Anxiety creeps up my throat as his machine produces three bags for every two of mine. If my output is a snow-fall, his is a blizzard.

Suddenly, the blizzard stops.

Cheers turn to gasps as Frank's feed jams. Moving faster than I've seen, Frank disengages power and yanks mangled paper from his machine's innards. As his Maryland compatriots holler encouragement, Mr. Yates calls out, "Twenty seconds past. One minute, forty seconds remaining."

My heart leaps. If his machine can't run continuously, I have a chance.

No sooner have I thought this than deep-throated hurrahs rise again to rock the room. Frank's machine has reengaged. Bags stream out, making up for lost time. I'm presently in the lead, but at the rate he's going, it won't last.

"Forty seconds past," yells Mr. Yates.

Suddenly, my machine's steady rattle turns erratic. My eyes dart away from Frank's growing output to see my pulley adapter edging out of alignment with the drive pulley. Before I can react, the pulley belt slips, then catches, jerking the machine—table and all—forward. That two-inch movement skews the alignment, causing the belt to flip off and slither to the floor.

Horror slices through me. I was so fixed on Frank's machine, I didn't notice my machine's vibrations gradually shifting the table to which it was strapped.

Drat! Why didn't I use weights to hold it in place? But there's no time for regret. Disengaging power, I snatch up the belt.

Sweat dampens my hands as I reposition my machine. Every second it sits idle is a second against me. I hasten to refasten the belt, and as I turn to loop it over the drive pulley, I realize that the other machine has also stopped.

Once more, Frank's snatching snarled paper out of his machine. For an instant, our eyes lock. Then we furiously plug away at our tasks, striving to be the first to resume the race.

In the midst of that frenzied scramble, I recall Frank's words at the river: *You know, Mattie, if we were working together . . .*

I squash the memory. Frank's distracted me enough. I need to concentrate on winning.

As if I needed another reminder, Frank's machine growls back to life, sending the men into ecstasies. Through their whooping, Mr. Yates yells, "One minute past. One minute remaining."

Meanwhile, I'm struggling to get my power system back in place. Unfortunately, I've had no practice at this, and on my first try, the belt slides uselessly over the pulley adapter, unable to grab it. Precious seconds tick away as I disengage power and reposition the machine for another attempt.

Dear God, please let this work . . . I throw the switch, and this time the belt catches. A relieved "Hallelujah" escapes me as the machine noisily resurrects. Unwilling to be derailed a second time, I grasp the sides of the table to hold it in place as the machine churns, steadily adding to my pile.

Unfortunately, my pile is half the size of Frank's.

"One minute, twenty seconds," shouts Mr. Yates.

How much time did I lose? Thirty seconds? More? From the women's agonized expressions, my situation must look impossible. But then a collective male groan resounds.

Frank's machine is down again. My spirits lift as he struggles with his third jam. Whatever mechanism he's devised hasn't been perfected, which means victory remains within my grasp.

I glance at my machine, still whipping the specially initialed paper into bags. With Frank delayed, the size of my pile creeps closer and closer to his. Perhaps mine is a tortoise's speed, but as the fable goes, "Slow and steady wins the race."

"One minute, forty seconds."

With a snarl, Frank's machine returns to the fray. The avalanche of bags resumes, and the gap between us expands once more.

No! Jam up again, you dratted contraption! Come on, jam! Just as I direct those unsporting thoughts towards Frank's machine, a sharp crack from my own machine seizes my attention.

The lever mechanism controlling the plate folder has snapped. No sooner have I registered this than the broken pieces tumble in the path of the other mechanisms, and the machine's rattling grinds into a sickening crunch.

I jump to disengage power. Tearing at the paper feed, I yank it aside to assess the damage, and my heart stops.

My machine is broken. Utterly broken. The meticulously arranged folders, the precisely harmonized gears, the painstakingly positioned follower are a jumble of ruined parts. Even the frame's cracked.

I look from the ravaged mechanisms to the tools in my apron, and helplessness swallows me whole. *I can't possibly fix this.*

As I stand paralyzed, I'm vaguely aware of men clamoring, of Frank stymied by a fourth jam. But whereas his efforts might reward him a chance to continue, all my chances are gone.

"Two minutes—time's up!"

The power halts, and applause erupts. "Well done," says Mr. Yates, clapping with the rest. "Truly an exhilarating spectacle. No doubt both contestants performed to the best of their ability."

To an uninvolved bystander, the words are a compliment. In my ears, they harbor an undercurrent of malice. No doubt Mr. Yates is delighted to point out that my best couldn't keep pace with Frank.

But I haven't the wherewithal to feel offense. In fact, I don't feel anything. Dazed, I woodenly follow the boss's instructions to bring my bin forward.

Two trestle tables are also carried to the platform. Frank and I each place our bins on a table, and Mr. Pope joins Mr. Yates to judge the results.

Mr. Yates rubs his hands together. "As the saying goes, 'Ladies first.' We'll begin with you, Miss Knight."

I nod, not trusting my voice to respond. My chest feels like lead as Mr. Yates and Mr. Pope take bags from the bin, open them up, and stand them on the tabletop in rows of ten. Meanwhile, Mrs. Yates and Daniel wait on the sidelines with their tankard and sand. I sense the two sneaking me sympathetic looks, but I'm past comfort. I risked everything, and I lost.

The last bag is inspected, and Mr. Yates booms, "One hundred fifty bags. That's the total for Miss Knight."

"And not a single defective bag," adds Mr. Pope. "The quality was impeccable. An excellent effort."

I wince. I doubt the old boss intends to be cruel, but his remark is a fistful of salt on the wounds of defeat. People can compliment my workmanship all they like, but that doesn't do a thing to increase my bag count.

Mr. Yates moves to Frank's table. "Next, Mr. Niebuhr."

I fix my eyes on the ceiling beams. I can't bear to look at the women's disappointment or the men's sneers. I certainly do not want to witness the boss's glee as he shows off Frank's work.

"Aurelia, Mr. Mowe, your assistance, please."

Mr. Pope's request startles me out of my misery. Mrs. Yates and Daniel immediately go to the old boss, who frowns at a bag in his hands. Next to Mr. Pope, Mr. Yates stares into Frank's bin, his brow furrowed with consternation.

Confusion rustles the room as Mrs. Yates scoops a measure of sand and empties it into the bag Mr. Pope holds.

A thin stream leaks out, just above the bag bottom.

I blink and readjust my glasses. Sure enough, a small tear–no more than a half inch–splits an "F" and an "N" printed on the paper.

I glance at Frank, but his features reveal nothing. He merely faces the muttering throng, his back ramrod straight.

Mr. Yates, on the other hand, is unable to completely hide his agitation. He engages in a hushed conversation with his grandfather, glancing now and then into the bag bin. Meanwhile, Mrs. Yates hovers nearby. Her back is to me, so I can't see her expression, but whatever it is, I sense it will keep the proceedings honest.

At last, Mr. Pope sets aside the torn bag and returns his attention to those waiting in the bin. But instead of opening and standing them in rows, he stacks the still-folded bags tidily upon the tabletop. Meanwhile, Mr. Yates plucks a bag from a stack and impatiently beckons to his wife for a test.

It holds tight.

He stands the bag upon the table and takes another. The tension eases from Frank's pals when it also passes, and confidence returns to their eyes as the next twenty bags pass muster.

The twenty-third bag leaks.

Hope rises in my chest. Judging from the stacks on the table, Frank produced well over two hundred bags, but if their quality is inconsistent, the final outcome is anyone's guess. As such, my spirits soar when the twenty-fourth bag leaks—and plummet as the next dozen pass.

When the thirty-seventh bag fails, hope sparks again, but I'm afraid to kindle it. If things continue in this vein, I'll lose for certain.

But it's not certain it'll continue this way. Waiting in those stacks could be a spate of bad bags.

However, those bad bags don't materialize. They continue to pass, and when Frank's count reaches forty-five, I tear my eyes away.

This is insufferable. It's my duty to witness the results, but the prolonged assessment is worse than the contest itself.

The sand runs low. Daniel, who's been in a constant scamper to keep the pail filled, starts heading out for more, but Mr. Yates says, "That won't be necessary, Mr. Mowe. The evaluation has concluded."

My head jerks up. Stacks of untested bags remain. "Mr. Yates," I say, as onlookers exchange perplexed looks, "what about the rest?"

"My grandfather has already assessed those," he replies, placing a forty-sixth sound bag on the table. "The sand test was only necessary for those whose integrity was uncertain."

My eyes dart back to the stacks. *Those bags didn't need testing? That means they're all sound?*

Judging from their height, they number well over a hundred. And Frank only needs one hundred and five more to claim victory.

Mr. Pope's voice plows through my distraught calculations. "Ladies and gentlemen, it is with great pleasure that I announce the final results."

The crowd hushes. I hang my head, resigning myself to defeat.

"Miss Knight, one hundred fifty bags. Mr. Niebuhr, forty-six. Congratulations, Miss Knight!"

Chapter 17

WHOOPING AND STOMPING ROCK THE MILL ADDITION AS women cavort to the strains of Mrs. Yates's hired fiddler. The Maryland men only stayed long enough to wolf down a sandwich or two; the overseers tarried longer but also excused themselves as soon as they could. The female hands, however, have whirled me about the floor all afternoon and show no signs of flagging.

So it's the fiddler who brings our romp to a close as he ends with a flourish. "Thank you, everyone, but my time is done. Good night, ladies."

He exits to our applause, and I collapse onto a bench to catch my breath. "Mattie," Ida asks, dropping beside me, "need a hand getting home?"

I shake my head. "Daniel's bringing the handcart round once he's done helping Mr. Pope to his carriage."

She chuckles at the mention of the old boss. "Mr. Pope couldn't have been prouder of you if you were his own grand-daughter, Mattie."

Indeed, he'd bragged over and over about how he'd recognized my talent. The contest validated his decision to make me a mechanic, and everyone, including Mr. Yates, could only affirm it.

"I'm proud of you, too," Ida murmurs, patting my wrist. "And grateful. Took grit to do what you did. Till the day I die, I'll never forget it."

My cheeks warm. I'm not used to folks getting sentimental on me. Fortunately, I'm spared having to make a response by Fannie's hollering.

"Hey!" She waves from the door where the others have already gathered to leave. "You coming with us?"

Ida rises. "I am. You got your souvenirs?"

The group laughs, raising white bags printed with my initials. "You bet," shouts Fannie.

Mrs. Yates is one shrewd lady. Although Frank produced an astounding two hundred thirty-eight bags in two minutes, less than a quarter proved salable. That immediately sparked mutterings about the soundness of my bags. But before they could sour my victory, Mrs. Yates announced that she was filling my one hundred fifty bags with sand and distributing them as party souvenirs.

In one fell swoop, she eliminated doubts about my bag quality and extolled my achievement. And because she was our hostess, none could gainsay her. Courtesy compelled the men to take a "souvenir." Even Frank accepted one—though he disappeared soon thereafter. The women snatched theirs like hotcakes.

They brandish them now like trophies as they leave for home. I wave goodbye as they punctuate the dusk with congratulations and hip-hoorays, continuing the barrage until they drop out of sight.

A hush falls. With the celebration over, the giddiness that pulsed in my veins dissipates. Exhaustion weighs my bones, and I slump against the doorjamb.

It's over. After all these months, it's finally over. I accomplished my goal, showing Mr. Yates, Frank, everyone what I could do. Yet victory isn't entirely sweet.

Lighting a lantern against the deepening gloom, I turn toward my machine. I avoided looking at it while we celebrated. I refused to think about it while the women toasted me. But now, as the lantern illuminates the machine's remnants, my heart breaks all over again.

My finger traces the cracked slats, the bent follower wire, the snapped side folders. They are objects of wood and metal, parts I can replicate. But having labored so long over its creation, I feel a kinship with it, and grief wells up.

"I'm sorry . . ." I whisper. The machine served the purpose for which it was built, yet I can't stop feeling as if I've sacrificed a friend.

Footsteps sound at the entrance, and I quickly wipe my eyes. Pulling myself together, I say, "Daniel, I—oh, Mrs. Yates."

My cheeks flush hot as the tiny lady approaches. "Pardon me, ma'am," I stammer. "I thought you left."

She chuckles. "A good hostess is always the last to leave her party. It just took longer than expected to see Grandfather Pope off in his carriage. He had such a wonderful time, after all. But I'm glad you're still here, Miss Knight. My husband would like a word in the mill office."

The boss? Now? But I don't exactly have a choice. "Yes, ma'am. I'll go right away."

Mrs. Yates thrusts an arm in my path. "First things first." She pulls a scented handkerchief from her handbag and offers it. "Go ahead and cry. Better to get it out now than meet him while you're unsettled."

I start at her words. "Mrs. Yates?"

Her expression softens. "I saw your face when your machine broke," she says, lowering her gaze to its pitiful remains. "And I saw how you were looking at it just now. I can't say I understand, but I realize it's no small loss. And I realize victory doesn't necessarily erase the pain of your sacrifices."

She presses the handkerchief into my hands. At her touch, my breath hitches, and my precariously restrained emotions burst forth.

As I sob into her handkerchief, Mrs. Yates pats my back. "So many people think tears are weak," she murmurs. "I believe they point to how strongly you feel about something. You and your machine fought the good fight honorably and courageously with all that you had. Don't let anyone contradict that."

I sniffle. "Yes, ma'am."

❄ ❄ ❄

Ten minutes later, with my eyes dried and nose wiped, I stand before the mill office door. Considering the way Mr. Yates kept his distance after the contest, I assumed he wanted to avoid me for a spell. Squaring my shoulders, I steel myself for his worst and knock.

"Enter," he calls.

The office is quiet and illuminated by a single oil lamp on a corner desk, where the boss scribbles into a ledger. As I approach, I wonder if his intention is petty vengeance. Like keeping me standing and waiting while he pretends to be busy. Or browbeating me with a convoluted reason as to why Frank's loss was actually a win.

"Miss Knight." Mr. Yates sets down his pen. "It's late, so I'll be brief." Withdrawing an envelope from his frock coat, he places it on the desktop and slides it toward me. "Nine dollars, your wages for the week."

He leans back in his chair and looks at me directly. "The bookkeepers need time to adjust accounts to increase wages for the rest of the West Workroom workforce," he continues, "but they should finish by next week's payroll. Do you have any objections to that?"

"I . . ." Mr. Yates's prompt compliance puts me at a momentary loss for words. "No. No objections, sir."

He raises an eyebrow. "Was there more you wished to say, Miss Knight?"

I hesitate. I might have won our bet, but an employee needs to choose words carefully before her employer. Clearing my throat, I say, "I only wish to say I am glad you are proceeding so swiftly and . . . amicably."

"Instead of disputing the results in an unsportsmanlike manner?"

My jaw drops. Before I can protest, he cuts me off with a wave. "I spoke the words, not you, Miss Knight. It's no secret our relations have been contentious. However, while you may accuse me of being an ogre, you cannot accuse me of being dishonorable. Tell me, in the last seven months, have I ever violated the terms we agreed upon?"

I shake my head. When I first declared I could build a bag machine, we mutually understood I'd do it without his help. Although it was infuriating to scrape for material while he gave Frank free access to company stock, that was his right. Even the day Mr. Yates punished me for tardiness was within his authority as my employer.

"I've told you before. I'm a man of my word, and I honor my agreements." His fingers tap the envelope on the desk. "Moreover, you taught me a lesson, and I'd be a fool to discount it."

"Sir?" I'm astounded that the boss would confess such a thing, least of all to me.

His mouth twists wryly. "The battlefield taught me that ignoring an undeniable truth—no matter how outrageous—only leads to ruin. You have confronted me with such a truth, and rather than close my eyes to it, I'm beholden to reconsider my preconceptions about employees for this company's sake."

"I see." As usual, things boil down to his bottom line, although now he's forced to value women's labor equal to men's.

"On that note . . ." His gaze turns stern. "I'm informing you that I fully expect you to finish what you started and proceed to patent. Posthaste. I have need for your machine and will be the first to order one."

My brain stalls. "I beg your pardon?"

"I realize you've suffered a setback. But having built your machine once, you can do it again—with appropriate modifications, of course. It goes without saying that industrial equipment must withstand the rigors of a factory."

"Of course," I say, feeling like I've stumbled into Alice's Wonderland. After all, my adversary of the last several months is now treating me like a prospective business collaborator.

Mr. Yates pauses as if reading my thoughts and heaves a sigh. "Given recent circumstances, I suppose it's natural to assume I harbor . . . prejudices. Certainly, my wife has deemed it necessary to hail your machine's merits all afternoon. But even without her wheedling and cajoling, I'm convinced of its benefits, and as a businessman, I'm prepared to compensate its inventor fairly for it."

He rises to offer a handshake. "Our wager may have increased my expenses, but your machine bears the promise of greater company profits. So, shall we let bygones be bygones?"

Bygones be bygones . . . I never expected Mr. Yates to bury the hatchet. Yet as his employee, I'm better off making peace even if I'm not convinced of his sincerity. And on the off chance he's speaking honestly, it would be a tremendous change for the better.

I clasp his hand, and we shake like equals. But amid the euphoria of having gained the boss's respect, the question arises:

How on earth do I get a patent?

Chapter 18

THE NEXT MORNING, REVEREND PARSONS PREACHES ON THE Scripture: "Ask and it shall be given you; seek and ye shall find." The words are an encouragement to ponder the divine, but right now, I'm ashamed to say that all my prayers are for enlightenment on a worldly matter.

Namely, the patent process.

"Is that something you need to bother with, Mattie?" Fannie asks as we sip coffee in the Fellowship Hall after the Sunday sermon. "Why not start building your machines for the factory? The boss said he'd pay. That's money right there."

"Ninny." Ida cuffs Fannie on the head. "If she does that, what's to stop the boss from copying her machine and selling them himself? Nothing. That's what patents are for. They make sure inventors like Mattie get their due off the inventions they make."

"That's right," says Eliza, frowning over her cup. "Mattie invented that shuttle guard, and she didn't get a cent for it."

"Exactly," says Ida, so vehemently that several heads turn. "Every Manchester loom got a shuttle guard, but the factory owners paid Mattie nothing, even though she spent weeks inventing it."

"Calm down, Ida," I say. "You don't need to get riled up."

"Yes, I do. You say you've no regrets about the shuttle guard because it was about protecting people. I can accept that. But this is different." She huffs like an aggravated mule. "That bag machine is about nothing except making money. You need to get what's rightly yours. Heaven knows you and your kin need it."

"You don't need to remind me." Although Charlie hasn't worsened since his brush with trouble last summer, neither has he improved enough to take a job. I wholeheartedly agree that my family's lot could change for the better if I play my cards right.

Unfortunately, this is a game I know nothing about.

"The problem is, I'm just a mechanic. I built the machine to prove Mr. Yates wrong. I wasn't out to get a patent. I don't know the first thing about them."

Fannie's brow wrinkles. "What about Daniel? He's smart."

I shake my head. I asked him the night prior, while we were taking my things home from the mill. "Daniel knows bookkeeping and sales, but he's as ignorant about patents as I am. And I've got another problem to tend to first, before I can try to patent."

"What's that?" Fannie asks.

"I don't actually have a machine. It broke, remember?" My shoulders slump. "I can't patent something that doesn't exist."

The collective mood dampens. "How long will it take to rebuild?" Ida asks.

"I don't know. Three months? Maybe two?" Although all my folding mechanisms have to be remade, I did salvage most of the gear train. Plus, my diary notes will eliminate the guesswork that plagued me before.

Even so, re-creating parts takes time and attention. I won't have the luxury to think about anything else while I rebuild. "Daniel says he'll see what he can find out about patents, but he's also helping make parts like before." I set my coffee down with a sigh. "I know it's important to learn about patenting, but our hands are full."

"Your hands are full," says Eliza, "but mine aren't. I'll do it for you."

"You?" exclaims Fannie, as Ida and I blink. "You're not an inventor. You don't know anything about patents."

"Neither does anyone else," Eliza retorts, tossing her head. "That means I'm as qualified as any person here to learn about them."

That's true . . . I know how good Eliza is at booklearning. Even if patents are complicated, she's certain to figure it out.

"I have a library subscription, and I'm friends with the librarian," she continues. "I might not become an expert, but I can get Mattie off to a start."

"Are you sure?" I ask. After all, Eliza has her own work. "You just agreed to alter a gown for—"

She waves away my concern. "I'll finish that before the week is over, and I won't take more sewing jobs until I'm done helping you."

When I hesitate, Eliza puts down her cup and takes my hand. "Mattie, let me do this. I want to do this. You don't know how vexing it's been, being unable to help you like Daniel has."

Eliza's fervor takes me aback. In the last several months, the machine's demanded so much of me, I haven't done a thing for her. I even neglected to get her a souvenir bag from the contest. Yet she remains my staunchest supporter, and this opportunity to help has her chomping at the bit.

Ask and it shall be given you; seek and ye shall find. Perhaps my friend's zeal is the answer to my prayers. In this instant, I can't help but see her as an instrument of Providence.

I squeeze her hand back. "You're an angel, Eliza, and I'm grateful for it. I'll be even more grateful if you help with this."

Eliza beams. "You can rely on me."

❊ ❊ ❊

I thought that once the contest ended, my life would resume as before, with the exception of an increased wage. Instead, my after-work hours continue in the pattern of making parts in the kitchen—minus the pressure of competition, of course.

Another thing missing from these evenings is Eliza's company. Whereas before she'd sew or crack nuts at the table while Daniel and I fitted out the machine, she now haunts the city library. The nights she's at home, she sits in the parlor studying periodicals like *Scientific American* or penning requests for information. Her stack of notes grows by the day, and I trust she's sounding out the patent process more thoroughly than I could myself.

Which is why discouragement hits hard when she reports her findings three weeks later.

"Thirty dollars for the application fee?" I exclaim. If I wasn't seated, I would collapse to the floor.

Daniel grimaces. "That . . . is a steep sum."

"There's no way around it," says Eliza. "It's required of all patent applications. No exceptions."

I slump over the kitchen table. My mind's struggling to grasp that staggering amount when Eliza's pinched expression tells me she's not finished. "There's more?" I ask, dreading her reply.

"Unfortunately, yes. Apart from the fee, there's the application itself. You can hire a patent agent or lawyer to prepare and send it to the Patent Office. Or you can submit it yourself. The paperwork will take time, but I believe it's possible to prepare the application ourselves, save for two things."

"Which are?" asks Daniel. I fervently pray they're something I can afford.

"Drawings and an iron model. The application won't be complete without them."

"An iron model?" I glance at the wooden mechanisms of my partially reconstructed machine. Wood parts require a knife and patience. Metal parts require specialized power-driven tools and a trained machinist. "What about a wooden one?"

Eliza shakes her head. "It must be iron. The Patent Office instituted the requirement after a terrible fire. The model also must be scaled to certain dimensions for their archives. Engaging a drafter for drawings shouldn't be difficult, but the closest machinist shops capable of patent models are in Boston. You'd need to stay close or visit frequently to oversee the work, which will require at least a month."

"A month!" Blood rushes from my head, leaving me faint. I've no idea what a machinist costs, but I know I can't afford a single ticket to Boston. And I definitely can't afford to stop working, even temporarily. Not with Mother and Charlie depending on me.

I've heard it said that it takes money to make money. In this instant, I feel the truth of that saying. And the unfairness of it.

"The challenge is considerable. However, I'm certain you'll surmount it, Mattie." Eliza smiles beatifically.

She might as well have told me to hoist a locomotive with only my two arms. "How am I to surmount it?" I say, my voice grating like a faulty gear.

"Mr. Yates increased your wages, didn't he? With the extra money—"

"Eliza," I snap, making her jump. "I haven't fully repaid the four of you for my glasses. It will take an eternity to save up the application fee, let alone the cost of an iron model."

"Then ask Mr. Yates for an advance," says Eliza. "He said he would buy a machine."

"I would caution against that," says Daniel soberly. "Mattie built the machine on her own time with her own materials. Therefore, no one else has a claim to it. If she goes to Mr. Yates for funds, he'll not only want a share of royalties, he'll likely want control over sales and licensing. After all, anyone else who gets your machine creates competition for his business."

Eliza falters momentarily but counters brightly, "Mattie could approach the banks instead—"

A derisive snort resounds from Uncle Thomas's room. "No banker alive would extend credit to a girl with only ideas for collateral," he barks through the wall. "If Margaret wants to borrow, her only options are kin and friends, and you can count me out. Spectacles are one thing, but I'm not selling my late wife's silver to fund a contraption that has no guarantee of profit."

Uncle Thomas's words sting, but he's right. I could pour sweat and savings into this endeavor and gain nothing for my trouble. Worse, I could fall into debt.

As the specter of debt collectors sends my flesh crawling, Daniel says, "Your uncle's right that Mattie's only option for funds is kin and friends, but I believe it is a viable one. Even if he's not willing to contribute, I am."

I cringe. Gambling my own money would be folly. Losing my friends' money would be unforgivable. Cradling my head in my hands, I groan, "Stop it."

"I'll contribute also," cries Eliza, raising her hand. "I'm certain others will, too, once we tell them."

"First things first, Eliza. Mattie must first rebuild the machine. Then she can start asking for money—"

"I said stop it!" My fists slam the tabletop, startling Eliza and Daniel both.

"M-Mattie," Eliza stammers, "what's w-wrong?"

My anger redoubles at her confusion, her utter disregard for my reality. "I don't need this," I bite out. "I never sought a patent in the first place. I have enough burdens without taking an additional one."

"B-but—"

Daniel's hand whips up to silence Eliza. "I think we ought to respect Mattie's feelings and end this discussion for the time being. And I think it best I go now." He rises to his feet. "I can let myself out."

No one says a word as he leaves. The instant the front door shuts, Eliza blurts, "Mattie, you can't g-give up—"

I storm off, unwilling to tolerate any more. Proving my skill to Mr. Yates was a fight I chose, because it was one I could win. But this patent business . . . from all I've heard, it's an endeavor for which I'm poorly equipped that could possibly ruin me.

Yet Eliza won't back down. As I stomp upstairs, she dogs my heels. "This is a once-in-a-lifetime opportunity," she insists. "You can't a-afford to let it go."

I whirl upon her. "I can't afford to take it up!"

Eliza begins to argue back, but I cut her off. "I have dependents, Eliza. If I don't work, they don't eat. That means I can't leave my job to go to Boston, and I can't throw money away on a whim."

"It's not th-throwing money away. Mattie, you m-must—"

"I must?" I scoff. "Easy for you to say. You're not risking a thing."

My venom forces Eliza to step back. Shame colors her cheeks, and the sight incenses me further. I never thought I'd regard my best friend with disdain, but in this instant, I'm sick of her folly and the unfairness of everything.

"Must be nice to have kin who keep a roof over your head and food on your plate," I spit. "So why don't you do something with your life? The last thing I need are orders from a coward too afraid to follow her own dreams."

Eliza gasps, her hand flying over her mouth. The soft sound jolts me out of my fury and back to my senses. *I went too far . . .*

I must make amends, ask for forgiveness. But as I grasp for words, tears trickle down her cheeks.

Shame strangles my throat. The next instant, I'm running.

I flee upstairs, past our room, and up the attic rungs. Slamming the hatch behind me, I collapse on an old pallet, my chest heaving.

Not only have obstacles overrun my path, but I've wounded my dearest friend. Someone who's only ever had my best interest in mind. Even the grim tidings she delivered tonight was at my behest.

God in Heaven, what have I done? And what do I do now? I take pride in fixing things, but this . . . I'm not certain it's reparable.

Everything I've built is crashing down. My last vestiges of self-control collapse, too, and I burst into tears.

Chapter 19

IDA'S SON STRIPS THE LAST BIT OF BARK FROM THE STICK AND hands it over. "How's this look?"

The little boy fidgets as I evaluate his handiwork. The cuts are crooked, but the wood is smooth beneath my fingertips. "Very good, Sam," I declare. "No splinters. I daresay you're ready for kite-making."

Sam flings up his arms with a whoop. Having reached the venerable age of six, he's decided to make his toys by himself, and begged me to teach him. Fortunately, he's proven an apt and delightful pupil.

Over his crowing, Ida says, "That's splendid, Sam, but kite-making will have to wait for another day. It's almost nine o'clock. Say goodnight and go upstairs with Nana."

Sam obeys, and as he and Mrs. Leavilte leave the kitchen, Ida says, "You'd best go, too, Mattie. I'm sorry he kept you so late."

"No rush. I'll sweep the peelings before I go."

I'm reaching for the broom when Ida lets out a huff. "It's not my nature to be a busybody, but isn't it high time you and Eliza made up?"

I freeze like a thief caught red-handed.

"Mattie, I appreciate you playing with the kids the last four nights, truly I do," Ida goes on. "But you shouldn't keep coming here to hide from her."

I sink into my seat with a sigh. I haven't breathed a word to Ida about our falling-out, and I doubt Eliza has, either. But Ida knows us too well for me to play dumb.

"You're right, Ida. I know you're right, and I want to make things right, but . . . how?" My shoulders hunch. "Where do I start?"

"Start by going home," says Ida, as if it were that simple. "You share a room, don't you?"

"Actually . . . I've been sleeping in the attic."

The admission makes me burn with shame. I never thought I'd be such a coward, but I haven't been able to muster the courage to face Eliza. So I've holed up in the attic, leaving early and returning late. Eliza, for her part, has made no attempt to flush me out.

I brace for a rebuke, but Ida gives me a sympathetic pat. "It's not unheard of for friends to quarrel. But if you want to stay friends, don't let this drag. Not to mention, tomorrow's the Sabbath, and the Good Book commands us to reconcile before approaching God's altar."

My conscience twinges. How can I enter the Lord's house with hard feelings lingering between me and my best friend? "Right," I mumble.

"And pray. The Good Lord will guide you if you ask."

I nod at Ida's advice, but inwardly I groan. Because I *have* been praying. If I ever needed divine wisdom, it's now. Guilt racks me every time I remember the terrible things I said, and I've been begging God to tell me how to undo the damage I wrought. But despite my repeated asking, He's been tightlipped on the matter.

As I leave Ida's house, I wonder how Eliza will receive me. Given her character, she'll readily forgive.

However, she was also adamant about my pursuing a patent. I recall her zeal for my paper bags and the way she hounded me to patent. Even if we make amends tonight, will the matter resurge to sow discord like a tenacious weed? I don't want to lose Eliza's friendship, but I cannot risk a venture that costs money and guarantees nothing.

At my wits' end, I halt amid Mrs. Leavilte's laundry lines and raise yet another prayer. *Dear God, help me please. Tell me what to do.*

My eyes scrutinize the stars for an answer. But the night sky bears only indifferent twinkling and silence.

I lower my gaze with disappointment. I don't expect anything as grand as a message conveyed by burning bush, but I had hoped for some response by now. *A note with directions would be nice . . .*

I shake off that wishful thought. The Good Lord has a universe to run; no doubt He's busy with more important problems. I must figure this out on my own. Straightening up, I resume weaving through the laundry lines to the front gate. Then I freeze.

Across the street, beneath the streetlamp by Uncle Thomas's gate, is Frank.

He and I haven't spoken since the contest. We've kept to our respective workrooms, and on the occasion that our paths cross, we avoid eye contact. For him to show up unannounced at my doorstep puts my every fiber on guard.

I briefly contemplate running to the police but decide against it. Frank's stance isn't hostile, nor is he in ambush like a railway bandit. Moreover, my life is complicated enough without creating a commotion for the neighbors to gossip over.

And if he does try something, I've got my birthday jackknife ready in my pocket.

Frank's head snaps up at the clomp of my boots against the pavement. Despite the strangeness of this late encounter, he tips his hat, all courtesy. "Good evening, Mattie."

I halt on the sidewalk, eight feet away. "To what do I owe this sudden visit?"

His expression turns sheepish at my prickly tone. "I suppose this is sudden. Sorry about that. But I owe you something and wanted to give it right away."

My brow knits. What could he possibly give me? A belated congratulations? An apology for blockheaded notions about women's wages?

He reaches into his coat pocket for a small rectangle of paper and holds it out. I squint to read the text printed upon it:

Boston and Albany Railway
1 Second-Class Fare to Boston

A train ticket? "Are you running me out of town?" I snap.

He chuckles. "I'm not telling you to leave. I'm giving you the means should you choose to go. See, I was at the post office Wednesday and overheard Daniel Mowe and Miss Eliza talking about you there."

My spine stiffens. "What exactly did you overhear?"

"That patenting is expensive and troublesome. Quit looking daggers at me, Mattie. It's not like I meant to eavesdrop. Anyway, after that, I made up my mind to get you a train ticket. I just had to wait till payday to do it."

I glance at the ticket. *So he got his pay this evening, bought the ticket, and has been waiting here since to give it to me?*

I can't comprehend his intentions, so I settle for flinging sarcasm. "You want to send me to Boston so I can fail?"

He rolls his eyes. "No, I want to give you a choice. If you want to go to Boston, your fare's paid."

"And it's a gift out of the goodness of your heart, no strings attached?" Frank's a man with dependents. I can't see why he'd spend his money like this.

"It's no gift." His expression hardens. "I told you, I owe you."

"How so?"

He presses a fist to his forehead, seemingly frustrated by my doltishness. "You had a bet with the boss, but you also had one with me. Remember what you said you'd do for me if you lost?"

Comprehension hits like a pail of cold water. "I . . . said I'd bring you coffee every morning."

"And I planned to hold you to that when I won. Only I didn't." His gaze locks on mine. "I never said what I'd do for you if I lost."

"You didn't," I say, remembering how I flung that gauntlet between us, "but I didn't demand anything either. So it's not like you broke your word."

"Maybe, but it doesn't sit well with me." He frowns, folding his arms. "Ever since the contest, my spirit hasn't been at peace. Sure, you got your raise. But the whole West Workroom got a raise. Didn't seem right that you didn't get something especially for you. So when I heard what I heard, I knew this was the right thing."

He presses the ticket into my palm. "You beat me fair and square. Not only that, you made a fine machine. I can say that because I tried for months to do the same. Whether you patent is up to you, but if you ask me, you can make a success of it. And though this isn't much, I hope it starts you on your way."

His hands squeeze mine. Then he lets go and hobbles off.

I stare after him. Once he disappears around the corner, my eyes drop to the ticket in my hand.

Did someone put him up to this? I can't imagine who would. Mr. Yates is impatient for my patent, but I doubt he'd humiliate Frank by asking him to persuade me like this. And Eliza and Daniel would never be so brazen as to ask my former rival to support my endeavors.

Then . . . could this be a sign? I've been desperate for direction, and the ticket indicates a very specific destination.

The notion of Frank bringing a divine message seems utterly contrary, yet I can't shake the sense that this is the answer I've been praying for. And though my circumstances haven't changed, I feel suddenly obliged to reconsider patenting.

Clutching the ticket to my heart, I look toward Heaven and say, "Well, if You're telling me to walk through the Red Sea, I'll be counting on You to part the waters."

I don't know how my attempt to patent will end, but I know it begins with making amends with Eliza. I felt compelled to reconcile before; now I'm doubly convicted. But that doesn't lessen the shame weighing my steps as I approach our bedroom.

Light shines beneath the door. She's still awake. Summoning my nerve, I raise my fist and knock.

Immediately, footsteps rush over, and Eliza flings the door open. "Mattie!"

Relief and guilt surge up at her glad tone. Relief because I'd anticipated anger or at least resentment. Guilt because her warm welcome makes me feel worse about avoiding her all week. Anxious to put things to rights, I blurt, "Eliza, I'm sorry for getting angry. I wrongly blamed you—"

"No, it was my fault," Eliza interjects, waving her hands. "You were right to lose patience with me."

I shake my head. "You were only giving the information you collected for me. I can't fault you for that."

"But you can fault me for insisting on what you should do." Eliza's head droops. "And . . . you were right to call me a coward."

That last word pangs my conscience. "Eliza, that's not true."

"It is. But I intend to change that." Drawing up to her full height, she says, "Mattie, let's move to Boston together."

Her proposal hits like a bolt from the blue. "Move? What do you mean?"

"My family's in Boston, remember?" she says, reaching for her handbag. "I've figured a way for you to live there without having to worry about rent."

She fishes out an opened letter and shows it to me. "The cousin who's living with my grandmother on Beacon Hill is getting married in December, and the family's been searching for a replacement companion. So I wrote to Nana and got her reply today. She says if I'm willing to be her companion, you're welcome to share my room, and if you help with chores, you can share meals, too."

The round script on the page confirms Eliza's statement. The arrangement would eliminate a massive obstacle. Yet concern nags me. After all, Eliza has deliberately used Uncle Thomas as an excuse to linger in Springfield for a reason.

"Eliza, are you truly prepared to go home?" I ask, recalling how the mere mention of the teachers' examination reduced her to tears. "Once you're back, won't your father press you to become a teacher?"

"Absolutely—if I returned solely to help you, Mattie. But this move is as much about my dreams as it is about yours."

My brow furrows. "How?"

"Because . . . here, it's easier to show you," she says, throwing on her housecoat.

Eliza leads me downstairs to the parlor, where she lights a lamp and opens the lid to the secretary. Inside is a score of sealed envelopes with Eliza's tidy handwriting. At first I think they're additional patent-related correspondences. Then I notice that the addresses say "Dressmaker," "Modiste," and "Fine Fashions."

She taps the envelopes with a finger. "These are inquiries for dress shop apprenticeships. Once I'm home, I intend to work toward becoming a dressmaker, and I'll convince my parents to accept it."

"Eliza, that—that's wonderful!" I know better than anyone the courage it took for her to make this decision. "I'm so proud of you."

"No. This was a long time coming. Too long." She looks up sharply, her features taut. "I've always admired you, Mattie. The way you accomplished whatever you put your hand to. I told myself it was because you were special, that you possessed something that made everything possible. And because I didn't have that gift, I was excused from trying. But I was wrong."

She lowers her head, abashed. "When you achieved what you did, you felt the blows and burdens as much as any other person. You've certainly borne more burdens than me. That means I need to stop making excuses, stop being a coward, and start moving forward."

She reaches out and grasps my hand. "You made me realize that I've been blessed with much. Blessed with things I can share with you. So say you'll go with me. Let's make both our dreams reality."

My heart pounds. Between Frank's ticket and Eliza's offer, I'm tempted to accept then and there. Yet duty holds me back. "Eliza . . . let me think about it. I'm not saying no, but I have Mother and Charlie to consider."

Eliza raps her temple with her knuckles. "I'm such a scatterbrain. I forgot to mention Daniel has an idea about that. He thinks we can ask Mrs. Yates for help."

"How can she help?" While Mrs. Yates is likely to be sympathetic, she's a married woman. That means she has no way to lend money without involving her husband.

"A lady like her is unquestionably engaged in charitable work. Even if she's not directly involved with veterans' aid groups, she must know ladies who are. If we ask, she's sure to know means of assisting your mother and brother." Eliza pauses, her expression wavering. "I realize accepting charity may be difficult. If you'd rather not—"

"No, I am. I am absolutely willing to accept it." I may have felt differently before, but after three years of single-handedly supporting my family, I welcome any and all the aid they can get. Especially since it'll free me to strive toward a future where we'll never need charity again.

Excitement lights Eliza's face. "You'd be willing then? To go to Boston together?"

I'm not one to be rash, but after tonight, everything points in that direction. Hugging Eliza tight, I answer with a resounding "Yes!"

Chapter 20

ALTHOUGH I ENJOY CELEBRATING CHRISTMAS, I'M NOT AS EN-thusiastic about hailing a new year. A factory worker's routine changes little with the seasons, so the close of one year and the beginning of the next bears no difference to me.

However, this New Year's Eve, I'm brimming with expectations for 1869.

A knock sounds at the front door. Leaving my half-packed valise, I scurry downstairs to open it for Daniel, who holds a large shipping box. "Special delivery," he says, tipping his battered felt hat.

I laugh, waving him inside from the freezing cold. "Special indeed. Come in."

"And a happy new year to you, Mr. MacFarland," Daniel calls out.

"Oh, Uncle Thomas isn't back yet. He's still supping at Ida's."

Daniel glances at the parlor clock, which reads five minutes past eight. "Seems the old fellow has gotten comfortable with the new arrangement."

"He has, which is good, because we shan't return to the old one."

Last month, Uncle Thomas accompanied Eliza to Boston. This was partly to attend their relative's wedding and celebrate Thanksgiving and Christmas with the rest of the MacFarlands. However, it was mainly so Eliza could move in with her grand-mother and begin her apprenticeship at Small and Martin's on Washington Street.

Uncle Thomas accepted Eliza's departure without complaint. After all, she was leaving to benefit a more aged relation. So he's arranged for Mrs. Leavilte to take care of his meals and laundry, and for little Sam to sweep his porch ramp until he engages a housekeeper. The arrangement, though, is working so well that it's likely to become permanent.

As Daniel takes off his hat and coat, he asks, "Speaking of arrangements, I don't suppose you've had word from your mother?"

A grin spreads across my face. "I was going to wait until you sat down, but since you asked . . ." Withdrawing my latest letter from my pocket, I hand it to Daniel.

He wipes the condensation from his glasses and reads. "Dearest Mattie, it is with greatest joy that I inform you Charlie's been accepted . . ." Daniel's gaze snaps up, alight with excitement. "Mattie, this is wonderful news!"

"It is," I say, clapping my hands. "And I have you to thank for it."

He shakes his head. "The credit belongs entirely to the Yateses."

As Daniel guessed, Mrs. Yates was acquainted with philanthropists, and one in particular who'd opened an asylum for veterans suffering Soldier's Heart. Once she learned about my family's circumstances, she immediately contacted that acquaintance regarding my brother. Not only that, she convinced Mr. Yates—the selfsame Mr. Yates who'd dismissed Charlie as a lazy degenerate—to appeal to the Pension Commission on his behalf.

As it turns out, Mr. Yates carries significant clout with the Commission. With a single letter, he sliced the red tape that had stymied my brother's application for years. Ultimately, Charlie was denied a pension because he sustains no permanent physical impairment. But the Commission also determined that he was entitled to a year and a half of retroactive pay for the months Mother nursed his war injuries.

While the settlement doesn't provide ongoing security, it's more than sufficient to sustain them while I leave Columbia Paper to pursue a patent. Moreover, Charlie's admittance for treatment kindles new hope for us. Yet none of this would've happened had Daniel not thought to approach Mrs. Yates in the first place.

"I am grateful to the Yateses, Mrs. Yates especially," I say. "But I wouldn't have dared ask their help without you." My throat grows tight with emotion. "So thank you. For not letting me give up."

Daniel returns a sweeping bow. "For you to go to Boston and obtain a patent is sufficient thanks. So let's hasten you on your way, shall we?"

He taps the box he brought, and I return a smile. "Yes, let's."

I lead the way to the kitchen table, whereupon sits my resurrected machine. Thanks to my diary notes and Daniel's assistance, I finished restoring it the day after Christmas. As Daniel sets the box beside the machine, he asks, "May I watch it run one more time before we prepare it for shipment?"

I beam like a proud mother. "By all means."

Daniel watches in rapt silence as I crank the machine, sending bags smoothly out its end. Once the last bag falls, he applauds. "Bravo, Mattie. Beautifully done."

Heat rushes to my cheeks. Daniel's complimented my work before, but tonight I'm oddly disconcerted by his praise. "I couldn't have done it without your help."

"Then let that be a lesson, Mattie Knight, of the astounding things that can happen when you rely on others," he teases. "Speaking of which . . ."

He holds out a slip of paper. "Remember my machine enthusiast friend Charles Annan? I wrote to ask if he knew any Boston machinists. He recommends this shop. In fact, he's already spoken to the proprietor, Mr. Burnham, on your behalf, and the man is expecting you."

Gratitude floods up at the name and address in Daniel's blocky script. I'd anticipated spending several days to find a machinist for my patent application model. Daniel has saved me the effort. "This is wonderful."

"Better yet, it seems you'll be able to afford his services. You said you could pay a hundred dollars, correct?"

"Yes. Once Mother receives payment from the Pension Commission, she'll send me a portion. Between that and my savings, I'll have a hundred dollars."

"Then my advice is to go straight to Burnham once you have the funds. If Charles recommends him, you can rely on his work. He'll likely know reputable drafters, too, and you'll get your patent before you know it."

Daniel speaks with conviction, and I'm reminded of how staunchly he's supported me this year. And how much it's meant to me.

"Mattie?" Daniel's eyebrows rise in alarm. "What's wrong?"

"What do you mean . . . oh." Without my noticing, tears have slipped from my eyes. Wiping them away with my fingers, I say, "I'm sorry. I don't know what's come over me."

"You're about to undertake a formidable task," says Daniel kindly. "It's understandable to feel overwrought."

That's not it. The challenge ahead isn't what's plunged me into turmoil. It's the person I'm leaving. The realization hits like a thunderbolt, and I'm suddenly compelled to confess my sentiments while I have the chance.

Daniel offers a handkerchief and jolts when I clasp his hand instead. "Daniel," I say, feeling strangely bold and shy at once, "I said before that I'm grateful to you. But more than that, I . . . I will miss you."

His expression softens. "Mattie, you're talking as if we'll never see each other again. That's absolutely not the case."

"I know. But—"

"Remember what I said about being your salesman?" His lips tug into a gentle smile. "Once you get your patent, I'll help you set up business. That is, if you still want my help."

"Of course I do." I clutch his hand tighter. "I can't dream of anyone I'd rather have."

"Then it's settled."

His free hand brushes the tears from my face. The light sensation sends a pleasant shiver up my spine. And when his palm cradles my cheek, the warmth of his skin against mine stirs a longing for more. My fingers intertwine with his, and we lean in . . .

Suddenly, the front door thuds open, and Daniel and I leap apart as if it were gunfire. Hurriedly wiping my eyes, I will the heat scalding my face to dissipate as Uncle Thomas calls from the entryway, "Daniel Mowe, is that you here?"

"Yes, Mr. MacFarland," replies Daniel, already composed and looking like innocence itself. "Happy new year, sir."

"A new year is certainly upon us," says Uncle Thomas, waddling into the kitchen. "As to whether or not it will be happy . . ."

The old man's eyes narrow at the machine and box on the table. Seeing his annoyance, I say, "Daniel came to help pack the machine. We'll move it out of the kitchen once we're done. He'll also be coming early the morning of the second to help take my things to the depot."

Uncle Thomas cuts me off with a thump of his cane. "Yes, yes, I understand that. What I don't understand is why your young man is content to send you off." Aiming his scowl at Daniel, he says, "I thought you had a genuine interest in Margaret."

My skin tingles where Daniel's hand lingered moments ago, and I struggle to keep my expression neutral as he replies, "I do have a genuine interest in her, sir. I've always wanted what's best for her."

The truth of those words makes my heart flutter. Uncle Thomas snorts. "Then why aren't you stopping her?" he growls. "What kind of beau lets his girl leave him and leave town to try to sell a harebrained contraption?"

I wince. Uncle Thomas has been witness to my building, tinkering, and whittling since the summer I constructed his porch ramp. But although my work has garnered even my boss's respect, Eliza's uncle still believes my highest priority should be finding a husband to honor and obey. And from the way he glares at Daniel, Uncle Thomas expects him to shove me into my proper place.

Daniel purses his lips as if mulling the question over. "When you put it that way, it does sound like a travesty."

"Then if you agree, do something!"

"I would, if Mattie had built a harebrained contraption. But this"—Daniel's finger taps the machine—"this is a contraption that actually works. And if my duty is to stop her when she's making a mistake, shouldn't it also be to support her if she's bound for success?"

My heart somersaults. Uncle Thomas harrumphs like a disgruntled mule. As he exits, muttering about the folly of young people nowadays, Daniel catches my gaze, and we share a smile behind the old man's back.

Chapter 21

RUTH MACFARLAND IS IN FINE FETTLE FOR A WOMAN IN HER eighties. Her eyes can no longer read anything smaller than three-inch letters, but she wrings laundry and kneads dough with vigor. Her hearing and wits remain sharp, too. As Eliza helps me maneuver my machine's crate past her grandmother's knickknacks to the front door, Mrs. MacFarland calls from her second-floor bedroom, "Are you girls leaving?"

"Yes, Nana," Eliza replies.

Mrs. MacFarland descends to remind us to bundle up, ask if we know which streetcars to take, and confirm that we have exact fare and the house key. Eliza responds to the barrage with a weary tone and long-suffering smile. I find the mothering endearing. After all, it's been years since anyone's fussed over me like this.

Once convinced we're sufficiently outfitted, Mrs. MacFarland reaches up to pat my cheek. "Mattie, stick close to Eliza. We don't want to trouble the police with a missing person report."

"Don't worry," I reply. "I'll hang onto her for dear life."

Having resided in Springfield and Manchester, I thought I was used to city living, but Boston's clamorous streets, suffocating throngs, and construction sites have reduced me to a bewildered bumpkin. After three weeks, I still can't find my way around our West Beacon Hill neighborhood. It amuses my Boston-bred housemates to no end, but I accept their teasing with good humor. My eyesight might be better than Mrs. MacFarland's, but when I accompany her on house calls and shopping trips, she's the one directing me through the avenues and alleyways.

That is why I've delayed visiting Mr. Burnham's shop, even though Mother's money order arrived a week ago. Any solo venture is bound to result in the missing person report Mrs.

MacFarland joked about. And a solo venture combined with icy sidewalks and a bulky crate is a recipe for disaster. Having Eliza guide me on her day off is unquestionably worth the wait.

However, I feel badly monopolizing her rare leisure time. As we exit her grandmother's cozy brick house into the cloudy late-January morning, I thank Eliza for her trouble.

"I don't mind," she replies. "I'm excited to do this. Besides, you've been taking care of Nana for me. I'm simply returning the favor."

Eliza's apprenticeship has had her busy as a beaver since her return to Boston. Because she loves the shop, she doesn't mind the ten- to fourteen-hour workdays, but she hadn't anticipated being detained past dinnertime with such frequency. So upon moving in, I took on the role of Mrs. MacFarland's companion. After all, I'm merely biding time until my patent model is finished.

Mrs. MacFarland's no invalid, which means my duties amount to completing a smattering of chores, accompanying her on walks, and reading the mail and newspaper to her in the afternoons. I'm happy to kindle fires and wash dishes, and our outings are acquainting me with Boston, if slowly. Reading aloud, though . . . that task has laid bare my disgraceful lack of schooling.

"I'm sure she'd much prefer you, Eliza," I say, embarrassed. "In fact, I'm surprised she hasn't lost patience with me. I haven't made it through a single newspaper reading without her correcting my pronunciation. The one time I penned a letter for her, I needed her to spell ten words for me."

Eliza laughs. "I think Nana enjoys correcting you. She taught at a girls seminary before she married, you know. It probably reminds her of her classroom days."

"If you say so," I mumble.

"And I know for a fact she adores you, Mattie. She said so the other day when she showed me the handrail you built for the basement stairs."

I shrug. "That was nothing."

"Then there was the loose shutter you repaired, that broken rocking chair, that squeaky cabinet door . . ." Eliza ticks off her fingers.

I huff, spewing white plumes into the frigid air. "Your grandmother is generously providing me room and board. It's the least I can do. And truly, it's as much for me as it is for her."

Eliza cocks her head. "What do you mean?"

I lower my gaze sheepishly. "I'm used to being busy, and waiting has got me antsy. If I've got something to occupy my hands, I don't feel as restless."

"Well then," says Eliza, tapping the box in my arms, "let's get this to the machinist before Nana runs out of things for you to fix."

❁ ❁ ❁

Two horse car rides and a short walk later, we reach our destination in Eastern South End. The neighborhood is a bustling mixture of residences and businesses, and 81 Dover Street is a combination of both. A brick house sits at the back of the property, and occupying what was once the front yard is a shop bearing the sign: Byron Burnham, Machinist.

Eliza skips up to the shop and gestures grandly to its stoop. "This is where your patent begins, Mattie."

She opens the door, and the familiar thick smell of machine oil floods my nostrils. Opposite the entrance is a long counter upon which sits a large ledger. Shelves holding mechanical drawings and machine parts line the walls, and behind the counter is a doorway through which I glimpse more shelves, a small steam engine, and a worktable covered with drills and reamers.

The grind of a power tool against metal emanates from the adjacent room. Setting my box upon the counter, I call over the din, "Excuse me."

The grinding stops, the whir of the tool fades, and a stout, balding man with a constellation of pockmarks on his jowly face appears. "Can I help you?" he asks, wiping oil off his sausagelike fingers with a rag.

"I'm looking for Mr. Byron Burnham," I reply. "It's regarding—"

"I'm Burnham. You must be that bag machine girl."

Eliza's eyes go wide at his surly tone. I'm equally perplexed, yet resolve to start things off on the right foot. Pasting on a smile, I offer a handshake. "Yes, I'm Margaret Knight. Pleased to meet you, Mr. Burnham."

He regards my outstretched hand like a diseased rat and reaches for the ledger instead. "Just so you know, Miss Knight, I take my work seriously," he says, flipping the book open. "I don't have time to waste on people playing at inventing."

I lower my hand as it clenches into a fist. "I'm not playing," I say as Eliza's panicked gaze darts between me and the machinist. "My machine can perform, and I mean to patent it."

He snorts. "Let's have a look then."

Burnham loans me a claw hammer and glowers over my shoulder as I pry open the box and remove the machine from its cocoon of wadded newspapers. Meanwhile, Eliza cowers by the door. No doubt, she's unsettled by the rude reception. I am as well, but Burnham's not the first to discount my ability. Once he sees my machine, he'll be forced to change his tune.

"This is the bag machine," I say, placing it on the counter. "Allow me to demonstrate." I grasp the crank to show its workings, but then I freeze.

The wooden finger is missing from the folding platform.

"Well?" Mr. Burnham barks. "I haven't got all day, girl."

"Just a moment," I stammer, craning my neck to see if the finger has tumbled inside the machine. Instead, I jolt to discover the follower is gone, too.

"Mattie," says Eliza, scurrying over. "Is something wrong?"

I push the shipping box toward her. "Some pieces came loose. See if you can find them."

She blanches and immediately begins searching the packaging. Meanwhile, I carefully examine the machine. To my relief, nothing is broken, though a few more parts are absent from their places. As I make note of what's missing, confusion assails me.

Everything was securely screwed or attached. Even if the machine was shaken during transport, they shouldn't have come off.

I shove my befuddlement aside. I can speculate later; right now, I need to get this machine working. Straightening up, I say, "Five parts came loose. Did you find them all?"

Eliza returns a stricken look. "I couldn't find a-any. Not a o-one."

Disbelief crashes over me. "That can't be right."

But the crate is empty, and Eliza's smoothed flat every scrap of newspaper it held.

What in Heaven's name? I gape at the box, whose sturdy, close-fitted slats show nary a crack. They wouldn't let daylight through, let alone a loose part. The lid showed no signs of tampering prior to my opening it. But I tested the machine before Daniel and I packed it, which means all the parts were present at the time.

Mr. Burnham clears his throat noisily. "I take it there won't be a demonstration?"

My face reddens beneath his scorn. "I-I'm afraid not. However, only five pieces are missing, and I know their exact dimensions, so I can sketch them for you." Snatching a pencil, I start outlining a wooden finger on a piece of newspaper.

Mr. Burnham yanks the pencil from my hand. "I told you I take my work seriously. That means I require a working prototype or a drawing of this quality."

He slams a mechanical drawing on the counter. The professionally rendered lines and symbols are breathtakingly precise. The sight of my clumsy sketch beside it makes me want to crawl into a hole.

I hang my head. "I apologize, sir."

The machinist regards me for a moment, then blows out his breath. "This isn't the first machine to arrive at my shop less than intact. You say you know what's missing, so make it. In the meantime, I've got room on the prototype shelf in the back, so you can leave your contraption here. That is, unless you prefer taking it home in that."

He points to the front window. Beyond its dingy panes, sleet falls beneath a darkening sky. The thought of carrying my machine in that weather—and possibly damaging it—stops me cold.

Before I can respond, Eliza tugs my sleeve, pulling me aside. "M-Mattie, are you certain you want to e-engage Mr. Burnham?" she whispers. "He's not very p-pleasant, and there are other m-machinists."

She has a point. Yet, despite Mr. Burnham's cranky demeanor, he's clearly top-notch at his trade. The intricate mechanical drawing beside my sorry sketch is but one of scores on his shelves. And I do respect the man for upholding standards. More importantly, Daniel recommended him.

"He is a grump, but I'm not here to make friends," I mutter back. "So long as he does a proper job—which he undoubtably can—he can grouse all he wants. Not to mention, Daniel and his friend went through the trouble of arranging this. I owe it to them to give Mr. Burnham a shot."

"I s-suppose," replies Eliza doubtfully.

Turning to Mr. Burnham, I say, "I will leave my machine in your care then, and we'll resume this discussion when I return."

"As you wish," he grunts, and sets about issuing a claim ticket.

Chapter 22

Friday, February 26, 1869

Dear Mattie,

I apologize for the tardiness of my response. When your letter arrived, things were in chaos because Frank Niebuhr had left for Maryland. His father suddenly took ill and unfortunately does not appear long for this world. As you might imagine, Frank's abrupt exit left us in a lurch. We've yet to find a replacement for you, and now the bag workrooms are without a single mechanic. If you appeared before Mr. Yates, I wager he'd offer double your previous wage to woo you back.

However, your priority is not Columbia Paper but patenting. Regarding Mr. Burnham, I am pained to hear you got off on the wrong foot. Even so, I advise you to be patient with the man. He may be a curmudgeon, but as Charles has written, his reputation is unparalleled. Moreover, I'm confident you will win him over. Once he gets a good look at your brilliant inventive ability, you're certain to get along.

As for the missing parts, I'm as perplexed as you are. I remember placing newspaper round the machine to guard against damage, and I recall how securely you nailed the lid. I can't fathom why they're gone.

Even so, do not let this happenstance discourage you, bizarre though it is. I know you will make up for the setback in no time. I will be awaiting word of good news from here.

Yours truly,
Daniel

I lower the letter to my lap. Slumping against the parlor sofa cushions, I stare at the flames dancing in the fireplace while I mull over what I've read.

Foremost in my mind is Frank's departure. He has my sympathies regarding his father, of course. But this news also precipitates an uncomfortable retrospection about the way he and I parted.

I didn't know what to make of him after he gave me that train ticket. He was no longer an enemy, but he wasn't quite a friend. My few attempts to figure it out made my head hurt, so I put it off. And kept putting it off. Ultimately, I left Springfield without bidding Frank goodbye.

I regret that now. Daniel didn't say whether Frank had left for good, but if family obligations keep him in Oak Creek, our paths may never cross again.

That saddens me in an unexpected way, and I wish I had resolved things one way or the other while I had the chance. I suppose I could send a letter, but given the prolonged silence that's stretched between us, I wouldn't know what to write.

I heave a sigh, then shake my head hard to clear it. Lamentable though it is, what's done is done. And as Daniel pointed out, my current priority is patenting.

I reread his response about Mr. Burnham. While I do not savor the prospect of collaborating with the old crank, Daniel's commendation fortifies my decision to stick with him. Daniel wouldn't urge me so unless I stood to benefit, and if Mr. Burnham gives me the best chance at a patent, I'll endure him.

My eyes linger on Daniel's declaration that I'll win Burnham over. The penned words bolster my resolve, but they also remind me how keenly I long for the sound of his voice. For his sympathetic ear. For his smile.

I trace his signature with a fingertip, my thoughts gravitating back to New Year's Eve, to the touch of his hand against my cheek and the headiness of his breath mingled with mine. I've wondered over and over what might've happened next—and curse myself for not having the nerve to find out.

But unlike Frank, Daniel remains in Springfield. That means

I have a second chance. Once I finish submitting my patent application, I'll return, and this time I'll—

The scrape of the front door jolts me from my musings. Slipping the letter into my apron pocket, I head for the entryway, where Eliza stands shaking snowflakes off her hat.

"Welcome home," I say, helping her out of her coat. "Your grandmother's gone to bed, but hot baked beans and Indian pudding are waiting in the kitchen."

"Wonderful. I'm starving."

We go to the kitchen, and Eliza inhales deep as I place steaming bowls before her. "Smells delicious," she says. "We'll make a cook out of you yet."

I scoff. "Credit for tonight's supper belongs entirely to your grandmother. I spent the better part of the day across the street with Mrs. Drew's broken sewing machine."

Eliza looks up from her meal. "Were you able to fix it?"

I plunk two silver coins on the tabletop. "Took a couple hours to figure the workings, but she flies like a breeze now."

Eliza hails me with her spoon. "Bravo! At this rate, you'll soon be the neighborhood handywoman."

"That would be something, but I'd rather finish this patent application business and move on."

"Of course, how silly of me," says Eliza with an embarrassed titter. "Speaking of which, is everything ready for our visit to South End?"

In response, I slide a cardboard box off a shelf to display the five parts within. "All present and accounted for."

Making these replacement pieces, unfortunately, took longer than I liked. The problem was that I needed key bits of hardware, and shopping in an unfamiliar town was like muddling through the Minotaur's labyrinth. However, once I got what I needed, actually creating the parts took less than a week.

As I silently stew about the month-long delay these pieces

caused, Eliza sighs. "I guess we'll never know what happened to the originals."

"I received a letter from Daniel today, and he confirms that the machine was whole and intact when we packed it," I say, dropping into the chair beside her. "Unless the Good Lord sends me a revelation, their disappearance will remain a mystery."

"No sense wondering any more about it, then." Eliza claps a hand on my shoulder. "You've got more important things at hand. Tomorrow Mr. Burnham will see what your machine can do, and we'll get that iron model started."

The thought of proving my know-how to the skeptical machinist rouses my spirits, and I reply, "Right."

❋ ❋ ❋

The five pieces fit perfectly. I turn the crank, and as the machine's parts whiz in harmony, I toss my head. "There you go, Mr. Burnham. One working prototype."

Eliza suppresses a smirk. Mr. Burnham, however, studies the machine with an expression blank as a brick wall. I wasn't so naïve as to hope for an astonished gasp or heartfelt apology, but I expected a reaction of some sort.

At last, he lifts his head. "Two hundred dollars," he says gruffly.

Confusion undercuts my triumph. "I beg your pardon?"

"You want a model, that's my price." Mr. Burnham thrusts out his hand, palm up.

"Wait," I stammer. "I understand I must pay, but I was told the price was one hundred dollars."

"Do you have a quote with my signature?"

My stomach churns. "No . . ."

"Then the price is two hundred."

Before I can negotiate, he takes a drawing and a small box and plunks them on the counter. "I charged one hundred dollars for this. Yours will take double the time and effort."

The drawing, labeled "S.C. Industries Gear Train No. 14," meticulously details an arrangement of cogs and shafts. And within the box gleams a clockwork creation that matches it with astonishing accuracy. Confronted with Mr. Burnham's work, which is better described as a sculpture than an industrial part, I recall Daniel's remark about his unparalleled skill and swallow my protests. "Fair is fair. I'll accept that price."

Mr. Burnham sniffs. "And I won't begin until I receive the full amount."

"Full amount?" exclaims Eliza as my jaw hits the floor. "It's c-customary to pay an advance and pay the remainder once the job is c-completed."

"True. I take a twenty percent advance from standard customers. But you . . ." Mr. Burnham regards us disdainfully. "You girls are not standard."

Eliza bristles. "If she hands over the entire fee, what g-guarantee does she have that you'll actually do the work?"

"A signed work order and receipt," he replies coolly. "A man's signature carries weight, after all."

Eliza's eyes narrow, then she yanks me aside. "Mattie, let's go," she hisses. "Clearly this unscrupulous cheat thinks all women are brainless ninnies he can swindle."

"I heard that," Mr. Burnham snaps. "Before you call me unscrupulous, know that you'll be hard-pressed to find another machinist who'll do business with a woman. And a woman without cash in hand or a male guarantor won't get a moment's consideration. We need assurance we'll be paid for our work, you know."

"That's what the advance is for!" Eliza fumes.

She and the machinist lock eyes, glaring hot enough to burn the shop down. I'm certain Mr. Burnham's going to throw us out when, finally, he huffs, flinging up his hands. "Fine. To prove I'm not the scoundrel you say I am, I'll take the twenty percent advance. Mind you, I'm bending over backwards. No man in his right mind would risk giving these terms to a mere girl."

Relief washes over me, and I reach to shake his hand. "Thank you."

"But," Mr. Burnham continues, looking down his nose with nostrils flaring, "I still need assurance that I'll get my money. Before I start, I must see with my own eyes that you have two hundred dollars in hand. Those are my terms, and you won't find any better in all Boston."

Chapter 23

STANDING BESIDE MY BED, I CONTEMPLATE THE MONEY I'VE laid atop the patchwork quilt. It's a combination of Columbia Paper earnings, funds my mother sent, and coins from odd jobs around the neighborhood. All told, it amounts to one hundred and five dollars. I've never possessed so much, yet it's not enough. At least, not for Mr. Burnham.

I bristle as I recall yesterday's confrontation. When Mr. Burnham laid his conditions, I was sorely tempted to take my machine and go. However, his assertions about machinists and female customers gave me pause. I've suffered contempt as a woman mechanic; I can't expect better as a girl seeking a patent. And if I burn the bridge with Mr. Burnham only to find no replacement, where would that leave me?

So my machine remains with Mr. Burnham for the time being. Best to keep the bird in my hand until I determine whether any others are in the bush. Eliza's positive another machinist will offer better terms. I hope she's right, but if she's not, I must conjure another ninety-five dollars.

"Mattie."

I jolt at Mrs. MacFarland's voice in my ear. As I'm wondering how she's suddenly materialized at my elbow, the parlor clock chimes three, and I jump, this time into a dither. "Our call to Mrs. Kerner! I'm sorry, I'll be ready in a moment."

Mrs. MacFarland whips up a hand. "My dear, as I have been trying to inform you for the last minute, I am canceling our visit, the weather being what it is." She points to the window, where a downpour assails the glass.

"Oh . . . yes, of course."

As embarrassment sears my cheeks, Mrs. MacFarland

glances at the money on my bedspread. "I take it your patent model weighs on your mind. I won't pry, but if you need a sympathetic ear, this old woman has one to lend."

My fluster dissipates. I'd resolved not to bother Mrs. MacFarland with my troubles. After all, she is Eliza's grandmother, not mine. But her kind expression beckons my heart to unburden itself, and I say, "Actually, I would very much welcome that ear."

We sit side by side on Eliza's bed. I don't know where to begin, so Mrs. MacFarland begins for me. "It's difficult for a woman to get money, isn't it?"

"Uncle Thomas said no banker would lend money to a girl with only ideas for collateral," I groan, "but it's worse than that. Women aren't trusted in business at all. I sent a letter this morning to my friend Daniel, asking if he can recommend another machinist or think of a way to convince Mr. Burnham to change his terms. I'm not very hopeful, though. Worst case, I'm stuck with Mr. Burnham and his two-hundred-dollar price."

"And you're obliged to collect the full amount before he lifts a finger?"

I nod. "I got his quote in writing so the price is fixed, and it includes all labor and material. But getting that amount . . ."

My gaze falls to the money on the quilt. "My family's given what they can, and I don't want to borrow from friends. That means I have to earn it, either here or in Springfield."

"Springfield?" Surprise flickers across Mrs. MacFarland's face. "You'd move back?"

I shrug. "The factory's shorthanded. The boss'll take me back and possibly pay extra, if I play my cards right. The problem is the costs involved."

"You mean the train fare."

"And lodging." I lower my head, abashed. "I got by before because I boarded with Eliza at Uncle Thomas's. Without her, it would be . . . improper for me to move back, and a boardinghouse would cost several dollars more per month."

"Whereas our arrangement provides room and board and proximity to machinists, but no pay," finishes Mrs. MacFarland.

"Please don't misunderstand," I blurt, hoping I haven't insulted her. "It's wonderful here, but I can only earn money through odd jobs and piecework out of home—with your permission, of course."

Unfortunately, piecework pays little, and I'm uncertain how much I can earn as a neighborhood handywoman. Whether I stay or return, saving up Mr. Burnham's fee will be slow going.

Mrs. MacFarland cocks her head. "Mattie, rather than fritter your time assembling hat boxes or the like in my house, why not work for Mr. Burnham?"

I gape as if she's gone daft. "How would I work for him?"

"Propose a labor exchange. He runs a shop, correct? Offer to work there, say, three afternoons a week in exchange for credit toward your model."

"I hadn't thought of that . . ." The idea, which would allow me to fulfill my obligations to Mrs. MacFarland, is certainly worth considering. "The only catch is that Mr. Burnham must accept my labor. I'm not sure he will. My sex aside, his is a one-man establishment; no one works in that shop but him."

"Even better," replies Mrs. MacFarland. "Every business has a thousand and one things to be done, and you're a clever, reliable girl. Start by sweeping the floor and carrying out rubbish. If you're canny about it, you'll figure a way to become his indispensable assistant."

"And if I manage that, perhaps . . . he'll set his condition aside and start on the model," I say, suddenly hopeful.

Mrs. MacFarland's wrinkled face splits into a grin. "As they say, my dear, it costs nothing to ask, and you have the world to gain."

❄ ❄ ❄

Through the South End hubbub, a steeple bell tolls six o'clock. I sigh, raising my umbrella higher to scan my rain-drenched surroundings. *This is what I get for being hasty.*

Mrs. MacFarland's suggestion so excited me, I left for Mr. Burnham's straightaway. I've lost enough time already, and having been to his shop twice, I figured I could find it on my own.

I figured wrong. Although I made it to the first streetcar and successfully transferred to the second, I missed my Dover Street stop. As such, what should've been an hour-long trip is now past its second hour.

Fortunately, I spot Mr. Burnham's shop on the next block. The "closed" sign hangs in front, but light glows from within.

My hopes rise. If he's so busy that he's working late, that might bode well for my labor exchange proposal. Praying that's the case, I hurry up to the stoop and knock.

The door nudges ajar.

I blink. Mr. Burnham doesn't strike me as the sort to leave the door unlatched after close of business.

No matter. I enter, leaning my umbrella against the counter and placing my handbag on the countertop. The reception area is dim; the only light trickles from the workroom, which is quiet save for a scuffling noise. "Mr. Burnham," I call, doing my best to sound like a competent assistant-to-be. "It's Margaret Knight. I'd like a word, please."

The noise stops. But Mr. Burnham doesn't respond, nor does he appear. "Mr. Burnham," I say, approaching the workroom. "Mr. Burn—"

Suddenly, someone slams into my middle. The impact sends me flying, and I crash into a shelf. As machine parts hail about me, a lanky silhouette—completely unlike Mr. Burnham's bulldog build—dashes for the exit.

A single word flashes to mind. "*Thief!*"

As my shout tears the air, the intruder trips over my umbrella.

He tumbles down, and without thinking, I lunge, seizing his ankle. "Stop, you," I yell. "Thief!"

A kick to the skull knocks the breath out of me. As stars spark in my vision, the villain breaks free and scrambles off. I attempt to give chase, but by the time I reach the door, he's long gone.

I crumple upon the stoop, cradling my head in my hands. My glasses are undamaged, thank God, but a bump swells over my eyebrow. That and my aching torso will bruise for certain. As my body and mind regain their steadiness, I wonder, *Should I get the police? Where do I find the police?*

"Girl! What in blazes are you doing?"

My gaze snaps up to see Mr. Burnham emerging from the house at the back of the lot. As he flounces across the gravel strip separating his home and shop, I stagger to my feet. "Mr. Burnham, it's terrible. A burglar—"

He shoves past me to look inside. There's a horrified gasp, then he rushes to the counter. A moment later, a lamp illuminates the room, and the machinist's eyes bug out.

The reception area is an unholy mess. Two shelves worth of parts and drawings litter the floor. A few sheets have been trampled; another smears beneath the wet folds of my mangled umbrella. Turning an apoplectic shade of purple, Mr. Burnham bellows, "What have you done to my shop?"

"It wasn't me," I cry. "I told you, there was a burglar. He knocked me over when I came in to find you. Look, see here."

The rim of a bowler juts amid the wreckage, and I snatch it up. "He dropped this when he ran. It's certainly not mine, and it can't be yours, either."

Mr. Burnham's eyes narrow at the dented hat. Even at a glance, it's clearly too small for his massive pate, and marked on the sweatband inside are the initials "CFA." But instead of relenting, he growls, "How do I know you didn't let the bastard in?"

The allegation is a slap to the face. "How dare you! That man was in there robbing you when I came in," I say, pointing to the rear room.

Mr. Burnham's brow darkens, then he stomps into the workroom. "You stay back," he snaps when I start to follow. "I don't need you underfoot while I take stock of my things."

Biting my tongue, I halt in the doorway. But as I watch him inspect equipment, scan worktables, and check drawers, I realize the room shows no signs of pilferage. No rummaged cabinets, no overturned boxes. In fact, a fifty-dollar note and stack of silver dollars sit in plain view on a tabletop, untouched by the thief.

As my mind boggles over this, Mr. Burnham goes to a shelf holding tagged boxes. Removing my crate, he takes it to the counter and plunks it down. "Hand over your claim ticket, take your contraption, and go before I call the cops."

I gape in incomprehension. "What?"

"Nothing's stolen. Nothing's even been touched back there."

"That can't be," I protest. "I saw—"

"What I see is the mess right here and the girl who probably caused it arsing about my shop." He shoves the box at me. "Enough's enough. They say a woman's bad luck on a ship. You're proof they're bad luck in shops, too. Leave and don't come back."

My vision goes red. I want to rail against him, plead my innocence, pound sense into his thick skull. But his glare tells me no amount of arguing will change his mind. Nor is this pigheaded fool worth convincing.

Snatching the ticket from my handbag, I slap it on the countertop. "Don't worry. It'll be a cold day in July before I set foot in here again."

Chapter 24

When I stormed out Mr. Burnham's shop, I was convinced he was the rudest, most asinine machinist in Boston, if not the world.

Three weeks later, I'm forced to reevaluate that sentiment.

My machine weighs me down as Eliza and I trudge home. But the fruitlessness of this afternoon weighs heavier.

"Chin up," says Eliza with forced cheer. "Over a hundred machinists are listed in the city directory. We only saw four today."

I attempt to return a smile, but can't quite manage it. What Eliza says is true: if I am to carry on, I must believe one of those hundred-odd machinists will accept my business. But if today is any indicator, this search will be the most degrading endeavor of my life.

Worse, my best friend's being dragged along. On her precious afternoon off, no less. Unwilling to abuse Eliza's goodwill further, I say, "You're right. There are plenty more fish in the sea. Given there are so many, it'll be more efficient to go by myself."

"Out of the question," snaps Eliza. "I don't want you inquiring alone."

"And I don't want people thinking you're a street—" I catch myself and lower my voice to an undertone. "A streetwalker."

Most men believe a woman's place is at home. Some further presume that any woman not at home must be of loose morals. Machinist Paul Upham and his assistants made that patently clear today as they leered and smirked and interpreted my inquiry for an iron model as a more unsavory proposition.

"It's one thing if those men look askance at me," I mutter on. "I'm the one seeking a machinist. There's no need for you to be insulted as well."

"There's no need for either of us to be insulted," Eliza hisses back. "But it's a wretched world, and you're more likely to be harassed if you're alone, so I'm going with you."

"But—"

"Mattie, please!" Eliza whirls on me with tears in her eyes. "You don't know how badly I felt when you came back from Mr. Burnham's with your poor face battered."

She chokes up, and I set down my box with a sigh. "Eliza, I'm fine," I say, handing her my handkerchief. "No one can even tell I was in a scrap." Although, admittedly, a good two weeks passed before I dared show my face to the world.

"But if I had been there, you might not have gotten hurt," she sniffles. "That thief might not have gotten away. At the very least, I'd have been a witness."

"I doubt that would've made a difference to Mr. Burnham," I mumble.

"It would've made a difference to me," Eliza declares, stomping her foot. "The Good Book says, 'Two are better than one. Though one may be overpowered, two can defend themselves.' I'm sticking to that, and I'm sticking to you. Once the Easter rush is over, I'll have two afternoons off each week, so don't you dare go without me."

I stifle a groan. Any attempt to dissuade her will only result in a public disturbance, so I pick up my box instead. "Well, if you insist on following me, step lively. I'm hungry, and I'd rather have my dinner sooner than later."

My response mollifies her, and we walk the rest of the way in silence, Eliza smiling in satisfaction and me praying our next machinist excursion isn't nearly as unpleasant.

We enter the house to the aroma of roasting potatoes. "Welcome back," calls Mrs. MacFarland, emerging from the kitchen. "How was it?"

"Not very well, Nana," replies Eliza. "One shop was a den of boors. Two wouldn't give us the time of day, and the fourth . . . he made Mr. Burnham seem like a bargain."

"How so?"

"Keniston and Sawyer wanted two hundred dollars for labor, plus another fifty for materials," I say, setting the machine down to stretch the ache from my muscles. "But that fifty was only an initial fee, and Mr. Sawyer wouldn't even attempt an estimate of the total cost. He would only say that I was responsible for buying whatever additional material he thought necessary."

Mrs. MacFarland clucks her tongue. "That's disheartening. I hope this bears good tidings then." She holds out a letter. "This came for you. The postman says it's from Springfield."

My heart leaps. Since the incident at Mr. Burnham's, I've sent three letters to Daniel, each urging a quick response, but received nothing back. His prolonged silence has had me on pins and needles, and I've pounced on the postman every time he comes by.

That wait is finally over. I take the envelope with eager fingers, but stop short.

"Mattie?" says Eliza. "Is something wrong?"

I hold up the envelope and point to the return address. "It's not from Daniel. It's from Ida."

"Ida?" Surprise wrinkles Eliza's brow. "That's unusual. Between work and mothering, she never has the time or inclination to put pen to paper. If she's written, it must be important."

My own curiosity piqued, I open the letter. "Dear Mattie," I read aloud. "I am writing because Daniel Mowe has disappeared . . ."

My vision swims. The ground seems to sway beneath my feet, and I'm vaguely aware of Eliza guiding me to sit on the parlor sofa. Gently plucking the letter from my grasp, she continues where I left off:

Daniel Mowe has disappeared from Springfield. He was present for payday March 13, but the following Monday, they found a resignation letter in the office. It only said he was obliged to return home, but they have no address other than his Springfield residence. Daniel's landlord received no notice either. The boss is fit to be tied.

You are Daniel's good friend, so perhaps you know his circumstances. If not, you should offer your support if you know his whereabouts.

God bless you. Ida.

Eliza's brow furrows. "March 13 . . . today's the twenty-third. He left Springfield over a week ago, but you haven't heard from him since February, right?"

"I haven't," I say, remembering the close of his last letter. *I will be awaiting word of good news from here.*

As worry threads my gut, Mrs. MacFarland asks, "Can you guess his whereabouts, dear? Could you write him?"

I shake my head. "He's from Newton Lower Falls, that's all I know. If his landlord and Mr. Yates don't have an address, I don't know anyone else who might."

The thought of Daniel vanishing into thin air turns my lungs to lead, and I'm imagining all manner of horrible fates when Eliza grips my hand. "Mattie, I'm positive he's fine. This is . . . out of the ordinary, but Daniel is a smart, sensible young man. He wouldn't abandon everything on a whim. There must be a good reason for this."

She's right. I recall how Frank rushed off to his father's deathbed. Something equally compelling must have forced Daniel to leave. I haven't the faintest idea what, but I trust Daniel's judgment. Whatever he's doing, it must be in everyone's best interest. A selfish part of me wishes he'd confided in me. But maybe this is his way of being considerate. He was so determined to see me succeed. Perhaps he didn't want his concerns to distract me from my own. If that's the case, I'm bound to do my level best to make my patent a reality until he reemerges.

I let out my breath in a long, shaky exhale.

"Mattie," says Eliza, "Are you all right?"

"I'm fine," I reply, squaring my shoulders. I have to be. Because I must forge ahead with one less ally.

Chapter 25

In our ongoing search for a machinist, Eliza and I have encountered a range of establishments. Some are tiny operations in the proprietor's basement. Others fill entire warehouses. On this gray May afternoon, we stand before 76 Sudbury, a four-story complex that clamors with industry.

"It appears the next five shops are housed there," says Eliza, glancing at our list.

"Sounds like it," I say, picking out the snarl of machine tools amid the racket. "They probably share a common boiler for power. With them clumped together, it'll make getting rejected all the quicker."

"Don't talk that way, Mattie," Eliza chides. "You must be positive."

"Right, right." But it's difficult to maintain faith in the wake of disappointment.

Earlier this month, shop nineteen on our list, Wyman and Sons, agreed to make my model. I was elated—until I returned two weeks later to discover they hadn't done a lick of work on it. When I demanded an explanation, the senior Mr. Wyman merely shrugged, saying other customers had priority and they would begin mine when it suited them. Whereupon it suited me to disengage the Wymans and take back my machine.

Disheartening though that was, letting that experience wreck my current efforts would be worse. Eliza's correct that I must put my best foot forward if I want any hope of progress. Firming my grip on my machine's box, I say, "Where first?"

"Lincoln and Graham in Number 2."

The medium-sized shop is on the ground level at the rear. It has an open floor, and amid the lathes, machine tools, and worktables are four machinists and an apprentice. As Eliza and I enter, the boy nearly spills his oil can. "Mr. Graham," he pipes, scurrying to a leather-aproned graybeard fitting a reamer. "We got two gals in the shop!"

"Probably a couple of damn drys," grumbles the machinist, not looking up. "Tell them we like our beer, and we're not giving it up."

I suppress the urge to roll my eyes. In addition to streetwalkers, Eliza and I have been presumed militant suffragists, religious fanatics, and zealous prohibitionists. If a machinist welcomed us as prospective customers, I'd probably faint from joy.

I set my box on the counter with a thunk. "Drink all you like, Mr. Graham," I say, loud enough for everyone to hear. "I'm not interested in banning beer. I am interested in an iron patent model. So may I have a word, please?"

Tools grind to a halt. The staff stare, holding their collective breath, as the boss regards me like an escaped sideshow freak.

"No," he says, and turns back to his tools.

"My prototype is right here," I say, refusing to be rebuffed. "And I have money—"

Mr. Graham slams his reamer down, making my heart leap out my chest. As I struggle to regain composure, the machinist speaks with chilling calm. "Now listen here, Miss . . ."

"M-Miss Knight," I stammer.

"Women should be seen, not heard, Miss Knight. But females nowadays can't seem to remember that. I got enough womenfolk squawking at home. I'll not deal with another fool female here."

"But—"

"Will." Mr. Graham gestures sharply to a young man with the build of a bull. "Show these girls out. The rest of you, back to work."

With that, the snarl of tools revives. Everyone returns to his task, save the bulbous-nosed bruiser who lumbers to the counter.

"Sorry, Miss Knight," he says, his voice a tremulous contrast to his brawny body. "Mr. Graham doesn't want you here, so please leave."

My mind races. Mr. Graham's already got his head down, steadfastly ignoring me, but the fellow tasked to oust me looks apologetic behind his curly red beard. Should I appeal for sympathy? Argue that I'm a legitimate customer? Or slink meekly away?

Eliza tugs my sleeve. "Mr. Graham's intractably prejudiced against our sex. We'd best move along, Mattie."

She's right. A man must be civil enough to listen for me to persuade him; Mr. Graham will throw me out before I can try.

As I reach for my box, the young machinist's brow knits. "Mattie . . . your name's Mattie Knight?"

His expression puckers as if on the brink of recognition. Wondering if we've crossed paths before, I reply, "Margaret Knight's my name, but friends call me Mattie."

His eyes flick to my box. "You work in Manchester five years ago?"

"I did." Now my wits are racing to place his face. "At the Amoskeag Mill, Building 3. How do you—"

"Name's William Abbott. Louisa Abbott's my sister."

"Louisa . . ." At once, his face overlaps with another in my memory, and I gasp. "You do look like her. You share the same nose."

He grins, rubbing his nose. "Runs in the family. Here, let's talk outside."

He tucks my box under his arm and ushers us onto the dingy stoop. Once the door shuts behind us, he taps the box with a fingernail. "You want an iron patent model for this, yeah?"

"Yes," I reply.

He thumps his fist on his chest. "I'll do it for you."

For a thunderstruck moment, Eliza and I gawp. Then Eliza squeals, throwing her arms aloft. "God be praised! Mattie, you found your machinist."

"Wait, wait, wait." I wave my hands, flabbergasted by the abrupt offer. "Mr. Abbott, are you certain? You haven't seen my prototype."

He flashes a dauntless smile. "You invented that shuttle restraint when you were twelve. Whatever you got now has got to be worth bringing into the world. And call me Will."

His voice rings with enthusiasm, and instinct tells me he's a man of his word. Still, I'm hesitant to get my hopes up. "What about your employer? He doesn't like me. Won't you get in trouble?"

He chuckles. "Mr. Graham's a partner, and he's got weight, but the real boss of the shop's him." He points to the "Lincoln" in the sign overhead. "Mr. Lincoln likes me, and I just did him a big favor. When he comes back this afternoon, I'll work something out, promise."

"Thank you," I say, touched. "I'd be much obliged if you do."

"And if you're content to let me do the work, I won't charge for labor. Only stock."

My jaw drops. I couldn't have been more astounded if he'd conjured up glass slippers and a pumpkin carriage. "You'd do that for me?"

He returns a puzzled look. "You did my sister a good turn making that shuttle restraint. It's only right I do you a good turn."

"But . . . I made it after Louisa got hurt, not before. I hardly deserve to be rewarded by you."

"That's not true. You did help. Which is more than I can say for myself."

I give him a questioning look and he sighs, regret clouding his features. "When the accident happened, I'd just started my apprenticeship here. I was worried sick about Louisa, but worrying was all I could do. I couldn't go home to care for her, and I didn't earn enough to keep her away from the mill. The minute she was well, our old man made her go back, even though she was terrified of another accident."

Will claps a hand on my shoulder. "But you made certain there wouldn't be another accident. Your invention gave all us Abbotts peace of mind, not just Louisa, and I'd be honored if you let me show our thanks."

I'm left speechless. Never in my wildest imaginings did I expect my shuttle restraint to lead to this. As my mind boggles, Eliza titters. "The Good Lord works in wonderful and mysterious ways, doesn't He, Mattie?"

"He does." I might have lost Daniel, but from the looks of it, a new skilled ally is on my side.

"So, Miss Knight," says Will, "what's your answer?"

I extend a handshake. "The answer's yes. And call me Mattie."

Chapter 26

WILL ABBOTT IS A GODSEND.

That thought crosses my mind every time I visit Lincoln and Graham, and it arises once more as Will demonstrates the motions of my half-finished model. The iron mechanisms are scaled slightly smaller than the originals but move better than my hand-carved parts ever did.

"What do you think, Mattie?" Will asks, still turning the crank.

I flash a grin. "I think you've done a bang-up job."

Will's not been long at his trade, but he's worked on a dozen patent models and knows their requirements. He's also got a talent for cams and gears. When he started on the patterns for my part castings, he suggested changes to smooth their motions. Some recommendations I took; others I declined. And one suggestion about lever arms led to a spirited discussion which, in turn, led to an improved plate folder mechanism.

"The swing of the plate folder is much sharper," I say, pleased with its performance. "And the gear train looks perfect. If you weren't such a heartbreaker, I'd kiss you, Will Abbott."

His coworkers guffaw at my joking. Will may be homely, but he's surprisingly popular thanks to his muscle and charm. When I reconnected with his sister Louisa, who's now happily married in Concord, she warned me he was a scamp and unlikely to settle down soon.

But I do wonder how I'd feel about Will if that wasn't so. In Springfield, the one mechanically inclined fellow I knew was my rival, and the one supporting my endeavors didn't have a mechanical bone in his body. Will encourages me and possesses mechanical know-how; if he wasn't a ladies' man, I'd probably fall in love.

It's better this way. Daniel's disappearance turned me topsy-turvy, and we weren't even courting. I must focus on patenting and keep romance out of business. That means maintaining a strictly customer and machinist relationship with Will.

Taking five silver dollars from my handbag, I place them on the counter. "There's one set of castings left, correct? Here's the payment."

He shakes his head. "I told you, you don't need to pay till the casting's—"

"Take it." I shove the coins toward him. "You're already doing the labor for free. Keep piling on favors, and your admirers will bludgeon me out of jealousy."

Indeed, Will's done so much, I feel guilty. He doesn't possess his own tools, so he was obliged to call in a favor from Mr. Lincoln. Not only did Will negotiate to make my model using the shop's equipment, he got permission for me to enter the place if Mr. Graham wasn't around.

Will frowns at the money, then throws up his hands. "Fine. I'll take care of those castings double-quick then."

"You've been plenty quick, Will." Part of Mr. Lincoln's agreement is that Will cannot neglect his regular workload. However, Will has plugged steadily away over the summer, lingering past closing three nights a week to work on my model. Moreover, we've never wasted time quarreling over particulars. Once I make a decision, he accepts it, no argument.

As far as I'm concerned, Will is progressing as fast as humanly possible, so I declare, "Haste makes waste. Cast and fit the last pieces in two weeks like you promised, and you'll have my undying gratitude."

"Yes, ma'am," says Will, pocketing the coins. "By the way, have you mentioned your bag machine to anyone?"

"Only half the town's machinists before I found you," I reply, thanking God once again for Will Abbott. "Why do you ask?"

"Someone came asking about it." Turning to the shop apprentice, he calls, "When was it that gangly guy came?"

The boy snickers. "The one that banged his head on the lintel? Last Monday."

"Monday?" My brow furrows. Since Will began my model, I've busied myself increasing my funds through odd jobs. I certainly haven't propositioned anyone about the machine and have only spoken to my housemates and Will about the model's progress. "What did he want, Will?"

"Said he heard a bag machine was at the shop and wanted a look at it."

Uneasiness creeps over me. "You didn't—"

Will snorts. "Of course not. It's against shop policy, not to mention he had a shifty look about him."

"Don't fret, Miss Mattie," the apprentice adds with a gaptoothed grin. "Your machine and model were covered up in the back. He couldn't get a look if he tried."

I smile back, relieved. "I suppose this speaks to the necessity of getting a patent in the first place. And since the model's nearly done, I better start looking for a draftsman."

"Oh, speaking of that." Will jerks a thumb toward one of his coworkers. "Theo's brother-in-law might be able to do your patent drawings. Right, Theo?"

Theo nods from his workbench. "My sister's man, George, is an assistant draftsman for a downtown firm, and he's been talking about taking side jobs. Good fellow, does good work. If you like, I'll take Will and see if George's interested."

"Please," I say, delighted for a referral. "I'd be grateful if you did."

"No trouble at all. It'd be helping my kin as much as you. Besides, you're the decent sort, Mattie. You know what you want, but you're not a flaming arse about it."

Will laughs. "Got that right. Compared to the usual cranks we get, Mattie's a breath of fresh air."

I smile as the shop chortles agreement. Will's coworkers initially gave me the cold shoulder, but their indifference gradually melted to grudging respect and, by summer's end, warmed into a comfortable rapport. Of course, Mr. Graham remains the intractable exception, but the acceptance I now enjoy in this shop is heaven.

Grateful to have attained their goodwill, I say, "I'll be counting on you two to put in a good word for me then."

❊ ❊ ❊

I leave Lincoln and Graham in high spirits. Upon arriving home, I discover a letter bearing gladness of a different sort.

Fannie Foster is getting married.

"My," exclaims Eliza when I show her the letter after dinner. "That was fast."

Fannie's beau is Columbia Paper's new assistant bookkeeper. They met when he started in April. Five months later, they're engaged.

"The courtship may have been quick, but the wedding won't be for a while," I say, fanning myself against the late summer mugginess. "The ceremony aside, Fannie's swamped with all she's got to do to set up house. Good thing the ladies from Sunday school class are helping her make linens and such."

"You've done your part, too, Mattie." Lifting the letter, Eliza reads, "'I was glad for the raise before. Now that I've a hundred and one things to buy, I'm truly grateful you won us that higher wage.'"

"That seems such a long time ago." The quarrel over pay, the machine contest, the long nights in Uncle Thomas's kitchen . . . memories swirl like the ice chips in our lemonade. "So much has happened since leaving Springfield, and nothing's gone the way I thought."

My voice catches, and concern fills Eliza's gaze. "Mattie, are you all right?" she asks, putting the letter down.

"Yes. No. I don't know." I slump over the kitchen table, chin propped on my arms. "I've soldiered this far thanks to you and your grandmother and Will Abbott. But I can't help wondering about Daniel . . ."

Eliza places a comforting hand on my shoulder. "You miss him."

"It's more complicated than that. I thought he was in for the long haul, that we would forge together through thick and thin. If we'd quarreled, if he'd died, I could make sense of it. But leaving without a word?" I bury my face with a groan. "I don't know how to feel about it."

"We were all confounded," says Eliza sympathetically. "Daniel was so sweet on you. I thought you two would surely—"

"No chance of that now." I sit up and read Fannie's postscript aloud: "'No one's heard from Daniel since he left for Newton Lower Falls. It's a crying shame, but I don't think you should expect him back. If you meet a nice man in Boston—and I'm certain you will—give him an honest chance. Good luck.'"

"She's right about that, you know," says Eliza.

"Of course she is," I snap. "It's been half a year. No one in her right mind should expect him back."

"No, I meant the other part. About giving someone else a chance."

I laugh, harsh as a raven's croak. "Eliza, I've got no time for romance. Even if I did, who would consider me?"

She returns a knowing look over her cup. "I believe Will Abbott qualifies as a nice fellow."

I nearly choke on my lemonade. For a well-learned person, my friend can conjure nonsensical notions. "Might I remind you, Will's a charmer? He's got a crowd of girls after him."

"For the right woman, a man will forsake all the rest."

"That won't be me," I say, fanning myself fiercely. "I'm a scarecrow compared to—"

Pounding resounds from the front door, giving us a start. It's past nine, and we're not expecting anyone. The knocking comes again, louder and more insistent, and Eliza rises. "We better get that before it wakes Nana."

We hasten to the entryway, and Eliza calls, "Who is it? What do you want?"

"It's Will Abbott," comes the muffled reply. "I need to speak with Mattie now. Please."

"Will?" I gasp.

Ignoring the triumphant smile blossoming on Eliza's face, I unlatch the door to reveal a winded and sweating Will. Wherever he's come from, he must have run the whole way. "Sorry about the late visit, ladies," he pants, mopping his brow with a kerchief, "but I got something important to tell Mattie."

Eliza's smirk deepens, and I reel like a kite in a storm. *He can't possibly be here because . . .*

As my brain plunges into romantic impossibilities, Eliza merrily ushers Will to a parlor seat. "No need to apologize. After all, some things can't wait."

"No, especially when it's bad news."

The muggy air turns chill. "What is it?" I say, dropping into the chair across from Will. "What happened?"

My apprehension mounts as he faces me with the gravity of an undertaker. "That bag machine of yours?" he says, his voice pained. "Someone's already submitted it for patent."

Nausea slams my stomach. As I clap a hand over my mouth, struggling to maintain composure, I hear Eliza sputter, "W-what do you mean, Will? Why are you s-saying such a thing?"

"Theo took me to meet his draftsman brother-in-law tonight. When we told George about the machine, he said it sounded like something he'd made patent drawings for. He had a copy in his house and showed it to us." Will lowers his head. "It was just like yours. It had the plate folder, the finger, the follower, everything."

My heart constricts. Will's worked on my model for four months. If he says it was the same, there's no mistake.

"Mattie," says Eliza, her soft voice sharpened to a vengeful growl, "someone's stolen your idea. Someone must have seen your machine at Mr. Burnham's or the Wymans' and copied it."

"Hush, Eliza." I'm thinking the same, but I can't jump to conclusions. Taking a steadying breath, I ask Will, "When was George engaged to do the drawings?"

"He said he started the first week of the year."

I blink. I arrived in Boston on January 2, but my machine stayed boxed in Mrs. MacFarland's basement until the end of the month when I took it to Mr. Burnham's. "Someone gave him a prototype to work off just after the new year?"

"No, he got loose pieces to begin detail drawings first. The inventor didn't send the complete assembly until March."

Loose pieces in early January . . . the complete assembly in March . . . I teeter on the verge of comprehension but can't quite grasp it.

"And who, pray tell, is this supposed inventor?" says Eliza, arms akimbo.

Will hands me a piece of paper. "This is what George knows about him."

I unfold it and gasp. Beside me, Eliza stammers, "Wait, that's the fellow D-Daniel brought . . ."

Printed at the top of the page is:

Charles F. Annan
Newton Lower Falls

Chapter 27

Every Saturday at midday, craftsmen, scientists, and investors gather at the Massachusetts Charitable Mechanic Association's building to exchange ideas and form partnerships. According to the draftsman, George, Charles Annan attends these "New Innovation Luncheons" whenever he's in town. Will's description of the gangly fellow who asked about my machine matches what George and I recollect of Annan, and if he's still in Boston, this is my best chance to find the scoundrel.

George had already planned to attend, and he agreed to bring Will along so both could keep watch for Annan. But while they would blend in seamlessly, my height and sex would make me stick out like a sore thumb. So while Will and George mingle in the second-floor banquet hall, I must lurk elsewhere.

Fortunately, the Mechanics Building lobby has an ideal place for spying.

I snap to attention as a new group enters the building. For the twelfth time, I scrutinize the men emerging through the front door, and for the twelfth time, I deflate in disappointment. None of them, however, notice my staring, hidden as I am behind the twisting pipes of "Swanson's Efficiency Steam Engine."

A carriage-sized machine isn't something typically found in a lobby, but the Mechanics Building is filled with displays touting the winners of the Association's mechanical craft competitions. I could spend hours marveling over the devices in the hallways, but because I'm keeping a lookout for Annan, I've spent the last half hour using Swanson's clever invention as a hunting blind.

I'm not entirely sure what I'll do if I succeed in capturing my prey, though. If Annan submitted an application last spring, its review has probably just begun. Once mine reaches the patent office, both applications will undoubtedly grind to a standstill while the patent examiners deliberate over the identical designs for Heaven knows how long.

The ideal scenario is for Annan to withdraw his fraudulent claim. However, I doubt an appeal to conscience will prompt him to right his wrong. Will has offered to convince Annan with his fists, but I wonder if even that will persuade someone so brazen.

If only I hadn't shown him the machine in the first place. In retrospect, I was foolish to trust Annan just because he was Daniel's friend, and he pulled my strings like an expert puppeteer with his recommendation of Mr. Burnham. No doubt he was diligently copying my machine while Mr. Burnham delayed me with excuses.

My teeth gnash at the memory of the mysterious "intruder" in Burnham's shop. Between the initials on the fallen hat and what I recall from our tussle, I'm positive he was Annan. The indignity galls me all over when I hear the front door open, followed by men's voices.

". . . Be along soon, Mr. Binney."

"Then we can wait for him here, Mr. Annan."

Entering the lobby is a portly graybeard with an ivory-handled walking stick, and holding the door for him is a lanky man with rust-colored hair. Recognition hits at Annan's caterpillar-like eyebrows, and I quickly duck my head.

My fingernails dig my palms as their conversation drifts into my ears. I'd like nothing more than to leap out and claw Annan's eyes, but I can't be rash. If anything, this is my chance to discover what he's up to. Unfurling the hand fan I borrowed from Eliza, I obscure my face and sidle closer to eavesdrop.

From my glimpse of Mr. Binney, I gather that he's an investor, and he confirms it when I hear, "I've colleagues who want to hear more. Once we get a few more interested parties, we should like a demonstration."

"Of course, Mr. Binney. We can bring the bag machine to your office whenever you like. Once you see what it can do, you'll have no doubts about lending support."

My hackles rise. *Already at work selling my machine, thief?*

"With your permission," Annan goes on, "we can discuss plans for distribution and rights at the demonstration. Ah, here comes Mr. Mowe."

My heart seizes. *Mr. Mowe? He couldn't possibly mean—*

"Apologies for the wait, gentlemen."

An all-too-familiar voice freezes the blood in my veins. I glance over my fan toward the door, and my world shatters.

Striding in with a portfolio and a businessman's demeanor is Daniel.

He shakes hands with Mr. Binney, and the sight drives a knife between my ribs. Until this instant, I'd dismissed the possibility that Daniel was involved. I knew he had ample opportunity to betray me, but I refused to presume he would. I trusted Daniel. I believed he cared about me—that, even apart, he wished for my success.

Daniel chuckles at something Mr. Binney says, and my blood boils. I once loved Daniel's laugh; the sound cheered me, warmed me. Now it mocks me as I imagine him laughing while he pulled the wool over my eyes.

But he hasn't gotten away with it yet.

"Well," says Mr. Binney, gesturing toward the stairs, "shall we? I'll introduce you to my partners."

"I'd advise against that, sir," I shout, snapping my fan shut. "Unless you wish to be associated with a liar and a thief."

I plant myself in their path. Mr. Binney raises an eyebrow, unsure of what to make of me. Annan's eyes bulge in their sockets.

Daniel also goggles, but only for an instant. With a deftness of a master actor, his expression smooths into a mildly aggrieved air. "I don't know who you are, miss," he says with a sniff, "but you shouldn't fling accusations like that."

My eyes narrow. *You want to play that game?*

Turning to Mr. Binney, Daniel murmurs, "Let's go. This maniac must be in the throes of some female hysteria."

"Charles F. Annan." I point at the fake inventor, making him flinch. "Hometown, Newton Lower Falls. Fraud, pretending to have invented my bag-making machine."

Annan flusters. "Wait just a—"

I jab my finger at Daniel. "Daniel S. Mowe. Age twenty-three. Also from Newton Lower Falls. Most recently employed as junior bookkeeper at Columbia Paper in Springfield, but abandoned his position last March. Presumably to promote Mr. Annan's efforts to sell the machine they stole from me."

I toss Mr. Binney a saccharine smile. "As a prudent businessman, I'm sure you'd like to confirm my assertions. Contact Columbia Paper's proprietor, Charles Yates. He'll be happy to tell you the particulars about the bag machine and his wayward employee."

Mr. Binney's mouth pinches as though I've dumped manure on his polished shoes. "I've heard quite enough," he huffs, stalking for the exit. "Good day, all of you."

Daniel and Annan chase after him. "Mr. Binney," Daniel pleads, "this isn't what you—"

The old man's cane whips up, cutting him off. "A word of advice. Have your dalliances if you must, but keep them hidden. In business, a man requires a spotless reputation. Even a hint of impropriety"—Mr. Binney's eyes slide meaningfully toward me—"and no one will have anything to do with you young bucks."

With that, he storms out the building. Annan hastens after him. I watch them go with a mixture of satisfaction and annoyance. Although my efforts bore the intended result, I'm vexed that Mr. Binney presumed my accusation the ravings of a jilted paramour.

I face Daniel. The mask he wore for Mr. Binney has shattered. Fury contorts his features beyond recognition, and it strikes me that this is the first time I've seen him for who he is.

His fists clench, looking ready to whale me. I meet his glare head on. Unlike the night my face got kicked, we're in a public place in broad daylight. Not to mention, Will Abbott and George are within screaming distance.

"The jig is up," I declare. "So quit this farce before I drag your name through the mud."

Daniel bursts into laughter, a crazed, defiant sound that raises goosebumps over my skin. Foreboding grips me as he doubles over, clutching his sides.

The fit ends as abruptly as it began. Daniel straightens, his lips twisted in a sneer. "My dear Mattie," he says, regarding me like a bug to be squashed. "Challenge me, and you'll be the only one dragged through the mud. With the full blessing of the law, I might add."

He opens his portfolio and thrusts it under my nose. Inside is a drawing of the bag machine beneath the title: "Bag Machine. Inventor Charles F. Annan. Patented August 31, 1869."

Chapter 28

IT'S RAINING PITCHFORKS AS ELIZA AND I ALIGHT FROM THE streetcar at Court Square. This October has been unusually stormy; between the resulting floods and the earthquake that rocked Boston on the twenty-second, some speculate the End Times are near. But even if Judgment Day isn't at hand, I am determined to bring judgment down on Daniel Mowe's head.

I always knew he was clever. I was just too besotted to realize he was also a thieving snake. And because Daniel slithered into my good graces, his accomplice got everything he needed to copy my machine without my realizing it.

Not only that, they had the cunning to expedite their patent application. Apparently, the lengthy process can be shortened through additional fees. How they covered the hefty cost is a mystery, but it paid off. A written exchange with the Patent Office confirmed that the patent certificate Daniel flaunted is legitimate—even if its claim is entirely false.

My only recourse now is a lawsuit. I don't know much about patents, but I know less about law. If I want any hope for success, I need an attorney.

Eliza, who's doing her best to shield us and my oil-cloth-wrapped box with her umbrella, peers through the down-pour. "There's the courthouse," she says, pointing toward its soaring pillars. "Pemberton Square is somewhere around here."

"It's that way." I tilt my chin toward the next corner. "We turn right and go another block."

As I take the lead, Eliza chuckles. "You seem to know your way."

I snort. "I should hope so by now."

Unlike Boston's machinist shops, which are scattered hither

and yon, her law firms cluster near the courthouse. As such, I've haunted these blocks the last several weeks in my search for a patent attorney.

But even though these offices contain fancy furniture and fancier staff, their reception is annoyingly similar to that of a machinist shop. When I ask to meet with an attorney, most smile condescendingly and oust me quickly, albeit politely. Of the three dozen law firms where I inquired, five deigned to offer an appointment. And once I explained that I sought counsel not for a patent application but a lawsuit, four of those five immediately withdrew their offer.

I don't know whether to be disheartened or grateful for that one lone appointment. Either way, today I meet that attorney. If he rejects me, too, I'll be at the end of my rope.

Our destination is a second-floor office in an ivy-draped building with curling wrought iron railings. As we enter the wood-paneled suite, my nervousness tugs up a notch. I come from the world of workshops and factories, and this landscape of leather-bound books and brass-studded cabinet letter files is a realm whose rules and customs I've yet to grasp.

The reception area also accommodates the lawyer's three assistants, who look up from their desks. The eldest, whose bushy black beard sports a sprinkling of white, rises to greet us while the younger two exchange clouded looks.

Ignoring their frowns, I say to their older cohort, "My name is Margaret Knight. I have an appointment."

"Yes, we've been expecting you. This way, please."

Eliza and I leave our wraps and umbrella at a coat stand and follow the bearded assistant to a door bearing the nameplate:

Charles F. Stansbury
Counselor at Law

He gives two sharp knocks, then opens the door.

Beyond is a room redolent of leather and cigar smoke. A square table and matching chairs sit at the center. By the brocade-curtained windows is a desk holding writing implements and tidy stacks of portfolios and papers. And at that desk is a man with a silk waistcoat, fitted jacket, and shock of gray hair.

"Your two o'clock appointment, sir," announces the assistant. "Miss Knight, you can set your box there." He gestures toward the table, which is empty save for a large wooden tray with a shallow rim.

As I place my box by the tray, the attorney crosses the grapevine-patterned rug to offer a handshake. "Charles Stansbury," he says, flashing a smile with prominent canines. "How do you do?"

A chill goes up my spine. The combination of his sharp teeth, gray hair, and wiry build give the unnerving impression that I've stepped into a wolf's den. However, if I'm to win against Daniel and Annan, I'll need a predator's ferocity on my side.

Steeling my nerve, I clasp his hand firmly. "Margaret Knight. Pleased to meet you."

I introduce Eliza, and we sit at the table. "My assistant has briefed me on the particulars of your inquiry," says Mr. Stansbury, glancing over a page of notes. "If I understand correctly, you invented a machine for making paper bags. While you were in the process of preparing your patent application, a fellow by the name of Annan copied and patented the design with the aid of your former coworker."

"That's right," I reply. Eliza nods emphatically.

I brace myself for a skeptical look. I garnered plenty during my rounds of law firms. But Mr. Stansbury merely nods toward the box. "That, I presume, is your machine. Would you demonstrate it for me?"

"Of course," I say, hastening to remove its oilcloth.

Within moments, it's out on the table. "This is the iron model we made for my patent application," I say, turning the crank. "The original prototype was of wood."

I'm about to explain its workings when Mr. Stansbury says, "Now if you please, Miss Knight, would you take the machine apart?"

I blink at the unexpected request. "I can try," I say uncertainly. "It'll be difficult without tools."

Eliza jumps up. "Lincoln and Graham's isn't far. I can dash over and—"

Mr. Stansbury whips out a large toolbox from a cabinet. "I believe these should suffice," he says, displaying its contents. "Disassemble what you can and place the pieces in the tray there."

As he sets it beside my model, his wolfish gaze scrutinizes me, and I realize: *It's a test.*

I smile. If that's the case, I'll take the opportunity to prove myself. "Very well."

Starting with the side folders, I dismantle the machine. Having built it from scratch twice, taking it apart is child's play. As I deftly remove pieces, I tell Mr. Stansbury each one's name and purpose.

I'm one quarter of the way done when he stops me. "That will be sufficient, Miss Knight. If you'll allow me."

He takes the tray. For a moment, he regards the neatly placed parts as if studying their design. Then he gives them a rough shake, startling Eliza and me both. "If you would, Miss Knight," he says, handing back the now-jumbled pieces. "Please return them to their places."

Eliza's brow darkens, but I feign a bored air. "As you wish," I say. "Forgive me if I'm not as swift with the reassembly. The pieces appear to have disordered themselves."

Mr. Stansbury watches intently as I get to work. I welcome it. I don't often get to show off before such an attentive audience. Although my pace is halved due to his hijinks, the machine comes together surely and steadily.

I'm in the homestretch, about to put together the side folder mechanism, when I stop short. "Mattie, what's the matter?" says Eliza, as I duck under the table.

"The two bevel gears for the side folders are missing," I say, readjusting my glasses to scan the carpet. "Mr. Stansbury, do you have a light?"

"Is this what you're looking for?" The attorney extends a hand and opens it. The two gears lie in his palm.

I sag in relief, grateful I don't have to comb his rug for lost pieces. Eliza, however, flushes with anger. "Mr. Stansbury, that wasn't very nice," she snaps.

"Perhaps not," he replies, returning the parts to the tray. "But you're not looking for someone 'nice.' You want a lawyer who will prevail against the thief who stole your invention, don't you?"

"That's true," I reply, as Eliza deflates sullenly in her chair. "And I imagine you want a client who meets particular standards." I tap a bevel gear with a finger.

He grins, pointed teeth gleaming. "I've a hard-earned reputation for success. I'm not risking that on an infringement lawsuit for an inventor who doesn't know her own machine."

"But you don't consider a female client a risk?"

Mr. Stansbury doesn't bat an eye. "You're not the first woman to seek my counsel, Miss Knight, although admittedly you're the first to have claimed to have invented an industrial machine. Twenty years in this profession have taught me women are just as capable of inventing as men, even if they don't always take credit for it."

I cock my head. "What do you mean, don't always take credit?"

"I can't give specifics," he replies, lacing his fingers over his lap. "So let's pretend a woman of standing invents something with the potential for profit. But within her circle, associating with a patent is so uncouth as to be unladylike. Hence, to uphold her good name yet reap the financial benefit, she may contrive with her husband or brother to patent the invention under his name."

My stomach turns. Crediting my achievement to another would be unbearable as hacking off a limb. Eliza, though, lowers her gaze sadly. "I can see that happening," she murmurs.

"However, for those who wish to patent under their own names, the door is wide open, and I've assisted dozens of women in obtaining patents," Mr. Stansbury continues. "As far as the Patent Office is concerned, so long as your application is in good order and you have indeed invented something new, your sex doesn't matter. Unfortunately, in a patent infringement lawsuit, your sex *will* count against you, Miss Knight."

Eliza and I prick up our ears as the attorney's demeanor turns serious. "They say Justice is blind, but she is administered by men who are not. It would be different if the invention in question were, say, a new type of corset. But because it is an industrial invention, your claim will draw double the skepticism than if you were a man."

"I'm prepared for that," I reply. "I've had plenty of experience convincing scoffers of my mechanical abilities."

"Then prepare yourself for one additional prejudice. Mr. Annan has a patent for the machine. Meaning he officially holds credit for its invention. That stacks the odds in his favor and places the burden of proof entirely on your shoulders."

I toss my head. "Fine by me. I got notes and witnesses to prove what I did."

He smiles. "I like your spirit, Miss Knight. Indeed, you'll need such spirit to endure the gauntlet known as the courtroom." He taps the tray. "My little test was no doubt unpleasant, but an opposing lawyer will subject you to worse under cross-examination. If you were a shrinking violet, I'd tell you to give up and go home. But from what I can see, you are capable of demonstrating you know this machine as intimately as its inventor should."

Hope flutters in my chest. "So do you think I can win?"

Mr. Stansbury strokes his beard. "This is only an initial consultation, but if you can indeed produce credible witnesses and dated notes detailing your inventing process, winning is a distinct possibility, provided you build your case properly. That means filing all pertinent legal documents and presenting the evidence in the most convincing way."

"Which would be your job if she engages you," says Eliza. "What would be your fee, Mr. Stansbury?"

I hold my breath as he mulls it over. "I estimate the paperwork and preparation for the trial to take three days of my time. The hearing itself will take at minimum two days. As such, I'd charge five days for a retaining fee. My daily rate is one hundred dollars, so five hundred dollars."

The sum shatters my wits. As I reel, Eliza stammers, "Would you consider l-lowering the fee? Perhaps for a share of f-future profits?"

"No." The reply is without malice, yet brooks no argument. "I am a patent attorney, not an investor. Not to mention, less than half of patents issued actually attain commercial profit. And my rate, by the way, is standard for all my clients. If you inquire with other firms, you'll find their charges are comparable."

"That may be the case, Mr. Stansbury," I say, finally regaining the power of speech, "but five hundred dollars is . . . considerable. May I have time to think this over?"

"Of course. This is not a decision to be made lightly. And I should mention, you are allowed to represent yourself in court, but that would be akin to performing surgery upon yourself. You save money up front, but come out the worse for it. Because in an infringement lawsuit, the prevailing party has the right to demand reimbursement for legal fees from the losing one."

My stomach sickens at the implications, and I swallow hard.

"I'll keep that in mind."

As I struggle not to be ill, Mr. Stansbury adds, "One last thing, Miss Knight. Do not drag your heels. Infringement charges must be submitted in what the court deems a timely manner. In other words, if you do not file within a half year of Mr. Annan's August patent date, consider your opportunity for retribution gone."

Chapter 29

OLD MRS. SHERMAN GUSHES AS SHE GIVES ME MY PAY. "YOU earned every cent. It's so wonderful to have a proper working washing machine again."

"My pleasure," I say, placing the coins in my handbag. "If you have anything else that needs fixing, please let me know."

"I will." Her wrinkled hand pats mine. "You're working as hard as Ruth says. I admire your grit. And I'll be praying for your success."

I muster a smile. "I appreciate that, Mrs. Sherman."

Despite the December chill, she insists on waving me off. Our cheery goodnights ring down the street as I leave. However, the instant she retreats into her house, my expression falls.

To say I've been busy as a bee is no exaggeration. With Christmas drawing near, Eliza's workplace has been in a frenzy, and I've spent every spare minute running errands for the dress shop when I'm not making repairs around the neighborhood. Between my varied jobs, I earned twelve dollars this week, a tidy amount by my usual standards.

But it is a drop in the pail compared to the remaining three hundred and ten dollars I must earn.

This would be easier if I were a man. I'd earn more as a mechanic, but without connections, applying for those jobs is a waste of time. Will and his coworkers would welcome my help in their shop, but Mr. Graham would never allow me to work there.

I don't want to believe my efforts will come to naught. I've sacrificed so much. But the fact of the matter is, time is running out.

My gaze lifts toward the Heavens. They're shrouded in heavy cover, a stark contrast to the sparkling night when I prayed for direction and received a one-way ticket to Boston. I wonder now if that revelation was all in my head. Or perhaps a cosmic joke.

A stiff breeze buffets my steps as doubt pummels my resolve. Is this worth it? Even if I scraped together the money to hire Mr. Stansbury, it doesn't guarantee victory against Annan. Returning to Columbia Paper would certainly be easier. I know and enjoy the work and have the entire factory's respect.

But could I respect myself if I gave up?

I'm exhausted from the thoughts running round my head when I arrive to a dark, empty house. Mrs. MacFarland's gone to Albany with Eliza's parents to attend a relative's funeral. As for Eliza, she and her coworkers are burning the midnight oil until Christmas Eve.

I drag myself inside, pausing only to take the mail. My brain feels as numb as my fingers as I fumble with the matches. After several tries, one strikes, and as I light the entryway lamp, I notice that the letter at the top of the mail pile is for me.

It's from my brother.

I jolt alert. The last time Charlie wrote was during the war, before he got hurt. After that, I only ever heard about him through Mother. To receive a letter now is like getting a message from beyond the grave.

It's terrible to think that way, but in many respects, Charlie has been dead the last four years. He's not sent me a single word through mail, Mother, or otherwise. He's certainly not lent any support. Everything I knew and loved as Charlie Knight disappeared, leaving only a husk my mother and I were duty-bound to care for.

I scrutinize the handwriting on the envelope. It's Charlie's, but not quite. I recognize the wide letters, but the lines are shaky, as if penned by an arthritic hand.

Is this the Charlie I once knew? Shortly after accompanying him to the asylum, Mother wrote to me about the place. Like many asylums, the countryside retreat employed a regimen of sedatives, light exercise, and prayer. Additionally, they used dogs and horses to lift patients' spirits—or so they claimed. Although I felt that the peace of the country would do Charlie good, I doubted a dog could help where my mother's loving care had failed.

However, this letter is evidence that whatever the asylum's done has wrought a change.

Not bothering to remove my hat and coat, I go to the parlor, light the lamp, and grab the letter opener. A quick slash, and the envelope's open.

My eyes go wide.

Nestled within the folded pages is a money order. Fingers trembling, I pluck it out and drop it when I see it's for ten dollars. *What on Earth?*

Curiosity consumes me, and I unfold the letter.

Thanksgiving Day, 1869

Dear Mattie,

How are you? I am doing good. That is something I thought I'd never say again, but I can honestly tell you I am doing good. The folks here have been good to me and helped me greatly. I have bad days, but nowadays, there are more good than bad.

It's still hard to remember things, but I do know I've not been able to care for myself for a long time. I also know the reason I didn't starve was your hard work. The faces and voices of the dead that haunt me are a trial worse than the war, yet I consider myself blessed because you never abandoned me. For that, I want to say thank you. And I'm sorry.

I'm sorry because you shouldn't have been burdened so. I am the man of the family. Caring for you and Mother was my responsibility. Instead, you carried us. Maybe you resent me for that. I don't blame you if you do. But I am doing my level best to become the reliable brother you deserve.

The doc has us try working when we feel steady. It's taken a while, but I can put in a day's work now if my mind is clear. I can't yet hold down a job, but the folks here give me hope that one day I will. Until then, I want you to have this.

I want to pay you back, Mattie. $10 isn't nearly enough, but I want to start. More than that, I want you to do all the things you couldn't because of me. I want your dreams to come true, whatever they are, and I pray that someday I can help you reach them.

Your brother,
Charlie

I'm sobbing by the time I finish the letter. For so long, I'd thought of Charlie as a responsibility, not a person. Now I've got my brother back.

Or partly back. The Charlie I knew was a strong, happy-go-lucky fellow, not one crippled by ghosts. From the sound of it, he's got a ways to go. Even so, he's determined to beat it. For my sake.

My gaze flits to the money order. *I want your dreams to come true, whatever they are . . .*

And if he's willing to carry my dreams forward, how can I lay them down?

I dry my tears and square my shoulders. "If you can keep up the fight, Charlie," I murmur, picking up the money order, "so can I."

※ ※ ※

Late the following week, Mrs. MacFarland returns. And she brings a guest.

"Uncle Thomas," I exclaim, hurrying outside to take the baggage from the cab driver. "I didn't realize you were coming."

Mrs. MacFarland snickers. "He didn't realize either. But when we stopped to call on him on the way home, the poor lamb seemed so forlorn in his empty house we were duty-bound to invite him for Christmas. Needless to say, he leapt at the offer."

Uncle Thomas's mustache twitches. "I do not leap, Aunt Ruth."

"As you say, Thomas," says Mrs. MacFarland, even as she gives me a surreptitious wink.

"Well, I'm glad to see you, Uncle Thomas," I say, setting the baggage inside before helping him up the steps. "Mrs. MacFarland, which room should I prepare for him?"

"I'm not staying, Margaret," says Uncle Thomas. "Too many stairs in this place. I'll be sojourning with Eliza's parents. I accompanied Aunt Ruth home because I have business with you."

I cock my head. "Me?"

As I wonder what business this could be, Mrs. MacFarland says, "The two of you talk in the parlor. I'll make tea. Ah, it's good to be home." Humming merrily, she disappears into the kitchen.

I usher Uncle Thomas to the parlor couch and perch on the seat across from him. My perplexity must show, because he says, "No need to make that face, Margaret. In truth, my business is better called a delivery. When the Leaviltes heard I was traveling to Boston, it suited Ida to make me their errand boy." Reaching into his tweed jacket, he withdraws a manila envelope. "This is for you. Open it."

I do so, emptying its contents onto the tea table. I gasp when a money order for one hundred and fifty dollars drops out.

That's not all. Five ten-dollar bills fall beside it. Flabbergasted, I stammer, "Uncle Thomas, what is this?"

He reaches inside the envelope to pluck out a smaller white one wedged at the bottom and hands it over. "This will explain it."

I tear it open and read.

December 8, 1869

Dear Mattie,

We heard from Eliza what happened. We felt compelled to act, so we each swore to contribute $1 a week for your lawyer. This is what we've collected since November plus what we got from the turquoise bracelet Mrs. Yates donated. (We don't know how she heard, but she did.)

This is not a gift. We owed you this when you won us our raise. Take it and fight for what's yours.

Also, this $150 is just a start. We will send another money order after Christmas.

God bless you and grant you the victory.

It's signed by the nineteen women of the West Workroom. A lump forms in my throat. "I can't take this," I murmur. "Why would they . . ."

"They did it because they thought it was the right thing to do," says Uncle Thomas matter-of-factly. "You've always done what you thought was right, no matter what anyone said, so you ought to respect their decision and accept it, Margaret."

I blink. Considering he deemed my patent aspirations foolhardy, I thought he'd declare a patent lawsuit further lunacy. But if he's telling me to take the money, I feel compelled to obey.

However, I am puzzled. "Something's strange, though. The letter says one hundred fifty dollars, but there's two hundred dollars here."

"That's because the money order is from the women," says Uncle Thomas with a huff. "The rest is from me."

My confusion jolts to shock, and I jump to my feet. "You can't afford that!"

Uncle Thomas isn't poor, but he's an old man on a fixed income with no surviving children. Fifty dollars is not an amount he can carelessly give away.

He sniffs. "Fear not. The principal in my savings account remains untouched. My brains haven't become so addled that I'd do something so foolish."

"Then how . . ."

He averts his eyes as if suddenly fascinated by the framed Scripture samplers to my right. "A widower has no need for a multitude of silver implements. Especially when he takes his meals out of home and rarely entertains. Now that I'm rid of them I'm rather glad to be freed from the never-ending task of polishing."

He sold his wife's silver? I sink to my chair in disbelief. This is the same man who downright refused to contemplate contributing toward my patent a year ago. "Uncle Thomas, why?"

"Because this is the right thing for me to do."

I shake my head. "The factory hands feel obligated because of their raise, but you don't owe me anything."

"I don't owe you anything, that's true, but I have failed you, Margaret."

His gaze meets mine, and I'm startled by the regret and self-loathing reflected there. "When you girls lived under my roof, you were my responsibility. As the man of the house, as your elder, it was my duty to provide guidance and protection from scoundrels who would take advantage of you."

He feels guilty because of Daniel? "Uncle Thomas, that wasn't your fault."

"It was," he snaps, his voice and color rising. "Not only did I fail to recognize the wolf in sheep's clothing, I approved him. I even encouraged his visits into my house. And not only did he break your heart, he broke your trust. He broke everyone's trust. If I was ten years younger, I'd hunt that weasel down and—"

Uncle Thomas catches himself, as if suddenly remembering he's a church elder and not a vigilante. "Anyway," he says, clearing his throat, "my neglect allowed that reprobate to steal from you. Theft is a violation of the Lord's Commandments, and that demands justice."

He slides the bills towards me. "The Good Book says, 'The Lord secures justice for the poor and upholds the cause of the needy.' God will uphold your cause, Margaret, and so will I."

Tears prick my eyes. Uncle Thomas is not my father or even a blood relation. "Uncle Thomas, I don't know what to say."

He cracks a smile. "Say you'll take it, Margaret. And that you'll win."

Chapter 30

MR. STANSBURY WASN'T MY LAWYER OF CHOICE INASMUCH as he was the only lawyer I could choose. However, he's given no cause for complaint. Shortly after the new year, we signed a contract, and the old wolf got straight to work. Within days, the necessary documents were mailed. Two weeks later, we received notice that my grievance was under review, and at the end of February, the Patent Commissioner approved my infringement suit and set a court date for May 5.

The news catapults my spirits, but Mr. Stansbury swiftly returns me to earth. "Understand, Miss Knight," he says, tapping the hearing notice on his desk. "Getting this was a crucial step, but it only gives you the right to enter the ring. The actual fight's yet to come."

I sober up at once. "Right, of course." After everything that's happened, I know better than to count my chickens before they're hatched.

"If Mr. Annan's got any brains at all, he'll hire his own counsel, and you know we lawyers can be a wicked bunch," he continues. "They'll do their damnedest to discredit your claim. That means poking holes in your testimony wherever they can."

"And we do the same to his."

"Maybe."

When I return a perplexed look, he explains, "Mr. Annan holds a patent. That in and of itself credits him with the wherewithal to have invented the machine on the date of his patent application, which was . . ." Mr. Stansbury searches his notes. "April 3, 1869. If he attempts to establish an earlier date of invention, *that* we can poke holes at. But even without presenting a shred of additional evidence, he can still win. That is because your capabilities have not been established."

I grimace. "So it's possible for him to win without doing a thing, but I must prove I have the know-how to build a machine."

"The burden is actually twofold," says Mr. Stansbury, raising two fingers. "We must convince the court that, one, you have the ability to invent, and two, you were actively developing your machine before Annan. And the tricky thing is, Miss Knight, even if you're telling the complete, unadulterated truth, a cunning adversary can turn your testimony against you. That is why we cannot walk in unprepared. Have you brought the items I requested?"

"Yes." I open the shopping sack on my lap and place my 1868 and 1869 diaries on Mr. Stansbury's desk. "My machine sketches and notes are on the daily entry pages, and the memo pages in the back I used to track the materials I bought."

"Excellent," says Mr. Stansbury, placing the diaries in a marked portfolio. "I'll review them, and we'll discuss how to present the contents at our next meeting. Moving on, the hearing is scheduled to begin May 5, and the names of those offering testimony must be submitted two weeks prior. As I explained before, we want witnesses who are sympathetic, but they must be credible and able to appear in court. Have you given it thought?"

I nod. "My roommate and my machinist already volunteered." Actually, it's more accurate to say they demanded to come. "They're both in Boston, so they won't have trouble getting to the courthouse."

Mr. Stansbury scans a sheaf of notes. "From what you've said previously, Miss MacFarland witnessed the machine's construction at your residence since its inception. However, she doesn't have any mechanical knowledge, does she?"

"Er, no. Will Abbott does, though."

"But you engaged his services in May '69. Nearly two months after Annan submitted his application to the Patent Office."

When my face falls, Mr. Stansbury quickly adds, "I'm not

rejecting them. Your roommate's testimony will be valuable in establishing your inception date, and Mr. Abbott's in establishing your mechanical competence. However, an additional witness who can testify to your mechanical abilities while you were in Springfield would significantly fortify your case. Ideally"—he flips through his notes—"one who was present at that machine competition at Columbia Paper in '68."

"There is someone," I say hesitantly. "My neighbor, Ida. She's a factory hand in my old division, and she saw the contest. I'll ask if she can come, but even if she can't, I'm sure another hand can."

I wanted to avoid making additional trouble for the West Workroom workers, but it appears there's no way around it. At least with everyone pitching in, whoever testifies won't be overly burdened by travel costs.

"A factory hand would suffice, but we could make a stronger case with . . ." Mr. Stansbury peers at his notes. "Ah, here's the name. Frank Niebuhr."

I give a start. "Frank?"

"Why not?" says Mr. Stansbury. "You were rivals for that contest, true, but you must've parted on good terms if he paid your way to Boston like you said."

"He did do that," I say, wondering if that qualifies as parting on good terms. I hadn't mentioned to Mr. Stansbury that I'd avoided Frank afterward.

"Mr. Niebuhr wasn't merely a coworker, he was a fellow mechanic. He attempted to automate the same process you did. That lends greater credence to his assessment of your skills and your machine than a factory hand."

"That is true," I admit. "But Frank's no longer at Columbia Paper. He left for Maryland last year. I'm not sure where he is now."

"Do you have acquaintances who might know?" Mr. Stansbury asks, undaunted.

"Probably." Frank left the factory, but his Oak Creek buddies are still there.

Mr. Stansbury pauses. Leveling his gaze at me, he says, "Miss Knight, it appears you have reservations about Mr. Niebuhr. Are you concerned he's predisposed against you? That he might testify in a manner that would damage your case?"

"What? No! Frank is honest to a fault. He'd never lie. It's just . . ." I fidget, a mix of emotions squirming in my chest. "Even if I track him down, I can't be sure he'll come."

Mr. Stansbury raises an eyebrow. "Is that all?"

His stare pries open my soul, and the truth comes out. "I . . . feel ashamed. He paid my fare to Boston so I could patent. Instead, I got mired in this." I gesture toward the court notice. "I feel like I wasted his money, and I don't know how to face him."

"I see," says Mr. Stansbury, steepling his fingers. "Well, clients have final say regarding witness selection, so the choice is ultimately yours. However, as your attorney, I strongly counsel you to include Mr. Niebuhr. As to whether he'll come, my rule is to always ask and let the individual decide. People can be surprisingly accommodating sometimes."

"Right," I murmur.

"As to your second point, humble pie is never pleasant, but ask yourself this. Does the embarrassment of that train fare outweigh the cost of my fee? Mr. Niebuhr's testimony might be key to your victory. If you forgo it out of pride only to suffer loss, not only will you have squandered Mr. Niebuhr's generosity, but also the five hundred dollars you paid me."

My breath hitches. Mr. Stansbury's right. I need all the help I can get, and I can't afford to be picky or proud about it.

Resigning myself to a large helping of humble pie, I say, "I'll figure out where Frank is then."

Chapter 31

Friday, April 15, 1870

Dear Frank,

I don't know if you got my other letters. If you haven't,

I tap the pen against the desktop as I struggle for my next words. I hate to beg. Worse, I feel Frank's already turned a deaf ear to me.

It's common for mail delivery to take upwards of a week in the country. It's not unheard of for letters to get lost. But over the last five weeks, I've sent three letters to the post office that serves the folks of Oak Creek and got nothing back.

To me, that silence means no. Mr. Stansbury interprets it differently. As he opined this afternoon: "If you haven't received a definitive response, a yes remains possible. Recall the parable of the widow in Luke's Gospel. She persisted unceasingly and thus obtained justice. So keep writing."

But what more can I write? I rise and pace the parlor so I don't have to stare at my pathetic opening line. My earlier letters explained how Daniel hoodwinked me and how grateful I would be for Frank's testimony. I've relayed the hearing's particulars, down to a map showing the route from the train station to the Boston courthouse. I even offered to advance a money order to cover travel costs.

The only new bit of information I've got is that the trial won't stretch beyond two days. This is because Annan's lawyer sent notice that they're presenting no witnesses. None, not even Annan. Mr. Stansbury expects my testimony to take the entirety of the first day, and the statements of my witnesses to take one additional day.

I had mixed feelings when Mr. Stansbury delivered that news today. In short, Annan's single claim to legitimacy is his patent application; that simplifies our task to proving I invented the machine before his April application date. But part of me wants Annan to squirm on the stand while we shred his lies in public. He humiliated me, and I want him to pay.

Perhaps I should take up Will's offer to give Annan a thrashing . . .

Stop that. I take a deep breath, pushing unlawful acts from my mind. As Mr. Stansbury is constantly reminding me, I'm the one at a disadvantage. That means I need to keep a cool head and prepare my own case right and proper.

Fortunately, I've three witnesses determined to testify, come hell or high water. Ida wrote last week that the West Workroom purchased her ticket to Boston. As for Will and Eliza, both got permission from their employers to take leave for the trial. Between the three of them, I believe we can prove beyond a doubt that I built my machine months before Annan's patent application.

Yet Mr. Stansbury insists that I continue reaching out to Frank. After three unanswered letters, doing so feels like wasted effort. But I hired Mr. Stansbury for his counsel, and if he wants to pursue every possible advantage, I shouldn't complain. Resolving to do my part, I return to the secretary and poise my pen over the paper. But no words are forthcoming.

The saddest thing is that I remember a time when I could say anything and everything to Frank.

I drop the pen and take out my jackknife. As Eliza likes to quip, I wouldn't be me without a tool in my pocket, and I keep this knife handy for odd tasks. However, I gaze at it now, not as my all-purpose tool, but a birthday gift.

As I recall the night Frank surprised me with his present,

other memories surge in its wake. Our conversations about factory machines. The cozy nights carving toys in Ida's kitchen. That Fourth of July waltz, far and away from everyone else.

This might sound strange to you, Mattie, but I don't want you to hate me. I never have.

The words ring in my mind with crystal clarity, and regret grips my heart.

Frank meant what he said. The train ticket he gave was proof of that. But suspicion clouded my judgment, keeping me from seeing his actions for what they were. Instead of taking the olive branch he held out, I moved on without a backward look.

Now I'm the one groping through the void for him.

My fingertip traces the initials carved into the jackknife handle. Once upon a time, Daniel had all of my esteem while Frank had all of my contempt. Now I've realized the Daniel I adored was an illusion, while what I had with Frank was special . . . and irretrievably lost.

My gaze returns to the unfinished letter. I'd intended to keep it polite and detached like the previous three, but not anymore. Rather, I feel compelled to pour out my remorse. Not as a means of manipulating Frank's cooperation, but to acknowledge that what we once shared was precious. That the feelings I abandoned in the storm of rivalry were not as trifling as I thought.

I'm not so simple-minded to think this will trigger a response when my other requests failed. I snubbed Frank, after all. He may burn my words without reading them, but I need to write them down nevertheless. Picking up my pen, I continue where I left off:

I want you to know I'm sorry.

Chapter 32

WHEN I CONTENDED AGAINST FRANK, IT WAS A FIGHT ON known ground. Yes, there were uncertainties, but I had a solid grasp of the rules, the risks, and my opponent's capabilities. My lawsuit with Annan, on the other hand, is entirely in foreign territory. And with the hearing less than an hour away, the unknown is frazzling my nerves.

"Mattie, wait! Your bag!"

"What?" I turn, halfway out the horsecar door, to see Eliza retrieving the handbag I left on the passenger bench.

I've scarcely registered my slip when Eliza's back at my side, taking my hand in hers. "Watch your step. We don't need you tumbling out."

Her grip grounds me, and I thank God once more for her steadying presence. Although Eliza's not taking the witness stand until tomorrow, she insisted on accompanying me today, and I'm glad she did. In addition to rescuing my bag, she's saved me from scorching my best clothes, leaving the house with my jacket misbuttoned, and getting onto the wrong streetcar.

I begin to thank Eliza, but she cuts me off. "Hush. I know you have a multitude of things on your mind. So concentrate on them, and I'll take care of navigating you."

She beams at me, and I muster a smile. "I'll rely on you, then." With that, I let her steer me through the Court Square throng while I review Mr. Stanbury's instructions in my head.

And those instructions are many. Over the past weeks, Mr. Stansbury's drilled me on a variety of scenarios to prepare for today's interrogation. Unfortunately, all that information feels about to burst out my skull like fish from an overloaded net.

"There you are, gentlemen. Good morning."

Eliza's call jolts me back to the present. While I was mired in thought, she maneuvered me into the courthouse foyer, where Mr. Stansbury waits with his black-bearded assistant, a portfolio, and two large boxes containing our trial evidence.

We exchange greetings, then Mr. Stansbury thumps me lightly on the back. "Relax, Miss Knight. You are facing an endeavor, but they're not attacking with pistols and pikes. So breathe. It'll allow you to circumvent the embarrassment of fainting in court." He smiles dryly.

I force a chuckle. I must look a wreck if the old wolf is attempting to lighten my mood.

"Now then, our courtroom is this way." Mr. Stansbury gestures toward a vaulted passageway. "Miss Knight, are you ready to enter the fray, or would you like time to collect yourself?"

I exhale a shaky breath and lift my chin. "I'm ready as I'll ever be."

The men gather their things, and Mr. Stansbury leads us to a pair of imposing doors that open into an oak-paneled courtroom. Two narrow tables face the judge's bench. One is already occupied by Annan and a barrel-shaped man I presume to be his attorney.

Indignation flares, but I bite my lip. Mr. Stansbury warned me to hold my tongue in the courtroom unless specifically directed to answer. So I settle for a silent glare.

Annan doesn't flinch. His eyes remain locked on the empty judge's bench. Meanwhile, his lawyer buries his nose in a stack of papers.

Fine. Pretend I'm not here. You can't ignore me much longer. With a toss of my head, I follow Mr. Stansbury and his assistant to the other table. While we three arrange our boxes and papers, Eliza makes her way to the public seating area, where a solitary graybeard sits reading a newspaper. The man's face strikes me as familiar, and I wonder where I've seen him.

Then my eyes fall on his ivory-handled walking stick, and I

gasp.

Mr. Stansbury, who's dismissing his assistant, gives me a side-long glance. "Miss Knight," he says in a low voice, "is something amiss?"

"The man with the newspaper," I hiss in his ear. "He's the investor, Mr. Binney."

"Hmm." Mr. Stansbury waves his assistant off, as if my frantic whisper was a mundane remark about the dampness of the room. He leafs idly through his portfolio, then says in an undertone, "No changes have been made to the list of witnesses. That means we can comfortably assume he's not here to testify on Annan's behalf."

"Then why is he here?"

"Probably because he has an interest in the bag machine. If that's the case, he has an interest in the trial's outcome."

Mr. Stansbury's logic extinguishes my panic. I'd heard through Will Abbott that Daniel and Annan attempted to solicit Mr. Binney's support after our fracas at the Mechanics Building. To no avail. Clearly the old man is too sensible to get himself ensnared in an ongoing dispute. But once that dispute is resolved, it will behoove him to act swiftly if the machine offers potential for profit.

As that thought sinks in, Mr. Stansbury, eyes still on his papers, murmurs, "From what you told me, that investor presumed you a spurned paramour. Care to prove him wrong?" A sly smile spreads across his lips.

Just then, a clerk strides into the room and announces, "All rise. Court is now in session, the Honorable Judge John M. Thacher presiding."

A doughy man with a frizzy halo of blonde hair enters in a billow of black robes, and I leap to my feet. My fidgets are gone. Rather, I'm chomping at the bit to start.

I invented my bag machine. I know it. My adversaries know

it. This is my chance to let everyone know it.

In a matter of minutes, I mount the witness stand and place my hand on the Bible the clerk holds out to me. "Margaret E. Knight," he intones, "do you solemnly swear that you will tell the truth, the whole truth, and nothing but the truth, so help you God?"

"I do." *And God help me get the credit I rightfully deserve.*

The opposing attorney, Mr. Clarke, possesses a peculiar build. His girth is considerable, but his arms and legs are spindly. The contrast between his round middle and skinny limbs remind me of a spider.

A spider who, at the moment, is ensnaring me in a web of words.

"From a gear of seventeen teeth revolving on a fixed pivot to a gear of seventeen teeth revolving on a fixed pivot, the motion being transmitted by intermediate gears set upon different fixed pivots, could you change the velocity of the second seventeen-tooth gear by changing the number of teeth in the intermediate gears?"

It takes every scrap of willpower to keep my jaw from hitting the floorboards. I can barely understand the long-winded terms, let alone interpret the actual problem behind the words.

The worst part is that victory seemed a sure thing a half hour ago. Per court procedure, my testimony began with direct examination. In other words, my counsel asked questions, and I answered them. We also produced my 1868 diary, my wooden machine, and the iron model as exhibits. Although Annan and his lawyer did not bat an eye, Mr. Binney, the judge, and even the court transcriber couldn't hide their surprise at the number of drawings and notes I presented.

Mr. Stansbury meticulously laid out the basis of my mechanical skills, my familiarity with paper bag manufacturing, and the process by which I invented my machine. Once his direct examination concluded, our case felt solid as a rock.

Until Mr. Clarke began his cross-examination. He started harmlessly enough with, "How have you acquired your knowledge of mechanics?" Somehow, that innocent question paved the way for a near-incomprehensible quiz about hypothetical gear teeth.

As my wits seize up, Mr. Stansbury takes out his handkerchief. Flicking the fabric, he dabs his forehead, and the fluttering linen makes me stop short. *That's right. I don't have to rush.*

Mr. Stansbury warned me that fluster often causes people to respond without thinking, and a cunning attorney can bully a witness into a discombobulating pace of question-and-answer. However, I am by no means beholden to let Mr. Clarke drag me as he likes, and Mr. Stansbury's handkerchief is his silent signal to remind me of that fact.

I inhale deeply to calm myself and say, "Would you please repeat the question?"

Because my every answer will be recorded, I'm entitled to have any question put again. Mr. Clarke sneers as if I'm a simpleton, but Mr. Stansbury puts his handkerchief neatly away, indicating I've done well.

Mr. Clarke repeats his gear teeth puzzle, making a great show of slowing his speech. Despite his insulting tone, this time I'm able to translate it to normal English and picture the problem. After mulling it over, I respond, "I should think you could."

"Then," Mr. Clarke plunges on, "it is your opinion that intermediate gears meshing with each other have an effect in transmitting motion upon the velocity transmitted independently of the relation of the number of teeth in the wheels at the beginning and end of a gear train, is it?"

The second avalanche of words engulfs me. My hands clench, itching to squash Mr. Clarke like the vile bug he is, and Mr.

Stansbury whips out his handkerchief a second time.

I wrestle my temper down. As Mr. Stansbury's reminded me a thousand times, I cannot afford to be rash. He's also warned me to answer only what I'm asked and not make additional comments. Unfortunately, if that spider continues spinning me in this direction, I'll wind up ensnared.

I straighten in my seat. Rather than allowing him to befuddle me with riddles, I'll simply state what I know is true. "As I understand, changing the number of teeth in the gears between the seventeen-teeth gears of the previous question could affect the velocity of the second seventeen-teeth gear."

Mr. Clarke opens his mouth to speak, but I cut him off. "Please understand, I never claimed to be a master mechanic. The way I got the movements of my machine was by continually experimenting with different-sized gears and numbers of teeth. Had I been formally trained in mechanical theory, it would have saved me a great amount of labor."

"Objection!" Mr. Clarke's interjection rips the air like cannon fire. He turns to the judge. "The witness's answer was irresponsive. I ask to put the question to her again."

My pulse races as Judge Thacher mulls it over. *Please don't let him, please don't let him . . .*

"Permission granted to put the question to the witness once more."

Mr. Clarke smirks. My heart sinks. I glance toward Mr. Stansbury for help—and find him looking calmly back.

As I blink at his unruffled expression and folded hands, his instructions echo in my head. *The worst thing I can do is confuse you with too many directions. So if I give no signal, take heart. Be confident in the stance you've taken.*

Judge Thacher halts the proceedings to give the clerk instructions regarding the transcription. While they speak, my mind races. Mr. Clarke's convoluted question will be forced on me again, but Mr. Stansbury showed no alarm. That means he approves of my response even though the outcome was contentious.

That being the case, I'll stick to my guns.

I glance at the judge. Mr. Clarke's question is intended to cast doubt over my ability to make a machine. I must convince the judge that I can figure out the answer, but not the way a formally trained person would.

The hearing restarts, and Mr. Clarke rattles off his question once more. Without hesitation, I reply, "I decline to answer."

Mr. Clarke's eyes gleam as though I've flown into his snare. "Why do you decline?"

"I decline, not because I am ignorant about the subject. I am well acquainted with the practical operation and workings of machinery, and I should like to demonstrate that knowledge to the court. However, I cannot answer because the words of the cross-interrogation are too confusing."

My response is steady, and so is the glare I aim at Mr. Clarke. He returns a patronizing sniff. "Since you are confused, would you like the examination to stop that you may recover your composure?"

I scowl back. He may try to paint me as a pretender who's overreached herself, but I refuse to give him that satisfaction. "I am perfectly willing to continue as long as the questions do not involve an undue amount of mechanical theory. And I am especially willing if the questions are about the actual machine I invented and not hypothetical gear trains."

"Well then," says Mr. Clarke with exaggerated forbearance, "we will change the subject."

He withdraws to consult his notes. After flipping through pages, he saunters to the clerk's desk where my exhibits sit. Pointing to my diary, he asks, "According to your so-called experiment notes in Exhibit A, you changed the shape of the cam for your folding plate mechanism several times, did you not?"

God be praised, a question I understand. "I changed it by making it fuller in some parts and taking off in some other part. This was done to get the timing right."

"By 'get the timing right,' you mean harmonizing the operations of the machine, don't you?"

I wring the folds of my skirt, wishing they were Mr. Clarke's neck. If there were a contest for irritating remarks, he would win hands down. "I do. I mean harmonizing the motions of the folding plate to fold the bottom fold of the bag."

"You changed the proportions of the same mechanism's jointed lever arms frequently, didn't you?"

"I changed the proportions a good many times until I got one that would traverse the required distance," I reply, wondering where Mr. Clarke is going with this.

"Without referring to the exhibits or any other notes, please state how these parts, the cam and jointed arms, operated the folding plate, if you can." Mr. Clarke hooks his thumbs into his waistcoat, looking down his nose at me. No doubt he expects me to squirm.

A cloying smile spreads on my lips. "The cam was attached to the feed shaft and revolved with it," I say. "One end of the longer jointed arm was attached to the frame and rotated on a pin passing through the hole, the arm working up and down freely. Another pin was placed in the center of the arm, or thereabouts—about two inches and five-eighths from the pin in the joint . . ."

The description spills from my lips as smoothly as a sonnet delivered by a well-rehearsed orator. As I continue relating the mechanism's operations in minute detail, Mr. Clarke's face twitches, and Annan pales.

I conclude my response. For several moments, there's only the scratching of the transcriber's pen as he hastens to put my answer to paper. Mr. Clarke scowls as if he's tripped into his own net. In the public seating area, Mr. Binney gawks while Eliza beams.

As for Mr. Stansbury, his features remain neutral, but I detect the twinkle of approval in his eyes.

It doesn't matter that I don't know formal terms. It doesn't matter that I don't know fancy calculations. What matters is I know my machine better than anyone, and I can prove it.

Chapter 33

Eliza frowns at my half-eaten lunch. "Mattie, you must eat," she wheedles, pushing the plate toward me. "You won't last the rest of the hearing if you don't."

With a sigh, I pick up my bread and cheese for a bite. Eliza's right, I know she is, but I'm so tired that chewing and swallowing feels like a chore. If Mr. Stansbury hadn't ushered us back to his office for the lunch recess, I would've fallen asleep where I sat in the courtroom.

As I wash the morsel down with the tea his assistants left us, Mr. Stansbury returns to the room. "We should leave for the courthouse soon," he says, gathering papers from his desk. "Miss Knight, are you ready for round two?"

"I'd be lying if I said round one didn't wear me out," I say, rubbing my temples, "but I've had twelve-hour workdays. I'll find a way to tolerate a few more hours of Mr. Clarke."

After my refusal to continue down the rabbit hole of theoretical gears, Mr. Clarke interrogated me about my machine's construction for the remainder of the morning. He covered everything from the number of gears connecting its shafts to the type of wood I used to carve parts. While his fancily phrased questions often gave me pause, once I clarified what he was actually asking, answering was a cinch.

"Enduring a cross-examination is more difficult than people realize," says Mr. Stansbury as he packs his portfolio. "You've held up well. In fact, you've done so well demonstrating your mechanical competency, Mr. Clarke is likely to switch to a different tack. So stay sharp."

Unfortunately, staying sharp is easier said than done. Between the noontime heat and my exhaustion, my brain is a drowsy slug.

It's all I can do to follow Mr. Stansbury's lead through the throngs to the courthouse. As we mount its front steps, my gaze drags up to the entrance, and I glimpse the back of a tall man disappearing through the building's double doors.

My eyes snap wide. *That height. That build.*

Daniel.

I sprint, taking the steps two at a time. Dodging a gaggle of clerks, I dive inside to see his lanky frame turning round a corner. Seven quick strides, and I seize his shoulder. "You—"

My cry ends in a choke as an unfamiliar harelipped face gawps at me. "I beg your pardon," says the startled stranger.

I snatch my hand back. "I'm sorry," I stammer. "I . . . mistook you for someone else."

Cheeks burning, I beat a hasty retreat. It wasn't Daniel. Of course it wasn't Daniel. There's no reason he should be here. Given the tale Mr. Clarke's spinning, that Annan has absolutely no connection to me, it behooves Daniel to make himself scarce.

"Mattie!" Eliza rushes to me as I return to the foyer. "You scared me running off like that. What happened?" Behind her, Mr. Stansbury's brow wrinkles with concern.

"I'm fine. I thought I saw—" I halt and shake my head. "It's nothing."

Eliza frowns. "Nothing?"

"All that matters today is that I focus on the enemy in there," I declare, whipping an arm toward the courtroom. "Isn't that right, Mr. Stansbury?"

The old wolf regards me a moment, then cracks a smile. "It is. And it's good to see you've caught your second wind, Miss Knight."

❄ ❄ ❄

Embarrassing though my mix-up was, the unexpected gale of emotions swept my lethargy away. That stranger might not have been Daniel, but he reminded me of wrongs I swore to set right. I retake the witness stand with renewed determination.

Which is a good thing, because Mr. Clarke sallies forth with a new plan of attack, as the wolf predicted.

"During your direct testimony," he begins, "you claimed to have begun work on a machine in February '68 for the purpose of a bag-making competition. You also claimed to have completed that machine in September '68, did you not?"

"I did," I reply.

He folds his skinny arms, oozing skepticism. "You claim, therefore, to have invented a working machine in seven months?"

"Yes."

"Yet you never submitted a patent application for this supposed invention. In fact, you submitted nothing to the Patent Office until the infringement charge filed in February '70, over a year later. Is this not so?"

My spine stiffens. *That's what he's getting at.*

At its core, a patent is an acknowledgment of being the first to conceive and execute an inventive idea. As such, the Patent Office places great store on expeditiousness, and on the surface, the fact I did not contact it sooner is a glaring shortfall.

Mr. Stansbury had prepared me for this, but practicing in his office is utterly unlike facing a hostile courtroom audience. Willing my nerves to steady, I say, "That is true, but I was diligently preparing a patent application those months."

Mr. Clarke scoffs. "If you were so diligent, how is it that so many months passed without that application's submittal?"

"So many months passed because I first had to move from Springfield," I retort. "My prototype was made of wood, and I required a machinist to make my iron model. However, the closest shops were in Boston. It may be a simple matter for you to change residences, sir, but moving to another town is a burdensome endeavor for a factory worker."

"Objection," bellows Mr. Clarke. "That last remark about burdensomeness is irrelevant."

The judge strokes his double chin. "Objection upheld."

But that remark is entirely relevant! I cast a silent plea to Mr. Stansbury, but he folds his hands upon the tabletop to signal there is nothing he can do. The judge's say is final.

After a brief exchange with the court transcriber, Judge Thacher instructs Mr. Clarke to resume. With the glee of a cat toying with a mouse, he continues, "When did you move from Springfield, Massachusetts, to Boston?"

"January 2, 1869," I reply through gritted teeth.

"You stated that your purpose was to hire a machinist to make a patent application model. That is, Exhibit C." Mr. Clarke points at my iron model. "When was Exhibit C completed?"

"The end of last September."

"Last September?" Mr. Clarke gasps in mock surprise and makes a show of ticking the months off his fingers. "You were in Boston nine months—nearly an entire year—before your model was made. You purport this to be the result of diligent effort?"

"I do," I say with a toss of my head, "because I was diligently seeking a machinist the first part of '69. Finding a competent machinist takes time and effort. It wasn't until May 28 that I found and engaged Will Abbott at Lincoln and Graham to build my model."

Mr. Clarke snorts. "What proof do you have that you were diligently seeking a machinist and not idling away those five months?"

"My roommate Eliza MacFarland accompanied me and can attest to my inquiries." As I reply, Eliza nods emphatically at the rear of the courtroom. "The shops and the dates we visited them are listed in my 1869 diary. In addition, I have two dated quotes pasted in the diary's memorandum pages."

I submit my 1869 diary as evidence. The clerk labels it "Exhibit D," then allows Mr. Clarke to examine it. As he studies its contents, I wonder how much he knows about his client's trickery, if he's aware of Annan's connection with the machinist Burnham.

I'd like nothing more than to rail about Annan's deception. Unfortunately, only Annan and Mr. Burnham can verify those facts, and neither has incentive to do so. If I hauled Mr. Burnham to the witness stand, who knows what falsehoods he'd spew. Vexing though it is, it's safest to treat Burnham simply as one of many machinists I sought out.

This is, of course, the stance Mr. Clarke takes when he resumes his cross-examination. "If your notes are to be believed, you inquired at two dozen machinist shops prior to Mr. Abbott and obtained a quote from a Byron Burnham dated March 4, 1869, and another from Wyman and Sons dated May 5, 1869, correct?"

"Yes."

Mr. Clarke pins me with his gaze. "Why did you not engage the services of Mr. Burnham or Wyman and Sons?"

"Mr. Burnham had a contentious personality," I reply, using the description Mr. Stansbury recommended for this occasion. "As for Wyman and Sons, I did engage their services on the date of their quote, but they failed to perform the work as promised. So I was obliged to take my prototype from their shop and seek the services of another."

"To summarize," Mr. Clarke says, "over a period of five months you approached two dozen establishments, only to obtain two quotes, and then had the terrible luck that neither of those machinists suited your needs, correct?"

The snide phrasing all but erodes my self-control. Unfortunately, his words are technically true, so I bite out, "Yes."

Mr. Clarke clicks his tongue. "Miss Knight, you fault these machinists for your delay, but would it not be more accurate to say these machinists simply could not do what you wished because something was fundamentally wrong with your prototype? Or perhaps"—his features darken into a leer—"something was fundamentally wrong with you as a customer?"

My hands clench the armrests to keep from snatching the judge's gavel and hurling it at Mr. Clarke. I knew he'd question my difficulties with machinists, but to cast such aspersions over my character? However, losing my composure will only play to his advantage, so I rein in my temper and say, "No."

My answer is the absolute truth, but I sense doubt rising in the courtroom. Mr. Clarke's eyes glitter. "To confirm," he continues, "you claim to have engaged a machinist to build your model May 28, and it was completed at the end of September, correct?"

"Yes," I say, praying that my honesty will shine through Mr. Clarke's slanderous clouds.

"Is it also true that on Saturday, September 11, 1869, you sought my client Charles Annan at the Mechanics Building in Boston?"

Surprise lances me even as Mr. Binney perks up in his seat. I hadn't expected Mr. Clarke to mention that encounter. I thought he'd avoid it entirely. "Yes," I reply.

"Why did you seek Mr. Annan?"

I hesitate. He wouldn't pursue this line of questioning unless his client stood to benefit. Unfortunately, the only answer I can conjure is the truth. "I suspected he'd stolen my machine design. See, a man tried to sneak looks at my machine while it was at Lincoln and Graham. Not long after that, I learned Mr. Annan was getting up a bag machine."

Mr. Clarke cocks an eyebrow. "That man at the shop could've been anyone. Why did you suspect Mr. Annan?"

"The staff's description matched Mr. Annan there." I point at Annan, who returns a blank look.

"The staff's description matched," Mr. Clarke echoes. "You didn't actually see Mr. Annan yourself?"

"No, but my machinist did," I retort. "He can tell you when he testifies tomorrow."

The attorney doesn't flinch. "When did this supposed

attempt to 'sneak looks' happen?"

"The end of August."

"And how did you learn Mr. Annan was getting up a bag machine?"

"I heard through my machinist Will Abbott—"

I catch myself just as I'm about to mention George May. *Wait, is he going to turn the connection between George and Annan against me? Accuse me of using the drawings George made for Annan?*

I snap my mouth shut, deciding to err on the side of caution. Unfortunately, Mr. Clarke has already collected sufficient rope to hang me with.

"You purport," he says, pacing with his hands clasped behind his back, "that you sought Mr. Annan on September 11 because you suspected him of stealing your design. Because some imagined look-alike tried to peek at whatever contraption you had at your machinist's shop. But . . ."

He halts, whirling on me with showman grandeur. "It was, in fact, the other way around! You heard of Mr. Annan's success, and your true intent was to steal the design he'd submitted to the Patent Office—and indeed, had already received a patent—when you waylaid him at the Mechanics Building. Isn't that so?"

My fist slams the armrest. "Absolutely not! I did not have to steal from him because I had a perfect working prototype. My machinist can attest to that."

My body trembles with righteous indignation, but the judge's gaze only narrows with skepticism. Mr. Binney and the court clerk also exude contempt, their stares decrying me a hysterical, deceitful female. Behind his attorney's gloating form, Annan curls his lip while Mr. Stansbury blots his forehead with his handkerchief.

As I sense Mr. Clarke's noose coiling around my neck, Mr. Stansbury's words ring in my mind. *Justice is blind, but she is administered by men who are not.*

Chapter 34

I REMEMBER LEARNING IN SUNDAY SCHOOL THAT FEMALE WIT-nesses were excluded at the time of Christ. The reason: a woman's testimony was deemed as reliable as a lunatic's. Hundreds of years later, things haven't improved much for our sex.

My day on the witness stand made it patently clear that my word doesn't carry the clout of a man's. While Judge Thacher nodded along to Mr. Clarke's conjectures, my explanations drew raised eyebrows. The disparity was enough to make me tear my hair out. Worse, I must watch my best friend subjected to the same on this second day of the hearing.

Eliza, however, isn't about to let anyone walk all over her.

"I witnessed her constructing her machine at home starting February '68," she declares without a hint of stutter. "She worked on it every night until she attained success at the end of summer."

Mr. Clarke snickers. "How did you, a seamstress, determine that your friend attained success with a machine?"

"Why, I used the bags the machine made, of course." Eliza cocks her head as if baffled by such a simplistic question. "There were hundreds in the house from her test runs, so I took them and filled them with meal and sand and even ashes. They worked so well, I took them to market for shopping."

Mr. Clarke sniffs, unamused by her theatrics. "Have you a specimen of one of these bags?"

"I regret to say I have not," she replies matter-of-factly.

"You haven't one?" The lawyer throws up his hands in mock surprise. "Even though there were 'hundreds' in the house?"

"When I moved from Springfield to my grandmother's Boston house at the end of '68, I could only bring bare necessities. I'm sure you'll agree, paper bags do not count as a necessity for a young woman changing residences."

I'm in awe as Eliza parries Mr. Clarke's jabs time and again. I feared her gentle disposition would crumble against his assaults, but in the past hour, my friend has proven a lioness. No one would guess she struggles with a stammer. And not only is she articulate, she's not allowing Mr. Clarke's tricky speech to befuddle her.

"You claim Mr. Annan visited your Springfield residence on September 1, 1868, with the intent of looking at Miss Knight's wooden machine, correct?"

"I fixed no date," says Eliza, "but Mr. Annan did visit that month, and it would've been a Friday because the contest the next day was on a Saturday."

Mr. Clarke's nose twitches. "You are positive that when Mr. Annan called at your residence, Miss Knight's wooden machine was present?" he plunges on.

"I am certain. She even demonstrated for him by turning out bags."

"At that time, did you hear Mr. Annan and Miss Knight exchange words?"

"I did."

"What did they say, specifically? Tell the exact words they exchanged, if you please."

Eliza's brow darkens. But rather than losing composure, she maintains the poise of a noblewoman miffed by a buzzing fly. "They said many things, mostly regarding the machine. However, if you wish for me to relate their exact words, I am unable to do so. I did not deem it necessary to memorize their conversation."

"Did Mr. Annan not say at that time that he had his own machine in his loft that turned out bags by the thousands?"

Eliza's nostrils flare. "He did not."

"Did he not say that he had full-size drawings of the machine for making such bags for a long time, got up by other parties, and that he had built such a machine from such drawings?"

"He did not."

Mr. Clarke folds his arms. "You don't remember what Mr. Annan said at this supposed demonstration, but do remember what he did not say, do you?"

My teeth gnash. Eliza, however, counters his nastiness with aplomb. "I remember that he said nothing of that sort which your questions imply."

Mr. Clarke glowers, but Eliza meets him glare for glare. Seconds tick past as the two engage in a silent contest of wills.

Finally, Mr. Clarke breaks his gaze. "That concludes the cross-examination, Your Honor," he says to the judge.

Judge Thacher glances at the clock on the wall. "Court adjourned at ten o'clock. We will resume in a half hour with the next witness."

His gavel strikes. The courtroom empties—Judge Thacher and the clerk heading for the judge's chamber, and Mr. Clarke and Annan going Heaven knows where—leaving me, Mr. Stansbury, Eliza, and Mr. Binney, who has returned to observe the second day of the hearing. As the old investor buries his nose in a newspaper, Mr. Stansbury and I welcome Eliza back from the witness stand.

"You were splendid," I say, wrapping her in an embrace. "I daresay you've nerves of steel."

She chuckles. "I couldn't let that scoundrel twist facts, not with your invention and your honor at stake." She turns to Mr. Stansbury. "Do you think my testimony helped? To tip the scales in Mattie's favor, I mean."

"Hmm . . ." Mr. Stansbury rests his chin in his hands. "Regarding your testimony, Miss MacFarland, I couldn't have asked for better. However, you are Miss Knight's bosom friend, and you have no mechanical background to speak of, so the court will regard your testimony with a grain of salt. While it's evened the scale somewhat, for things to actually swing in Miss Knight's favor will depend on our next witnesses. Speaking of which, it appears Mr. Abbott has arrived."

He nods toward the door, where Will Abbott's nose pokes into the courtroom. Catching sight of us, Will calls, "I'm not late, am I?"

"No," I say, waving him over, "you're a half hour early."

As he joins us, I realize he's drenched in sweat. "You're soaked, Will," I say, pouring him water from the pitcher on our table. "Did something happen?"

He downs the drink in one gulp. "Mr. Lincoln asked me to send a telegram before I came here," he said, wiping his mouth with the back of his hand. "Normally it takes a few minutes, but today the line went out the door." He shakes his head. "Apparently, there's a huge delay on the Boston and Albany line, so a bunch of folks were sending messages out."

I nearly drop the pitcher. "The Boston and Albany? What happened?"

"They say the first train out of Albany broke down in Worcester," he says, causing the color to drain from Eliza's face. "Is something wrong?"

"That's Ida's train," Eliza wails.

I clutch my head. Ida was supposed to arrive at the depot about now so she could testify on my behalf. Instead, she's stuck on the railroad tracks.

"Ladies, calm down." Mr. Stansbury's command slices through our panic. Turning to Will, he asks, "Mr. Abbott, you said the train broke down. Do you know if it was repaired?"

He nods. "Folks I talked to said the train's on its way, but they're expecting it two and a half, maybe three hours late."

Three hours . . . That means Ida's ten o'clock train could arrive as late as one o'clock, and the afternoon session in which Ida's testimony is scheduled begins at half past one.

Mr. Stansbury frowns, drumming his pencil against the

tabletop. "This isn't ideal, but it isn't a disaster. Short of the Boston and Albany setting a new speed record on the tracks, we won't have time to prepare Mrs. Leavilte at the office as planned. That means we must do our best to ready her here before the afternoon session commences. Miss MacFarland?"

Eliza jumps at her name. "Yes?"

"You know Mrs. Leavilte. Go to the depot. When her train arrives, bring her here posthaste. She's already delayed; we can't afford her getting lost in the streets of Boston on top of that."

"Understood." Eliza snatches her handbag, then grasps my hand. "Don't worry, Mattie. This may be cutting things close, but I'll get Ida here in time, I swear."

The determination in her eyes quells my anxieties, and I squeeze back. "I know you will."

❉ ❉ ❉

Though Will was the bearer of bad news this morning, I've had no complaints about anything he's said on the witness stand. Will's a well-spoken fellow, and in the courtroom, his natural charm translates to utter persuasiveness. I daresay he's got the judge eating out of his hand. The fact that Will is a man might also factor in the ready acceptance of his testimony. At any rate, I'm simply grateful he hasn't been pooh-poohed the way Eliza and I were.

This, of course, puts a crease on Mr. Clarke's brow. When he saw my machinist's name on the witness list, he probably expected a man cut from the same cloth as Mr. Burnham or Mr. Graham. Will's glowing testimony about the shuttle guard I invented in Manchester so stunned Mr. Clarke, he sat slack-jawed for most of Mr. Stansbury's direct examination.

Even so, the spider's still bent on wresting an advantage when it's his turn to question Will.

"Mr. Abbott," he begins, "you stated that Mr. Annan inquired about Miss Knight's machine at the Lincoln and Graham shop in August '69, correct?"

"Yes."

"Did you not, in this conversation, ask Mr. Annan whether he had been experimenting on or getting up his own machine to make square-bottom bags?"

Will taps his chin, mulling the question over. "I think I did. I know I asked if he was interested in purchasing rights to Miss Knight's machine."

"Objection," roars Mr. Clarke. "The last sentence of the response was uncalled for."

Mr. Clarke and Will turn to the judge. Caught beneath their blazing looks, Judge Thacher wavers, hemming and hawing. Finally, he coughs and says, "Objection upheld."

Mr. Clarke smirks. My fists clench, itching to punch through his teeth. Will, for his part, regards the round lawyer like a misaligned joint that needs to be whacked.

The cross-examination resumes. "Was not the language of your question to Mr. Annan: 'I understand you are getting up a machine to make square-bottom paper bags?'"

I repress the urge to roll my eyes. Mr. Stansbury warned me the opposition would try to distort testimony, but Mr. Clarke's falsehood is such rubbish, I'm surprised his breath doesn't reek like a dung heap.

Will, of course, is not about to tolerate such nonsense. "No."

His reply is firm, decisive. And it does not deter Mr. Clarke in the least. Bold as brass, he leans over the witness stand railing. "Are you certain you did not say that?"

Will inclines his head toward Mr. Clarke. "I. Am. Very. Certain."

The menace in his tone would've made most fellows quake in their boots, but Mr. Clarke is unflinching. "Did you not tell Mr. Annan that Miss Knight's machine was very poorly arrayed, that you had to alter it all over, and expected to be obliged to change its whole organization, and almost despaired of doing anything with it?"

I nearly gag. Thank Heaven it is not Mr. Burnham on the witness stand. No doubt he would've affirmed that and worse.

Will, on the other hand, has gone from indignant to bewildered, stupefied by Mr. Clarke's audacity. Shaking his head, he replies, "No. Never."

"Are you certain?" presses Mr. Clarke, perceiving Will's shock as weakness.

Will's mouth presses into a firm line. "I am very certain I never used those terms."

"Then did you say anything to the same effect?"

Silence hangs as Will gawps at Mr. Clarke. Then he reclines against his backrest. "If I did tell Mr. Annan anything about Miss Knight," he says, cracking his knuckles, "it was that I have nothing but the greatest respect for her abilities, and that all the machinists that refused her business missed the opportunity to work with a fine customer."

Mr. Clarke sniffs. Looking as if he's swigged vinegar, the lawyer sidles off to pace the floor, and Mr. Stansbury stifles a chuckle. "Mr. Abbott's a tougher nut than Mr. Clarke anticipated," he whispers into my ear. "He won't drag the cross-examination much longer."

He's right. After a few failed attempts to attribute my machine's workings to Will's inventive ability, Mr. Clarke concludes his querying.

Judge Thacher strikes his gavel. "Court adjourned at half past noon. We reconvene in one hour."

As the judge exits with the clerk in tow, Mr. Stansbury shakes Will's hand. "Excellent job, son. I couldn't have asked for better."

Will's ruddy complexion deepens two shades. "I only wish I could've helped more," he says, rubbing the back of his neck.

"You still need someone to speak to Mattie's inventing while she was in Springfield."

"True," says Mr. Stansbury. "God willing, Mrs. Leavilte will supply that testimony. Speaking of whom, perhaps we should relocate outside to await her arrival." His gaze slides to a corner of the courtroom, where Annan and his lawyer are holding a hushed conversation.

"Good idea," I say. Lingering in the same room as those low-lifes can only bring trouble.

Will accompanies us to the courthouse porch. Then, with a wink and a flourish of his hat, he takes his leave. "Send word to the shop once it's over," he calls as he jogs back to work. "Everyone's got fingers crossed for you."

"I will," I shout, waving him off.

No sooner has he rounded a corner than I spy Eliza's hat bobbing through the crowd below. My heart leaps—and then crashes when I see she's alone.

"Eliza," I yell, rushing to the sidewalk with Mr. Stansbury close behind. "Where's Ida?"

We practically collide at the base of the stairs, and Eliza's heaving body collapses in my arms. At first I think she's fainted from exertion and her corset stays. But then her head snaps up, and I realize her gasps are sobs. "Sh-she wasn't there, Mattie," she cries. "The tr-train came, but Ida wasn't there!"

My fingers dig into her shoulders. "Are you absolutely certain? She had a second-class ticket. Did you check those cars?"

"I did. All of them. I even checked the lavatories. I called her name a good ten minutes on the platform, but . . ." Her voice trails off, her tears streaming afresh.

My eyes dart to Mr. Stansbury, whose sunny mood has clouded. "Mr. Stansbury," I say, "What should we do?"

His reply is calm but grim. "A person does not disappear into thin air. If Mrs. Leavilte was not on that train, my guess is she is either on the next train or she is not coming at all."

My stomach drops at his second guess. *Ida wouldn't fail me. She promised* . . .

Mr. Stansbury turns to Eliza. "Do you know when the next train is expected to arrive?"

She nods. "Three o'clock."

Mr. Stansbury's frown deepens. "The court does not like to wait, but I can argue for extenuating circumstances. However, it'll reflect badly on us if we delay proceedings and the witness never arrives. Miss Knight, is there anyone we can telegram to confirm Mrs. Leavilte is on her way?"

"Ida's mother-in-law and children are always at home," I reply, praying that there's no line at the telegram office. "I'll send a telegram to her house and—"

"Don't trouble yourself, Miss Knight," booms a voice over the sidewalk bustle. "I can tell you now Ida Leavilte has been unavoidably detained in Springfield."

Our eyes leap toward the speaker, and my jaw drops at a familiar hooked nose and stovepipe hat.

"Mr. Yates!"

Chapter 35

Mr. Stansbury cocks his head. "Yates? This man is your former employer, Miss Knight?"

"I am," Mr. Yates interjects, striding over to give Mr. Stansbury a business card. "You are Miss Knight's attorney, I presume."

"Charles Stansbury, counselor-at-law," he affirms, exchanging a handshake.

"Well, Mr. Stansbury," says Mr. Yates, "you should know I've come to testify in Ida Leavilte's place."

"What about I-Ida?" Eliza blurts. "What h-happened to her?"

"Her daughter contracted the croup the night before last." When our eyes widen in alarm, he adds, "Fret not, the child is expected to recover. But because Mrs. Leavilte was thus occupied, the West Workroom was in a tizzy yesterday over who might testify in her place." He shakes his head. "It had such an adverse effect on productivity, I put a stop to it by declaring I would go."

"You did?" I gasp.

He raises an eyebrow. "Do you have an objection?"

I gulp, realizing how rude I sounded. "No, sir. It's just . . . er . . ."

"We gladly welcome your assistance," Mr. Stansbury cuts in. "Your testimony as an employer will be invaluable. However, the court must be informed of the change. Moreover, I should brief you on certain matters prior to the hearing."

"By all means. And Miss Knight." Mr. Yates turns to me. "Don't misconstrue this as special effort on my part. Columbia Paper's biggest clients are in Boston, and I've been intending to visit them. It was merely convenient to aid you in your business while I see to mine."

"I understand," I say, although I don't. Mr. Yates was Frank's champion, not mine. Even if it was "convenient," a favor from Mr. Yates is unimaginable as a flying pig.

"By the way," says Mr. Yates, scanning the courthouse entrance, "is Daniel Mowe attending the proceedings?"

I start at the mention of Daniel. "No, sir. I've not seen him since I filed my lawsuit."

Annoyance wrinkles his brow. "The Lord deal with the scalawag, then," he says, though his tone indicates he'd rather deal with Daniel himself. "Meanwhile, we shall ensure any royalties I pay for your machine don't line Mr. Mowe's pockets."

So that's it. It's strange to find myself on the same side as Mr. Yates, but since we've both got a bone to pick with Daniel, I've no complaints.

Mr. Stansbury gestures towards the courthouse. "Mr. Yates, if you'll come this way."

"One moment," says Mr. Yates as a stout woman in servant livery trots up with a leather valise and a large, thin box.

"Here are the things you requested, Mr. Yates," she says, handing them over. "Do you need anything else?"

"No, Martha. I'll join you and the missus at the hotel for dinner once I'm finished."

The missus? My gaze darts in the direction from which the servant came to see two waiting cabs. One groans with luggage. The other sports Mrs. Yates's stylish figure in the passenger seat.

Mr. Yates heaves a long-suffering sigh as the servant returns to her mistress. "Women," he mutters to Mr. Stansbury. "Leave it to my wife to turn business travel into an excuse for a shopping spree."

Mr. Stansbury offers words of commiseration, but I suspect Mrs. Yates isn't merely interested in buying up Boston's latest fashions. I have no proof, but instinct screams that she had a hand in her husband's decision to act on my behalf.

Her eyes meet mine and she smiles, waving a gloved hand.

I don't know what I did to earn her favor, but I'm grateful for it. Returning the wave, I mouth, "Thank you."

While I worked for Mr. Yates, he treated me at best with icy civility, at worst with disdain. Thus, hearing the man speak positively of me—before a judge, no less—is a bizarre experience.

"During the two years I employed her, the machines under her purview ran without a hitch. Her skills are top-notch. I've never had issue with the quality of her work."

"Would you say with confidence as a paper bag manufacturer that Miss Knight is well acquainted with the manufacture of paper bags?" asks Mr. Stansbury.

"I say with confidence that she is an expert," replies Mr. Yates. "When I added a second bag workroom to the business, she set up the equipment and trained the new mechanic I brought."

As the direct examination proceeds, Mr. Clarke scribbles furiously on a notepad while Annan sits stiffly beside him. The last-minute change has clearly taken them off guard.

Admittedly, I'm not certain how things will unfold with Mr. Yates, either. I'd informed Ida weeks ago what she could expect at the hearing, and Mr. Stansbury had planned to spend the lunch hour in his office preparing her for the witness stand. With Mr. Yates, Mr. Stansbury could only manage an eight-minute consultation in a lavatory (the only place of privacy available in the courthouse).

Yet the men emerged from their rushed meeting looking confident. And so far, the direct examination has gone smoothly as a well-tuned locomotive.

"Are you aware of Miss Knight's endeavors to build a machine to fold square-bottom bags?" asks Mr. Stansbury.

"Yes. I am the one she first proposed it to in February 1868."

"How do you fix the month and year?"

My stomach turns as I remember the argument that birthed our wager. Although Mr. Yates has portrayed me favorably thus far, that instant must be fraught with hard feelings for him.

"Because that was the month we received an order for an unprecedented volume of square-bottom bags. When Miss Knight heard, she suggested completely automating the bag-making process to meet the demand. She was willing to devise such a machine on her own time, so I told her to proceed. I also invited Frank Niebuhr, the division's other mechanic, to try building one to turn the endeavor into a contest." Mr. Yates smiles affably. "After all, there's nothing like a little competition to spark ingenuity."

I blink. Everything he said was true, but it painted me as a helpful employee rather than a thorn in his side.

Mr. Stansbury gestures to the wooden machine on the clerk's desk. "Are you familiar with Exhibit B?"

Mr. Yates regards it. "It strongly resembles the machine Miss Knight built for our contest."

"Did you witness Miss Knight making square-bottom bags with such a machine?"

"I did," replies Mr. Yates. "For the contest, her machine and Mr. Niebuhr's were connected to power for a span of two minutes. Ultimately, her machine produced one hundred fifty bags while Mr. Niebuhr's produced forty-six."

"Did anyone else witness this event?" asks Mr. Stansbury.

"The contest took place during Columbia Paper's tenth anniversary celebration in September '68. All one hundred and twenty factory workers were in attendance."

"Do you have proof this contest took place during your party?"

"I do."

Curiosity fills the room as Mr. Yates produces the box he brought to the courthouse. The lid comes off, and he lifts a large framed photograph. I'm too far away to make out all the details, but across the top is a banner that reads: COLUMBIA PAPER 10 YEARS.

The anniversary picture! This is the first I've seen it. After all, it was intended for the boss's enjoyment, not the eyes of the factory rabble.

As I adjust my glasses for a better look, Mr. Yates says, "I wish to submit this photograph as evidence to the court. It was taken minutes before the machine contest. Please observe the two objects at the lower right edge. The larger is Mr. Niebuhr's machine. The smaller is Miss Knight's."

The photograph passes to the judge with a magnifying glass. As he studies the picture, occasionally glancing to the wooden model for comparison, I feel Heaven has intervened. Mrs. Yates intended for this photograph to commemorate the anniversary, and Mrs. Townsend hadn't so much as glanced at the bag machines when she arranged us before her camera. Yet her lens captured the machines, binding them to that moment. And the fact that Mr. Yates, who wasn't even supposed to come, thought to bring it . . . it's as if the events were prearranged by a divine hand.

The judge gives a satisfied grunt, and the photograph joins the exhibits on the clerk's desk. Mr. Stansbury declares he has no further questions and clears the floor for Mr. Clarke.

Mr. Clarke, however, doesn't dive into the cross-examination. He requests a moment to study the newest exhibit. As he squints at the photograph, I suspect he's stalling for time.

After all, the doubts over my mechanical and inventive abilities have been refuted, and not by just anyone. Mr. Clarke might have pooh-poohed Ida as an ignorant female hand, but Mr. Yates was my employer. A factory owner, former Army captain, and all-around pillar of society isn't the sort to be treated lightly, and Mr. Clarke knows this.

Thus, he begins in a congenial tone. "You say you witnessed

Miss Knight making square-bottom bags with a wooden machine she brought to your company celebration in September '68, correct?"

"I did."

"Can you say with utter certainty that the machine she brought was her own design? In other words, is it not possible someone else built the machine, and Miss Knight claimed it was her work?"

Mr. Yates's answer is immediate. "Miss Knight built the machine, no question."

His decisiveness takes Mr. Clarke by surprise. "You seem terribly certain of this," says the attorney, recovering quickly. "Do you have solid grounds for your certainty?"

Mr. Yates arches an eyebrow. "You, sir, appear to be under the impression that a factory head is above supervising the workers under his employ. However, I adhere to a traditional Puritan work ethic. That means I personally oversee my company's matters, especially those concerning the bag workrooms, which are steps away from my office door."

Mr. Clarke coughs, a nervous sheen spreading over his forehead. "Well then—"

"As to the grounds for my certainty," Mr. Yates plows on, "the machine Miss Knight submitted for the contest was of wood, like Exhibit B." He nods towards the wooden machine. "In the months preceding the contest, I observed her whittling pieces during factory breaks several times."

Mr. Clarke's expression turns sly. "You say you observed Miss Knight several times," he says in an oily tone. "Is not such interest in a young, female employee inordinate for an upstanding man as yourself?"

Disgust sours my mouth. The lewd insinuation is not only absurd, it is repugnant.

"I suppose it would be inordinate if she were the only one I was observing thus," Mr. Yates responds blandly. "But I subjected Mr. Niebuhr to the same scrutiny. Being company owner, I was concerned that their enthusiasm for competition might inadvertently cause them to neglect their factory duties. As the health of my machinery fell under their purview, it behooved me to ensure both fulfilled their usual responsibilities."

"I see," says Mr. Clarke, deflating. "And did Miss Knight fulfill her responsibilities?"

"She did, save for a single instance of tardiness some weeks before the contest. She arrived twelve minutes late, for which I publicly reprimanded her and docked her pay."

My face warms at the mention of that humiliating morning. Still, it dispels Mr. Clarke's insinuations of undue favoritism. Having failed with that snare, he attempts another. "Regarding this contest, you stated that Miss Knight produced one hundred fifty bags and her rival produced forty-six. How were these numbers determined?"

"The bags were subjected to a sand test to verify soundness," replies Mr. Yates. "Those that passed were counted. This was performed in full view of the gathering by myself, my wife, and my grandfather, the company's retired head."

"Is it possible those numbers were inaccurate?" prods Mr. Clarke. "In other words, might a bag attributed to Miss Knight actually be the work of her opponent?"

"Absolutely not. The machines ran with different rolls of paper. Miss Knight's used paper printed with her initials; Mr. Niebuhr's bore his."

"You used custom paper for this contest?" asks Mr. Clarke with exaggerated astonishment.

Mr. Yates shrugs. "Manufacturing paper and paper goods is my business. Moreover, my wife has a penchant for spectacle. She ordered the paper to make the contest more memorable. Once it was over, she distributed the bags as souvenirs."

"Can you produce one of these initialed bags?"

"No."

"You haven't one?" Mr. Clarke's eyes glitter.

My stomach drops as I realize what he's seized upon. Although I've brought key pieces of evidence, I've not presented any bags. Neither have my witnesses. It may be minor compared to my notes and models, but Mr. Clarke's determined to turn it into a point of contention as he presses, "You hosted this party, yet did not keep a souvenir for yourself?"

"My family had the photograph to commemorate the event." Mr. Yates nods at the picture he brought. "We could afford to let my employees have the bags as keepsakes."

"But one hundred and twenty people were in attendance," says Mr. Clarke, consulting his notes. "If Miss Knight indeed produced one hundred fifty bags, shouldn't there have been excess for you to keep one?"

Mr. Yates's features tighten with distaste, but he replies evenly. "Perhaps. But I was not in charge of distributing the souvenirs, nor did I think it necessary to keep one for myself."

"You are saying then that you went through the tremendous trouble of organizing this event, even making specialized paper for the contest, yet couldn't be troubled to keep one bag for yourself?" Mr. Clarke's lips tug into a smirk. "Or . . . isn't it actually the case that the results of this contest were greatly exaggerated? That in fact Miss Knight's contraption failed to produce bags at all?"

A storm darkens Mr. Yates's brow. The attorney's practically accused him of lying. Eyes flashing, he begins to respond when the door suddenly bangs open and a shout rings through the room: "It's not exaggerated, and if you want a bag, I'll show you one!"

Chapter 36

FRANK NIEBUHR STANDS AT THE THRESHOLD, PANTING AS IF he's run all the way from Maryland. Opening the knapsack on his shoulder, he whips out two square-bottom bags.

My eyes goggle at his initials and mine printed on the dingy white paper. I don't know whether I'm more shocked over his arrival or the bags in his grasp.

A sharp "ahem" breaks the stunned silence. "How convenient," says Mr. Yates dryly. "But you've spoken out of turn. I'm still giving my testimony, Frank."

As Frank blushes, Mr. Stansbury snatches my ear. "Frank? As in Frank Niebuhr?"

I nod. The old wolf immediately sizes Frank up. I doubt Frank notices. He's too busy sputtering an apology to Mr. Yates.

Mr. Yates hushes Frank with a wave and turns to the dumbstruck judge. "This is Frank Niebuhr, my former employee, the mechanic Miss Knight contended against. I apologize on his behalf. He meant no disrespect, I assure you. His enthusiasm simply got the better of him. However, I should like to submit the bags in his possession as evidence."

"Actually, Your Honor . . ." Mr. Stansbury rises with his hand raised. "If I may have permission to speak?"

The judge motions impatiently, granting his approval, and Mr. Stansbury says, "Mr. Niebuhr is scheduled to testify after Mr. Yates. I believe it would be more appropriate to submit the bags in his possession as evidence to the court at that time."

Mr. Stansbury's statement takes me by surprise, but Judge Thacher merely grunts his assent. As he orders the clerk to show Frank to a seat, I tug Mr. Stansbury's sleeve. "What do you mean he's scheduled after Mr. Yates?" I hiss.

He responds by sliding a stamped sheet from his stack of court forms. Beneath the heading "Witnesses on Behalf of Margaret E. Knight" is written:

Margaret E. Knight, inventor and mechanic
Eliza G. MacFarland, apprentice dressmaker
William W. Abbott, machinist
Ida Leavilte, factory employee
Charles H. Yates, factory owner
Frank Niebuhr, mechanic

"Now that that's settled," says Judge Thacher, jolting my attention back to the proceedings, "let's resume the cross-examination."

He gestures to Mr. Clarke, who looks as if the ground's been cut from under his feet. After an awkward minute of paper shuffling, he says, "I have no additional questions for the witness, Your Honor."

The court adjourns for a half-hour break. The instant the gavel strikes, I pounce on Mr. Stansbury. "Why is Frank on the list? He never confirmed he was coming."

"He never declined, either," comes the simple reply. "There's no penalty if a witness fails to appear, so we risked nothing putting his name down. Besides, I had a feeling he would come."

"You did?" I knew Mr. Stansbury was a force to contend with, but now I am truly awed. "Because of your experience as a lawyer?"

"No. Because of my experience as father to three daughters. A man who pays for a lady's train fare rarely harbors purely platonic feelings." He winks. "Now if you'll excuse me, I have another witness I must escort to the lavatory."

The tide has turned against Mr. Clarke. He maintains composure, but his swagger is gone. Compared to the way he bullied me, his cross-examination of Frank gives the impression of a man grasping at straws.

"Your machine produced two hundred thirty-eight bags compared to Miss Knight's one hundred fifty. Did you not wish to challenge the results of the contest?"

Frank responds with military brevity. "No, sir. I'd agreed that only sound bags got counted."

"You had no issue with the method used to determine sound bags?"

"No, sir."

"You are absolutely certain?" Mr. Clarke's persistence carries a note of desperation. "You had not even a particle of discontent?"

Frank's features harden. "Sand doesn't lie. It stays in the bag, or it doesn't."

Indeed. My gaze shifts to the two square-bottom bags now among the court exhibits. Why Frank kept them remains a mystery, but a greater mystery is why he chose the particular bag that bears his initials. A two-inch tear mars the paper. Anyone else might have attributed the slight damage to months of wear. But its position—smack between an F and N—tells me otherwise.

I'd understand him keeping a passing bag from his machine. But a failed one?

"I have no additional questions for the witness, Your Honor."

I blink as Mr. Clarke takes his seat. "He's done?" I whisper to Mr. Stansbury. "It's only been ten minutes."

"He might've hounded Mr. Niebuhr longer had Mr. Yates not testified. As it stands, your old employer brought credence to our assertions, and Mr. Niebuhr further strengthened that testimony. Dragging the cross-examination would only weaken what remains of Mr. Annan's case." Mr. Stansbury grins. "Considering we had no opportunity to coordinate statements, this worked astonishingly well. I'd say victory is as good as yours, Miss Knight."

As my spirits leap, the judge says, "Court adjourned for deliberation at half past three. We will reconvene shortly for the verdict."

The gavel strikes, and Judge Thacher sweeps off to his chamber with the clerk carrying the transcript and court exhibits after him. Annan and his lawyer withdraw to a corner for a subdued conversation. A more animated discussion erupts in the public viewing area between Mr. Binney and Mr. Yates. Eliza sits primly nearby, no doubt noting the details of their exchange to relate to me later.

As for Frank, the stern mask he wore for the cross-examination crumbles into exhaustion. He rises shakily and stumbles as he exits the witness stand.

"Easy there," says Mr. Stansbury, catching him before he falls. "You all right, son?"

Frank returns a weary smile. "Bit tuckered, is all."

"Little wonder. You spent the better part of three days rushing here to stave off a deceitful buzzard. Which you did magnificently, by the way." Mr. Stansbury pats him on the back. "If I had to hazard a guess, I'd say you haven't had a bite all day. Am I right?"

Frank ducks his head sheepishly. Turning to me, Mr. Stansbury says, "We've a few minutes before the verdict. Take Mr. Niebuhr and reward him with a sandwich. Pushcart vendors should still be making rounds outside."

"Of course," I say, reaching for my handbag.

My smile, however, belies the nervousness quaking my gut. Frank and I have been in the same room for a half hour, but this is the first chance we've had to talk.

What do I say? Mr. Stansbury opined that Frank is soft on me, but if that's so, why did he never write? I suspect he still bears hard feelings, but then why would he rush here? Perhaps out of a sense of honor? His principles might have spurred him to testify, even if he resents me. Or maybe he wants me in his debt?

These thoughts spin round and round as we head out of the room. I'm wondering how to break the silence when Frank pauses at the courtroom door. "Mattie," he says, his voice low. "That beanpole in the corner's the bastard who stole your machine, right?"

The glare he aims toward Annan is lethal. "He is," I reply, taken aback.

Frank snorts. "Anyone who steals your hard work ought to be strung up and left for the crows. And if I ever catch sight of that cowardly cheat Mowe . . ."

He smacks a fist against his palm, and the sound clears my head. The next instant, a snicker bursts from my lips. I double over giggling, and the fire in Frank's eyes turns to bewilderment. "Mattie, you all right?"

I nod, hand clapped over my mouth, but I can't manage to collect myself. After days—no, months of overwrought nerves, all that tension has broken into a torrent of laughter. My muffled gasps draw stares, and I let Frank lead me away from the courtroom to a foyer bench.

When I regain composure at last, my insides ache, and tears stain my cheeks. However, the world feels right in a way it hasn't in ages.

"Better?" Concern shadows Frank's face.

"Much," I say, dabbing my eyes with a handkerchief. "I just . . . I'm so glad you came. When you didn't write back, I thought—"

"I'm sorry about that." Frank averts his gaze, hands running restlessly over his lap. "I wanted to help the instant I heard, I did. But . . ."

As he grasps for words, it strikes me how much he's changed. I'd been too distracted to notice earlier, but he's thinner. His skin is more leathery, his clothes more threadbare.

His voice, though, is as I remember. Melodic and deeply

resonant as a church organ.

I lay a hand on his weather-roughened one. "It's been hard since you returned home?" The words come out as more of a statement than a question.

His shoulders hunch. "You could say that."

"Is your farm in trouble?" I ask, brow furrowing.

He shakes his head. "Much as I hate to say it, now that we don't have doctor bills for Pa, the family's better off than it's been in a long time. It's just . . ." He sags against the backrest. "It was easier when I was just a brother to my brothers."

My heart goes out to him. "It is hard being responsible for everyone," I say, knowing exactly what that feels like.

"It's not that. Not exactly. I don't begrudge being family head. I'd do anything for my brothers and our home. But . . ." His eyes squeeze shut. "I miss the factory. I miss being a mechanic. Only time I heard anything close to machine talk was when letters came from the guys in Springfield."

The softly uttered words knock me for a loop. I can't imagine a Frank Niebuhr who doesn't prattle constantly about engines and gadgets. "Even if there isn't a factory in Oak Creek, there must've been someone you could talk to about machines," I say.

"My brothers only ever talk about horses and hunting. The few times I tried talking about machines . . ." He chuckles ruefully. "They really made me miss our talks."

My heart skips a beat. Then it pounds double-time when Frank locks eyes with me. "I got a confession to make, Mattie. Those bags . . . I kept them so I wouldn't forget how awful it felt to lose. See, after the contest, I swore never to lose again. I figured if I ever needed a kick in the pants to work twice as good or as hard, one look at them would do the trick."

I wince inwardly. *That explains it.*

"But after Pa died, my hands got full, and I forgot about the bags," Frank goes on. "Then last winter, we got word that a lumber outfit was being built the next county over. They were looking for mechanics to get up the engines and such that they were bringing in."

"So you ran over?" I guess.

"No. I put it out of my head."

His response throws me off. I wonder if he meant it as a joke, but his gaze is serious as he continues, "My mind was wrapped up with spring planting, on getting the farm off on the right foot. But more than that, I felt I couldn't go."

"Why not?"

"I hadn't touched a machine in months. All the things I knew and did as a mechanic felt rusted in my brain. So I put it behind me and set my mind on plowing and planting. Until one night, when I was going through my things and found our bags. And as I held them, I remembered. Not how it felt to lose, but how I loved putting parts together. How amazing it was to watch them work. And how nothing else in the world made me feel that way."

A smile tugs my lips. "The bags gave you a kick in the pants?"

"And how." Frank chuckles. "By then, the worst of the planting was done, and my brothers . . . they didn't really understand, but they knew I had to go. Truth be told, I had no hopes of getting hired. I left on April 2, and they'd wanted men in March. But I figured I'd at least get a look at their engines."

"That sounds like the Frank Niebuhr I know," I say, recalling how he'd cajoled his way into every engine and boiler room in Springfield. "I daresay I know the answer, but was it worth it?"

He grins. "More. Got hired on the spot. I won't lie, the place was bedlam, but it made me feel alive again. Better yet, everything I thought I forgot came right back. When we finished, the head mechanic asked if I'd come to his next job."

My elbow pokes his ribs. "Of course he did. What did you say?"

"Had to say no. I promised my brothers I'd be back for haying.

Though I did tell him to write if he had work around Oak Creek. So I headed home. That's when I got your letters." Embarrassment colors his cheeks. "Mattie, I swear I lit for Boston the moment—"

"You have nothing to be sorry for," I interject. "In fact, I owe you for getting here in the nick of time. I didn't get to say it before, but thank you, from the bottom of my heart."

He shakes his head. "I should be thanking you."

Confusion ripples up. "What for?"

"Writing." Reaching into his jacket, he withdraws my four letters, now creased and travel-stained. His fingers smooth the rumpled paper as he says, "I thought you hated me. Thought you'd never speak to me again, no matter what. So you asking for my help, it made me really happy. And what you wrote in that last letter—"

"I meant every word," I blurt, hanging my head. "I treated you awful. I was prideful and pigheaded."

My breath catches as Frank tilts my chin up with a fingertip. "Truth be told, I thought you were right to treat me like trash," he murmurs. "Because I was prideful and pigheaded, too. When the Captain told me about your bet, putting you in your place became the most important thing. I regret that. After the contest was done, I wanted to make up for the awful things I did and said, but I didn't know how. And once you left Springfield, I figured it was over."

His remorse resonates with my own regrets. I'd turned my back on our friendship, and by the time I realized my mistake, it seemed irrecoverable. He'd done the same. But Providence had brought us together again, perhaps for reasons beyond my lawsuit.

"Well," I say, suddenly bashful, "it would be terribly sad if this was it for us."

"I agree." Frank returns a timid smile. "Friends?"

He extends a handshake, and I recall the one we exchanged

the day we met. Hoping to reclaim that rapport, I clasp his hand firmly. "Friends."

"Mattie, Frank! There you are."

The two of us jolt to see Eliza waving frantically from down the corridor. "The judge is back. Hurry!"

Frank lurches to his feet, his weariness eclipsed by excitement. "Come on, Mattie. Time to get your due."

And I get it indeed.

"The court rules in favor of the plaintiff. The right to the letters patent of the bag-making machine in question are hereby awarded to Margaret E. Knight."

More words follow, but they don't register. Judge Thacher's nasal voice and the courtroom fade against one brilliant, all-consuming thought:

I won.

After eight months of sacrifice, after countless sleepless nights and prayers, after hundreds of dollars and more legal gibberish than I care to think of, justice is done. Moreover, I got the patent I came to Boston for.

And I couldn't have done it alone.

The gavel strikes, startling me back to the present. Next thing I know, I'm surrounded—by Mr. Stansbury shaking my hand, Eliza clutching my arm, Frank thumping my back. Even Mr. Yates hovers an arm's length away. As my old boss looks on approvingly, I'm reminded of the folks back in Springfield, and Uncle Thomas's words rise to mind.

God will uphold your cause, Margaret, and so will I.

That sentiment wasn't his alone. Along this twisting road, I'd somehow amassed a host of allies. Each one of them acknowledged me long before this. And thanks to their efforts, everyone had to acknowledge me now.

Including Annan, who's retreating from the courtroom with Mr. Clarke. Frank smirks at their disappearing backs. "Look at them go with their tails between their legs," he says, giving me an extra-hard smack. "You gave them what-for, Mattie."

"No," I say, heart swelling with gratitude. "*We* did." Flinging my arms around him and Eliza, I hug them tight.

Chapter 37

IN THE TEN MONTHS SINCE EASTERN PAPER BAG COMPANY opened for business, all sorts have walked through our door. Businessmen and foremen, suppliers and machinists. And today, one year after I won the rights to my patent, we welcome our first royal official.

"You have quite the den of industry here, Miss Knight," remarks Sir Roger.

As the stout gentleman admires the partly completed machines in the workshop, Will and our two assistants stand at attention. Our English guest wears an ordinary frock coat and top hat, rather than the gold braid and epaulets he sported at the Mechanics Building last week, but he still exudes an authoritative air.

After a brief consultation with his photographer, Sir Roger says, "Might we photograph you with your employees against that wall? The lighting would be best, and we'd have your company sign in the background."

"Certainly," I reply. "If you like, we can move a machine there, too."

"Would you? That would be splendid."

"Anything for Her Majesty is no trouble at all."

As I speak, I can scarcely believe that I'm talking about the Queen of the British Empire. That she's taken notice of me, an unschooled mechanic. And that she's deemed my accomplishments worthy of the Decoration of the Royal Legion of Honor.

When I first got the notice, I thought it was a prank. During the Mechanics Building ceremony, where three other inventors and I received our medals, I kept pinching myself, wondering when I was going to wake up. A week later, it still doesn't seem real. Then again, I often gaze around the workshop and feel like

I'm dreaming, too.

As Will and the photographer discuss where to place the machine, Sir Roger says, "I spoke with a Mr. Binney at the award ceremony. He mentioned he'd offered fifty thousand dollars to purchase your patent outright, but you declined. Would you tell me why, if you don't mind?"

"I don't mind." I'd be more surprised if he didn't ask. Combined with the lawsuit settlement from Annan, that sum would've afforded a comfortable life for me and my family without further effort.

"I chose to go into business because I wanted the satisfaction. See, when I was inventing my machine, folks said I couldn't do it because I was a girl. After I built it, they said it couldn't have been my work because I was a girl. Maybe I'm being prideful, but if Mr. Binney bought the rights, I doubt he'd tell anyone a woman invented it."

"You're probably correct," Sir Roger muses, twirling his mustache.

"I also figured that if he offered fifty thousand, there had to be demand for it."

I figured right. Mr. Yates placed Eastern Paper's first order, and it was by no means the last. The path's not been easy, but compared to the patent lawsuit, it's been less rocky. I had my settlement money to start, Mr. Stansbury introduced me to a contracts expert, and the fellows at Lincoln and Graham helped me find this shop. By far, the greatest boon was Will. When I was setting things up, he lent a hand whenever I needed it, and when machine orders flooded in, he came to work full time.

"You're content with your decision, even though you must remain at the grindstone?" Sir Roger asks.

I laugh. "I don't know what I'd do with myself if I didn't. I'm just satisfied I got the acknowledgment I want and my family's provided for."

Indeed, Mother's no longer beholden to do piecework. She now lodges near Charlie's asylum. Once he improves enough, they'll join me in Boston. Until that day, I have the means to cover their needs and more.

"Your family must be proud to have such a conscientious, diligent daughter," remarks Sir Roger. "But shouldn't a young woman allow herself some leisure time?"

"I got plenty of that. I spend Sundays at church and reading, and Saturdays tinkering."

The old gentleman cocks his head. "Tinkering?"

I point to a corner, where a jumble of metal parts sits on a worktable beside a shelf of tools and drawings. "Monday through Friday I take care of orders. Saturdays I try making new things."

Sir Roger chuckles. "Well, you're young. Perhaps you'll manage a second patent before you retire."

"Oh, I already got it."

I trot to the shop counter to retrieve the manila envelope Mr. Stansbury sent yesterday. I slide out its contents, and the Englishman drops his monocle at the heading:

United States Patent Office
Margaret E. Knight, of Boston, Massachusetts
Letters Patent No. 109,224
Pneumatic Paper-Feeder

"I got the idea after a printing press maker from the Mechanic Association showed me his shop," I say, flipping to the drawings. "Until then, I didn't realize how alike press feeds and bag machine feeds were. Anyway, with Will's help, I got the application to the Patent Office lickety-split."

"My," Sir Roger stammers. "You're not one to rest on your laurels, are you?"

"If you'd like a demonstration, I have a prototype—"

Just then, the front door bursts open, and Eliza rushes in with a dress box in her arms. "Mattie," she cries, "did they take the photograph?"

"Er, no," I say, as Sir Roger jolts at the interruption. "They're still setting up."

"Thank Heavens." She heaves a sigh, then flashes her best smile at Sir Roger. "Don't mind me. I'm just here to make certain Miss Knight looks her best for your photograph. If you'll excuse us." Grabbing my arm, she hauls me to the shop's tiny office and shuts the door.

"Honestly, Eliza," I say as she sets her box on a chair. "You didn't have to. I know how busy you've been since Madame Martin promoted you to dress finisher."

"And I say it was no trouble at all." Eliza pulls down the window shades and gestures at my stained apron and calico workdress. "Now off with those. We need to make you presentable for a queen."

We're not actually meeting in person. I keep that thought to myself. Eliza earnestly wished to outfit me in something new for the award ceremony, but work obligations prevented her from doing so. When she learned Sir Roger was tarrying a week to photograph the recipients in their workplaces, she seized the chance for redemption.

Judging by the shadows under her eyes, she's burned the midnight oil all week. Her smile, however, is radiant as she opens the box to reveal a snowy blouse, frilled with lace. Beneath it lie a matching skirt and jacket of fine blue wool, trimmed with navy piping and brass buttons.

Eliza helps me dress, and the sensation of brand-new garments is a novel one. I've only ever bought clothes secondhand. Running my hand over the skirt's crisp weave, I say, "It's strange wearing something no one's worn before."

"Get used to it," says Eliza, adjusting my collar and cuffs.

"You're a successful proprietress. You must dress like one. Now sit and let me fix your hair. Have you got a comb?"

"Top drawer," I reply, pointing to my desk.

As Eliza retrieves the comb, she eyes the newspapers and clippings cluttering the desktop. "Are these the articles about your award?"

I nod. "Will said I should frame them for the shop, and Mother wants them for a scrapbook. Plus I need another set for Frank when I write him about the award."

The comb falls from her fingers. "You haven't told Frank?" she gasps.

I shrug. "I scarcely believe it myself. I figure he won't take the news seriously without proof."

She shakes her head. "Mattie, if it's you, Frank Niebuhr is always serious."

Her words drip insinuation. Ever since the hearing, she's deemed Frank my knight in shining armor. Which means she anticipates a happily-ever-after for us.

My outlook is less fairytale-like. Frank and I rekindled our friendship, but a weekly exchange of letters is a far cry from wedding bells. As Eliza unpins my hair, I say, "I wish you'd quit thinking that Frank's languishing over me in Oak Creek."

"I wish you'd quit thinking that you're still competing. Is the thought of marrying Frank and working in the same shop so unbearable?"

"No, but it won't happen anytime soon."

Eliza combs at a snarl hard enough to make me wince. "How are you so sure?"

"Because I already asked—about him working for Eastern Paper," I reply. "His brother Joe turns eighteen next year. He's agreed to take charge of the farm then so Frank can do mechanic work again."

"So you offered him a position, and he said no?" Eliza is

flabbergasted.

"If it makes you feel better, he's not working for Mr. Yates, either. The mechanic he met in Maryland is doing railroad jobs now. Frank wants to join him."

Eliza goes stock-still, then stamps her foot. "Frank, you fool, what are you thinking?" she fumes. "And Mattie, why aren't you mad? You should be!"

"I'm not mad because I know why he doesn't want to come."

Eliza's anger dissipates to consternation. Hoping to make her understand, I continue, "By the time he leaves, it'll be three years he's been at Oak Creek. We aren't competing anymore, true, but he feels he's fallen behind. He wants to make something of himself. Not simply return to Columbia Paper or share my success. And the fastest way to do that is go out in the world."

Eliza's expression turns pained, but she nods. "Men have their pride. It makes sense that he wants to prove himself worthy of a woman with two patents to her name." With a huff, she resumes arranging my hair. "I only pray you aren't old and gray by the time you're done proving yourselves and start courting."

I chuckle. "Even if we did tie the knot, I doubt we'd stop trying to outdo each other."

Eliza groans. "I have a great deal more to say on that matter, but it will hold until your photography session concludes," she says, tucking the last hairpin in place. "Now, where's your medal?"

I take my handbag from its peg and withdraw a silver case engraved with the British royal emblem. The atmosphere turns almost reverent as I place it upon the desk and open it.

Resting on the indigo velvet lining is a gold medal affixed to a scarlet ribbon. The two-inch disc bears a heraldic design with the English lion to the left and a Greek goddess to the right. Arcing above them are the words: "The Decoration of the Royal Legion of Honor."

Eliza smiles as she lifts the medal by its bar. "Lovely though this side is, I'd almost rather show off the reverse." Turning it over, she reads the inscription on the back. "Bestowed by Her Royal Majesty Queen Victoria to Margaret E. Knight for her extraordinary achievements in technology."

"The fact that I have a medal implies that, doesn't it?"

"I suppose," she says, pinning it over my heart. "I just prefer it be absolutely clear to everyone. Although seeing you like this now . . ." She trails off, eyes growing misty. Grasping my shoulders, she turns me to face the office mirror.

A hush falls as we regard our reflections. Eliza looks as she always has, the picture of a refined young lady. I, on the other hand . . . the smartly dressed businesswoman gazing back at me is unrecognizable from the factory girl who once pestered the Bag Division mechanic.

Eliza leans against me. "You've come a long way, Mattie."

"I have," I say, fingering the medal. I doubt Old Jake imagined that his apprentice would one day receive a royal decoration.

"The best part is you still got a lifetime ahead." Eliza squeezes my forearm. "Who knows how far you'll go."

She's right. I'm not even twenty. With a laugh I say, "God willing, I'll get another five or six patents before I'm through."

Eliza tuts. "Balderdash. I say you get a dozen."

I gawp at my friend. "A dozen patents?"

"At least," she affirms with a toss of her head. "I'll even wager money on it."

She winks, and the room resounds with our laughter.

Appendix

Margaret E. Knight
Bag Machine
U.S. Patent Number 116842
Patented July 11, 1871

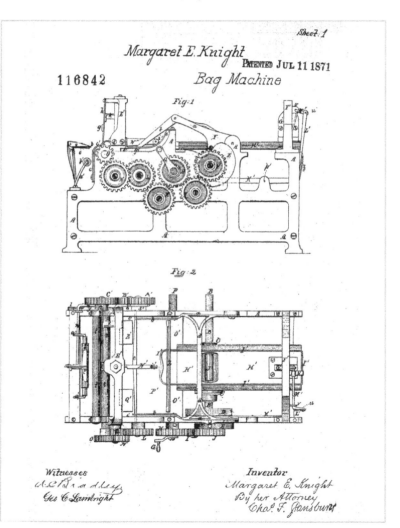

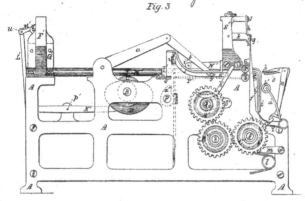

Margaret E. Knight

Bag Machine

Sheet 2

Fig. 3

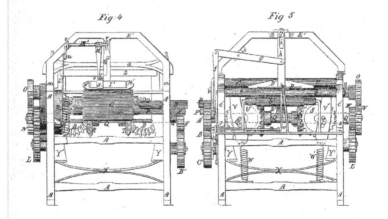

Fig. 4

Fig 5

Witnesses
J.C. Bradley
Geo C Lambright

Inventor
Margaret E. Knight
By her Attorney
Chas. F. Stansbury

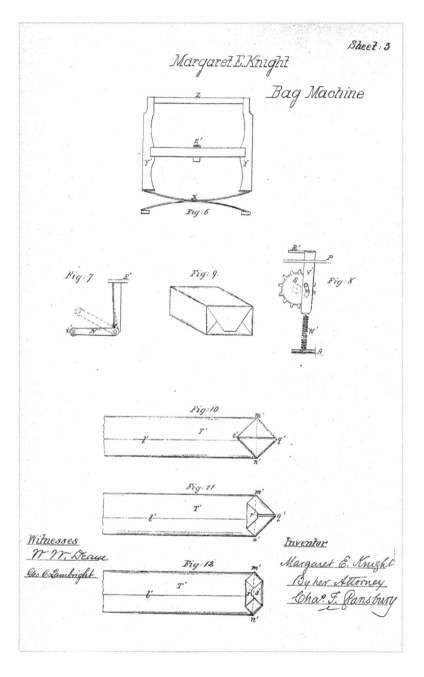

Margaret E. Knight

Bag Machine

Fig: 6

Fig: 7

Fig: 9.

Fig: 8

Fig: 10

Fig: 11

Fig: 12

Witnesses
W. W. Deaw.
Geo. C. Lambright.

Inventor
Margaret E. Knight
By her Attorney
Chas. F. Ransbury

116,842

UNITED STATES PATENT OFFICE.

MARGARETT E. KNIGHT, OF BOSTON, MASSACHUSETTS.

IMPROVEMENT IN PAPER-BAG MACHINES.

Specification forming part of Letters Patent No. 116,842, dated July 11, 1871.

To all whom it may concern:

Be it known that I, MARGARETT E. KNIGHT, of Boston, in the county of Suffolk and State of Massachusetts, have invented a new and Improved Machine for Making Paper Bags; and I do hereby declare the following to be a full and correct description of the same, reference being had to the accompanying drawing, in which—

Figure 1 is a front-side elevation of the machine. Fig. 2 is a plan or top view. Fig. 3 is a rear-side elevation. Fig. 4 is an elevation of the feed end, and Fig. 5 is an elevation of the delivery end of the machine. Fig. 6 is a front elevation of the severing-knife and frame. Fig. 7 is a side view of the guide-finger. Fig. 8 is a view of one of the side-folders and its operating parts. Fig. 9 is a perspective view of the finished bag. Figs. 10, 11, and 12 show the successive folds of the paper tube.

The same letter indicates the same part wherever it occurs.

The nature of this invention consists in the peculiar construction of a machine for the manufacture of flat or satchel-bottom bags from a continuous tube of paper fed from a roll over a former, and cut, folded, pasted, and delivered in the manner substantially as hereinafter described.

In the drawing, A marks the frame of the machine, which supports the operative parts. B is the feed-shaft, on which is a roller, C, which operates, in conjunction with a smaller roller, J′, in the former H′, to feed the paper. The paper is fed from a continuous roll, and is bent around the former H′, with the lap on the upper side of the former. The former H′ is an oblong piece of wood, attached, by a depending bracket, G′, to the gallows F′ on the rear end of the frame. Near its forward end the roller J′ is inserted in an opening formed to receive it, and co-operates with the larger roller C on shaft B in feeding the paper. Grooves or slits in the upper edge of the former H′ receive the side bars of the follower I′, which is an oblong metallic frame, the form and position of which are clearly shown in Fig. 2. A cam, D, on shaft B next the side framing operates a lever, K′, which is pivoted to the frame at p′. This lever is connected, by rod L′ and bent lever M′, to an arm, y, attached to the follower. (See Figs. 2 and 4.) A spiral spring, Z, is attached by its free end to rod L′ and by its fixed end to a cross-bar of the frame A, and reacts to

draw the rod L′ downward and throw the follower forward. On the outer end of shaft B, but turning loosely on it, is a cam, E, attached to a gear-wheel, J, which cam operates the plate-knife-folder F. I use the term "plate knife-folder" to indicate the device consisting of the arms *a b*, blade *c*, and cross-brace *d*, and mark the whole by the letter F. The blade *c* of this plate-knife-folder is attached to arm *b*, jointed to arms *a*, which are united by the cross-brace *d* and hinged or pivoted to the frame. A pin, *e*, projecting laterally from one of the arms *a*, rests on the face of the cam E and transmits motion to the knife. The ends of the blade *c* work in curved guide-ways *e′*, which give direction to the movements of the knife, carrying the blade downward and forward during half its stroke and backward and upward during the other half. The winch G indicates the point of application of the driving power, at the end of the shaft P, to the cogged gear H. This gear is connected with a train of gearing, by which the operation of the machine is effected. Gear H, by means of the reversing-gear I, imparts the proper motion to the gear J, carrying the cam E, which operates the plate-knife-folder F, as before stated. By means of reversing-gear K it gives the appropriate motion to gear L on the end of the principal shaft Q. On shaft P is a cam, Z′, Figs. 5 and 6, which operates to depress the frame of knife Z, the upward movement of said frame being given by the double spring X, which reacts in opposition to the downward motion of the cam. The spring X extends from side to side of the frame A, as shown in Figs. 4, 5, and 6, and receives the lower ends of the side pieces Y Y′ of the knife-frame. On the shaft Q are fixed the two bevel-gears R and T, engaging, respectively, with the bevel-gears S and U hung to brackets on the inside of the side framing of the machine. These gears S and U operate the side-folders Q′ R′ by means of eccentric pins working in the angular slots *u′ v′* in the downwardly-projecting shafts or stocks V V′ of those side-folders. Spiral springs W W′, reacting downward, give motion in that direction to the folder-stocks V V′ when released from the upward action of the pins on the gears S and U. This arrangement is clearly shown in Fig. 8. M, Fig. 5, marks a reversing-gear driven by gear L on end of shaft Q. On the same shaft as M, and attached to it, is a larger gear, N, which drives

116,842

cogged pinion O on the end of folding-roller S. The roller s is one of a series of rollers, $r s t$, at the delivering end of the machine, which receives motion from s. They are held in their places by the spring-guards c' d', which allow them the necessary amount of yielding play. In front of rollers $r s$, and between rollers s and t, plays the vertical knife D' attached to the rod h, having the slot i in its upper end, receiving the pin j, on which the rod h has vertical reciprocating motion. It is operated by lever g, having its fulcrum on end of stud k and pivoted to rod f, the lower end of which rod is bent around and operated downward by a cam on the inner side of gear-wheel C'. The lower end of f is pivoted to a vibrating arm, m, pivoted to the frame, and is forced upward by a coiled spring, l, the fixed end of which is attached to the side frame and its free end to the outer end of arm m. The gear C', which operates the knife D' by the mechanism just described, is itself driven by a reversing-gear, B', receiving motion from a gear, A', on the end of shaft Q. (See Fig. 3.) On the inner side of gear C' is a pin eccentrically placed, which operates bent arm or lever n, to which is attached the pasting-knife p. Spring q tends to keep arm n up. This paster works over a guide, o, which directs its movements, aided by a spring. A paste-roller, b', is supported upon arms a', projecting up from the frame. It is supplied with paste from a suitable reservoir, and supplies paste to the blade p. From gallows E' projects downward a standard, to the lower end of which is pivoted the guide-finger N', having the roller i' on its free end. A flat spring (see Fig. 7) attached to the standard and acting against a pin on the upper edge of the guide-finger tends to throw the finger downward. This spring is counteracted by the bent arm h', to which the finger is attached, and the outer end of which is operated by a cam, S', on the inside of gear A', on the end of shaft Q, as shown in Fig. 3. O', Fig. 2, marks the straight edge against which the severing-knife Z plays, and P' the metallic plate or table on which the folders operate.

Having thus described the construction of the machine, its operation is as follows: The paper from which the bags are to be made is drawn from a roll of indefinite length, suspended so as to be unwound and supplied to the machine as fast as required. It is folded around the former H', with the lap on the upper side, and the pasting, which makes it a continuous tube, is effected by suitable devices for that purpose. All these devices, being well known, are omitted from the drawing. The feed-shaft B receives intermittent motion, by means of intermediate gears, from an eccentric gear on the opposite end of shaft P from that to which the winch G is represented as attached, as in Fig. 2. This mode of producing a stop-motion, being a familiar one, is not represented in the drawing. The gearing is so adjusted as to arrest the motion of the shaft B, and consequently that of the paper tube, at the instant when, as hereinafter described, the folders Q' R' are holding down the forward end of the tube and the bag is being cut off from it by the severing-knife Z. The motion is resumed when the folders Q' R' are drawn back and the tube is released from their grasp. The feed of the tube is produced by the action of the two rollers C and J', the former turning in contact with the bottom of the paper tube and the latter on the inside of the tube, and the two nipping the paper between them and impelling it forward. The follower l' starts with the paper and moves with it until it reaches the guide-finger N', when it is drawn back by the operation of the spring z. The blade c of the plate-knife-folder F, operated by cam E, takes the paper, which is still held open by the guide-finger N', and carries it under that finger, which, as the paper passes under, pushes back the middle of the upper side of the tube, so as to give the peculiar form represented in Fig. 10 to the first fold. The blade c, still going with the paper as it feeds, passes under the side-folders Q' R' until the point q' of the paper is taken by the rolls $r s$. The plate-knife-folder F now draws back, the folders Q' R' close down upon the tube, and the feed-motion stops. The blade c now passes over the side-folders Q' R' again, making the second fold, as represented in Fig. 11, the guide-finger N' rising to let the fold of paper pass under it, and dropping again to hold it in its place. The blade c going back, the side-folders draw apart, and the first half of the bottom of the bag is made. The paper now passes between the rollers $r s$, the vertical knife D' descends and passes, with the paper, between the rolls s and t, making the third fold, represented in Fig. 12, and completing the other half of the bag bottom. At this point, and just before the fold is made, paste is applied to the bottom of the bag by the paster p, which receives paste from the small paste-roller b', and is operated by its connection with the gear C', as hereinbefore described. The severing of the bag from the paper tube is effected during the arrest of the feed-motion, as hereinbefore mentioned, by a vertical knife, Z, attached to a frame and operated by the cam Z on shaft P. It plays against a steel straight-edge, O', parallel to the edge of the table P', (see Fig. 2,) the two forming a species of shears, capable of cutting paper, cloth, or any other material applicable to the manufacture of bags.

I wish to have it understood that, believing myself to be the first to invent a device to hold back or push back a point or portion of one edge of the paper tube while the blade or tucking-knife forms the first fold, represented in Fig. 10, which is the basis of the flat-bottomed bag, I do not confine myself to any particular form, position, or mode of attaching the device referred to, which I have designated a "guide-finger," nor limit myself to making it fixed or movable, as long as it performs the function for which I have devised and use it. I have made it in various forms, and fixed as well as movable, and having a rearward projection like a heel. The guide-finger hereinbefore described I believe to be of the best form; but other forms will answer, with the necessary modifications of the accompanying mechanism, without altering the principle of operation by which the fold represented in Fig. 10 is made.

Having thus fully described my invention, what I claim, and desire to secure by Letters Patent, is—

1. The follower I', constructed and operating as and for the purpose specified.

2. The plate-knife-folder F, constructed, arranged, and operating as set forth.

3. The guide-finger N', or equivalent device, whether fixed or movable, the function of which is to hold or push back a portion of the edge of the paper tube while the fold represented in Fig. 10 is being formed.

4. The combination of a guide-finger with mechanism or a device for pushing the paper tube under said guide-finger, for the purpose of forming the fold represented in Fig. 10.

5. The side-folders Q' R', constructed, arranged, and operated by the means described, as and for the purpose specified.

The above specification of my said invention signed and witnessed at Boston this 9th day of November, A. D. 1869.

MARGARETT E. KNIGHT.

Witnesses:
SAML. C. MOORE,
JOHN WHEELOCK.

CPSIA information can be obtained
at www.ICGtesting.com
Printed in the USA
JSHW081959141022
31678JS00003B/3